GW00481010

RICHARD BUTCHER

The Pond at the Bottom of the Garden

REFLECTIONS ON AN ANGLING LIFE

The Pond at the Bottom of the Garden

First published in Great Britain in 2022

Copyright ©2022

Richard Butcher has asserted her right under the Copyright Designs and Patents Act 1988 to be identified as the author of this work.

A CIP catalogue record for this book is available from the British Library.
This book is sold subject to the condition that it shall not by way of trade or otherwise be lent, resold, hired out or otherwise circulated without the publisher's prior consent in any form of binding or cover, other than that in which it is published and without a similar condition, including this condition being imposed on the subsequent purchaser.

Printed and bound in Great Britain

This book is dedicated to my mum and dad, who gave me a childhood filled with happy memories and without whom I might have been condemned to a life on the golf course...

Richard Herbert Butcher, 1925 – 2004
Maureen Butcher, 1933 – 2017

Photo credits: Cover page, chapter one header, chapter two header, chapter five header and numbers 1, 2, 3 – John Kaye (my uncle)

CONTENTS

About the author
Foreword

ABOUT THE AUTHOR

Richard Butcher was brought up in Timperley, a suburb of south Manchester, and after a few false starts carved out a successful career in the waste industry, but fishing has played a central role in his life since he was a small boy. In his own words: "I could cast a fishing rod before I could write my own name. Why? Because both my parents were keen anglers and our little nondescript semi-detached house in Timperley had one feature which distinguished itself from virtually all the other houses in south Manchester. It had a pond at the bottom of the garden, and in this pond were roach, rudd, perch, tench and best of all, crucian carp. There was an inevitability that I would either embrace the fishing bug, or rebel against it. Thankfully, I embraced it completely and it has been the one constant feature of my entire life."

He is now retired and lives in the Cheshire countryside with his wife, their dog and two cats. Although he has written for *Total Sea Fishing* magazine and *Sea Angler* magazine, this is his first book.

FOREWORD

I have never considered myself to be anything more than a barely competent angler, but I do think I'm a lucky one. Lucky to be born to not one, but two, angling parents and also to have the ability to indulge my fledgling obsession quite literally on my doorstep. Lucky to have been able to retire in my mid-fifties and have the time to devote to, and to develop, these obsessions. In fact, my whole life has been an eclectic mix of angling obsessions, comprising both freshwater and sea angling and covering a whole range of different styles and target species. Each of these has been approached with a mixture of cack-handedness and, just occasionally, something almost akin to competence, which has enabled me to catch a few reasonably sized fish along the way.

There are many reasons why I wanted to write this book, which is in no way to be construed as a guide to better your angling abilities. However, if you can empathise with some of my obsessions, relate to a few of the tales and laugh or cry in the appropriate places, then I believe your hard-earned money will have been well spent.

So why did I want to write this book?

I have always enjoyed 'telling the tale' and reminiscing about angling successes and failures; indeed, the failures can often be more enriching than the successes.

Books have always played a big part in my life; when I was young my mother would go the library every week and bring home two books each for us all. Even now, our dining room and bedroom contains piles of books and I'm at my happiest when I can combine two of my favourite activities: fishing and book reading. When I was young some of my sporting heroes were angling writers, people such as Dick Walker, Clive Gammon and Ian Gillespie, and I marvelled at the way their prose could transport me to diverse places such as Redmire Pool or the Dingle Peninsula. Their influence on me will become apparent as you meander through these pages.

My favourite lesson at secondary school was English Literature – well, third favourite after lunch and rugby – which may make you wonder why I ended up choosing sciences for A levels and my degree: all I can say is, continue reading and you will eventually find out. I also remember a teacher telling us that we, as a country, were rubbish at football, rugby and cricket but were, and always would be, the world's best when it came to literature. Dickens, Shakespeare, Orwell, Carroll, he intoned; no other country had ever, or would ever, produce such a rich literary heritage. I wondered about sticking my hand up and adding Walker and Gammon to that list, but thought better of it; you kept your head down at my school as to do otherwise risked a swift belt from slipper or strap.

Being able to retire in my mid-fifties provided me with the opportunity to tentatively start my angling writing career without impacting too much on my ability to go fishing when the need has taken me, which is usually at least twice a week. In April 2016, I wrote and submitted an article for *Total Sea Fishing* magazine, partly as a way of keeping my mind active (my wife said I had to do something 'mentally stimulating') but also to fulfil a lifelong ambition of becoming an angling writer. I had an initial intention of getting just one article published; I was quite surprised when they asked me to provide an ongoing monthly contribution. Writing a book seemed a natural progression to further this fledgling career.

Retirement also gave me the opportunity to visit my elderly mother every week, my father having died over ten years before. During one of my weekly visits in the autumn of 2016, she asked me if I would mind taking her fishing to the little pond at the bottom of her garden – the same pond, at the same house, that provides the title for this book. I'm not sure how many years it had been since she last went fishing; and being in her eighties and requiring two sticks to get around meant that she couldn't fish by herself. So obviously, I said yes. I suggested that we wait till the spring when the weather would be a little warmer, although to be honest, the real reason for this delay was that I was particularly engrossed in beach fishing for small-eyed rays at the time and thought I could slot her in somewhere between the end of the winter and early spring thornback ray 'season' and the start of the bass and tench 'season'. With a broad date in the diary set for the following spring my mother brought out the battered old suitcase, the one held together with an old leather belt which contained all the old family photographs. Going through these hundreds of old photos while my mother plied me with tea and biscuits made me realise just how much fishing had coloured the backdrop to our family life, both in my early years and in the years when my parents were married before I came along. Put it this way: there were very few birthday or Christmas photos, but plenty containing either my mother, my father or myself plus an assortment of fish.

Some of these photographs took me into the province of incidental memories, fragments of which emerged from the back of my mind, having been forgotten for decades. Some photographs drew an immediate surge of emotion as I recalled their scenarios – sights, sounds, smells, but most of all how I *felt* - as if it were only yesterday; but others drew complete blanks.

It also started me wondering exactly why I became so obsessed with my fishing. There was a powerful resonance between the obsessions I felt then and those which I still feel. And why did some of these obsessions endure while others seemed only to occupy a specific time and place in my life? Why did I change from being a coarse fisherman into a predominantly sea-based one?

I asked my mother these questions but, not surprisingly, she could only answer the first question: 'it was the pond at the bottom of the garden'.

She also asked me if I'd ever considered writing a book…

CHAPTER ONE

THE POND

If there were such a thing as an angling gene, then this would explain perfectly everything that happens in the following pages. However, as a man of science, I know that there is no such thing and therefore the explanation must be more 'nurture' than 'nature'. This does, of course, make absolute sense too, as my early formative years were spent in the perfect angling environment.

My mother never tired of telling me how she and my father managed to acquire their three-bed semi-detached house in south Manchester. From living in a one bedroomed flat – little more than a bedsit – they both worked all the hours God sent to save up for a deposit. My father worked as a fitter making printing presses at Linotype and Machinery Ltd in Broadheath, Altrincham, whilst my mother worked as a nurse at Manchester Royal Infirmary. Some of the little spare time they had was spent fishing with two of my father's brothers-in-law, Dennis and John. Not only were they both keen anglers, they also had cars (neither of my parents could drive until I was seven) so they could transport them to a variety of waters that the newly formed Altrincham and District Angling Club had just acquired.

I asked my mother what initially attracted her to angling and she said that she would never have seen my father if she didn't go with him, but that she quickly came to enjoy going fishing almost as much as he did. Having been brought up in Barrow-in-Furness during the Second World War and in a family, like most families in Barrow, completely dependent on the local shipyard for work, catching sea fish either by netting or 'long lining' was a dietary necessity during the war years and periods of depression or strikes in the shipyard. This meant that my mother was never squeamish when it came to handling worms, maggots or the fish themselves. She had been expected to be able to gut and fillet sea fish from an early age. I suppose that being a nurse, worms or maggots held little terror for her compared to what she saw when on duty in Accident and Emergency.

My father loved float fishing, and although my mother didn't object to this, she preferred a more active approach to her fishing and liked spinning for pike above everything else. My Uncle, John Kaye – one of the angling brothers-in-law – was a sports photographer for the Express Group newspapers and I have him to thank for many of the photographs of my parents in these early days as well as the few fishless family portraits we have. He faithfully recorded the capture by my father of a fine net of roach and a large tench from the old wooden punt on Booths Mere, as well as the pike caught by my mother at places such as Tabley Mere and Lymm Dam.

My father's favourite fishing spot was a place called Astle Mere, deep in the heart of the Cheshire countryside. The mere was fed by two streams at one end and had a small dam with a plunge pool at the other, the outflowing river passing below the road which led up to the hall itself. The mere was surrounded, in those days, by mature beech trees, lily pads grew in its margins and it contained a good head of bream and perch, along with a few pike. One of my father's favourite stories concerned a day spent at Astle with his two brothers-in-law; they had been there since early morning with nothing but a few perch for sport. As dinnertime approached there was the ominous rumble of an approaching thunderstorm, so they decided to leave their tackle where it was (unthinkable these days!) and head for the local pub for something to eat and drink, but not before throwing in the remainder of their groundbait. Unfortunately, the beer at the first pub they arrived at was declared undrinkable, so a detour had to be made to a number of other public houses in that area, with the result that it was late afternoon before they returned to the mere. On arriving back at his swim, the first thing my father saw were bream rolling over his baited area and he then proceeded to have his biggest ever catch of bream, so many in fact that he had to stop putting them in his keepnet. These were fish of between 2–4lb and he continued to catch until he ran out of bait. Strangely enough, my two uncles didn't catch a single bream between them, despite fishing not more than ten or fifteen yards away from him!

In the spring of 1957, my parents had saved up enough money for a deposit and the next thing to do was to find a suitable house. After a number of unsatisfactory viewings my mother went to inspect a small three bed semi-detached house in Timperley, south Manchester; from the front, it was identical to thousands of other pre-Second World War semis that had sprung up all over south Manchester, maybe a little shabbier than some, but structurally still sound. From the back-bedroom window she looked out over a relatively large but somewhat overgrown garden – and a small pond. The pond provided a backdrop for fourteen houses and was no more than sixty yards long and maybe thirty yards wide; it was surrounded by yellow flag iris and appeared to have a small island at one end (in actual fact it wasn't an island but a shallower area where a large clump of iris grew). Much of the pond was covered in potamogeton – an aquatic plant whose leaves are shaped like a Zulu warrior's shield – and small splashes indicated the presence of fish, most likely small roach and rudd, she thought.

Although the presence of the pond would require a sturdy fence when children eventually arrived, she had no doubts that this was *their* house. It goes without saying that my father took one look at the pond and decided that this was the perfect house for him too, and after persuading a building society to lend them the rest of the money (no easy matter, according to my mother) they eventually parted with the princely sum of £1,350 and moved in during the summer of that year.

Why the pond survived the housing explosion in the 1930s is a story in itself. There was, apparently, much debate about whether this little pond, presumably an old farm pond, should be drained to make room for more houses, but because it was spring fed, the house builders were not able to empty it. They did, however, leave a gap between two of the semis for a road, should the source of the spring ever be found. In the end, they gave up on the idea and built a detached house in this gap.

Before the war, the pond was smaller than it became in the 60s, and a large tiled air raid shelter was constructed at 'our' end of the pond. At some point, so the rumour goes, a very small spring-fed stream behind the houses on the other side of the road was blocked off to stop the gardens flooding in wet weather, and overnight the level of the pond increased by about one or two feet. This caused the air raid shelter to flood, and to this day it remains there with its only access being from the pond itself. The only time we – my friends and I – got to see inside the shelter was when the pond froze over with ice sufficiently thick for us to walk across to it.

This pond wasn't unique in the area in my childhood. There was another one in the derelict grounds of Riddings Hall, which was only five minutes' walk away, as well as one near the Quarrybank pub in Timperley village. Unfortunately, these both disappeared before I was twelve to make room for more houses.

My parents wasted no time in exploring the fishing potential of the pond, although such time was limited. My father worked five days per week, with overtime on Tuesday and Thursday evenings plus Saturday mornings till midday. Sunday morning was church time, although sometimes the evening service could be attended instead, leaving the mornings free for fishing.

These fishing sessions produced, much to my father's delight, roach, rudd, perch and best of all, crucian carp. In hindsight, I suspect that some, or most, of these fish were not pure-bred crucian carp but hybrids with brown goldfish. Some looked like classical crucian carp with the dinner plate type shape – high bodied but wafer thin when compared to a normal carp – but others more resembled a 'normal' common carp but without the barbules. These crucian carp – for the purpose of this book, we'll call them that – normally varied in size between about two ounces and a pound and provided good sport on the light tackle my parents used.

A brief word on the tackle. My father had a fourteen-foot, four-piece rod, three sections of which were made out of bamboo with the top section being glass fibre. To this was attached a centre pin reel made by K. Dowling and Sons. My mother used an eight-foot fly rod and a small fixed spool reel. Small porcupine quill floats were used and the bait was usually bread paste, unless my father had made a detour to the tackle shop on Saturday dinner time on his way back from work and got his small aluminium bait tin filled with maggots. Groundbait was left-over bread that had been bagged and saved during the week, then mashed by hand until it was the consistency of a thick broth. My father sat on a willow creel – as every angler did in those days – and my mother sat on a small foldaway chair. Homemade rod rests (made from narrow-gauge copper piping), a small landing net and a keepnet, both made from heavy-duty cord, completed the set-up. There was no umbrella – if it rained they either got wet or went inside until the rain stopped – and no scales other than a Salter spring balance. This device was not particularly useful for fish of under a pound and, in fact, if a crucian carp of around that size was caught, the kitchen scales were summoned. These were the old-fashioned sort of scales with a long arm which pivoted in the middle. At one end was an enamel pan into which the fish would be placed with a flat plate at the other onto which lead weights of various sizes were added until the arm was balanced in the horizontal position. The exact weight of the fish could therefore be ascertained to the nearest ounce.

A couple of years later I decided to make an appearance, much to the joy of my parents. I have very few pre-school memories: a trip to Southport and a ride on a miniature railway is one hazy memory, but the most vivid one is the day my father returned home from work on a Saturday dinnertime with a fishing rod for me. I use the term 'fishing rod' in its loosest sense, as the rod itself was made of some kind of metal, permanently attached to which was a moulded plastic reel shaped like a mermaid. The set-up was completed with a bright red plastic float and a hook shaped like a circle which was attached to a material like thin kite string; certainly, there was no nylon involved. Rod, reel, float and hook were mounted on a lurid plastic-covered card on which was depicted a small boy attached to a huge fish of indeterminate species. I never asked either of my parents why on earth they acquired this contraption, as it was pretty useless as a piece of fishing kit. Maybe my father was given it by someone at work, or maybe it was cheap (money must have been tight, especially as my mother had given up work when I was born) and they thought a four-year-old boy would be quite happy with it anyway. In hindsight, I think the weather was warm and they both wanted to go fishing. This meant that I had to come down to the pond with them and they thought that having my own rod would provide enough of a distraction for them to at least get a modicum of fishing time in.

The following memories are supplemented by my mother's; when I talked with her in the autumn of 2016 she had limited memories of what had happened a year before, but could quite easily recall events of fifty years ago. I'm told that this is not uncommon for people 'of a certain age'.

Sunday morning arrived and it was still and very warm. I can't remember if we'd been to church or not but it must have been getting on for nine o'clock before we started fishing. The three of us sat alongside each other on the other side of a gated fence (to stop me wandering into the pond) on the grassy bank and in front of the dense beds of iris. Directly in front of us the iris had been cut down a little so that floats could be seen and in one area completely removed to allow for the landing of any larger fish. The water in front of us was mostly covered in potamogeton, although an area of maybe five yards by five had been cleared by my father to give some comfortable fishing space. I can't remember what bait we were using – I would assume bread paste – but I do remember both parents catching a succession of crucian carp, nothing huge; the biggest fish may have been half a pound in weight. I can recollect being transfixed by the disappearance of the float, soon to be followed by the appearance of these fish. I then became annoyed. Their floats were going under but mine wasn't: mainly because it was no more than a couple of yards out on the nearside of a clump of potamogeton, whereas they were fishing on the far side of this clump. When my mother caught yet another beautiful little crucian carp I decided I'd had enough. I threw my rod to the floor, burst into tears of frustration and stormed off up the garden.

My mother followed me, calmed me down and made a pot of tea for us all. We then returned to the pond with the tea and a plate of cup-cakes. I think it was the cake which had the major calming influence here. On sitting down by the water again, I noticed that my dad had made a few changes to my rod; he'd attached a length of nylon with a 'proper' hook and proceeded to show me how to cast 'properly'; 'pull a few handfuls of line of the reel with your left hand and cast with your right'. The little red plastic float sailed out just beyond the weedbed and a few minutes later it trembled and slid away...

I'd been instructed what to do if this happened, indeed I'd been watching my parents strike for the past couple of hours, so I yanked back hard on the rod. This only had the effect of depositing the float on the grass behind me. Cue yet more tears. My mother then put her own rod down and concentrated on helping me. It was now late morning, the bites had all but stopped as the sun started to make it uncomfortably warm and my father started to look at his watch. Sunday dinnertime was pub time for him and time for my mother to start the Sunday lunch.

'Time for one last cast,' he announced, and my bottom lip trembled as tears of frustration started to build again; life just wasn't fair, they'd caught fish and I hadn't. I've often wondered how my life would have been if what happened next hadn't occurred; would

I have been so frustrated that I would have fought against going again? I don't think so, but that's irrelevant anyway as the little red plastic float disappeared again with the minimum of fuss and with my mother's hand guiding mine I lifted into a small crucian.

Better writers than me have expressed their amazement at how their fishing rod 'came alive' in their hands with their first fish, but there really is no other way of explaining this feeling. The fish was only a couple of ounces in weight, but being a crucian carp, it fought better than most fish three or four times bigger than that, although it was soon unceremoniously swung into my mother's hand. Such a beautiful fish, and *my fish, not theirs!* (little did I know at the time that it would take many years to catch my next carp). My protestations about wanting another cast were ignored as my father 'had a serious thirst,' but the smile on his face was surely a reflection of my own happiness, something that was to happen many times over the coming years as he took more satisfaction in seeing me catch fish than he did in catching them himself.

I would like to say that this is where the obsession started, and that may be so, but strangely enough I have no more angling-related memories for the next couple of years, although my mother assured me that we did go fishing together many times. I do have other memories of the pond though, and I was immensely proud of its existence, especially as my circle of friends increased on going to school – no one else had a pond at the bottom of their garden!

Some of my earliest memories of the pond concern the swans that appeared each spring and stayed until midsummer. They built their nest in the same place – on the reedy island at the far end of the pond - and usually raised between two and five cygnets. Although they co-existed quite happily with the resident moorhens on the pond, their relationship with the human residents of the surrounding houses was a little more problematic, especially after the appearance of their young. I can remember my father staggering into the house holding his backside and explaining that one of the 'ruddy swans' (ruddy was the nearest my father ever came to swearing) had bitten him when he was bent over doing some weeding in the flower beds nearest the pond.

The swans were well known locally for other reasons too. Every year, at some point during the summer, they would decide that their brood had outgrown the confines of our little pond and needed a larger expanse of water on which to spread their wings. Hence, they would wander up one of the gardens, take to the road and head for the local canal, the Bridgewater canal, some third of a mile away. The first person to see them take to the road would call the local policeman, who promptly stopped the traffic to allow them free passage. It made for a strange sight – a policeman followed by an adult swan, a number of cygnets and another adult swan, behind which was a line of cars with doubtless some very frustrated drivers!

When I was six or seven, I was given a whole new fishing outfit for my birthday and Christmas presents. Having a birthday just before Christmas meant that presents were often combined in this manner, not that I ever felt at all deprived. The new ensemble consisted of a white two-piece solid glass fibre rod with a wooden handle, about seven feet in length. The reel was an Intrepid Elite, which was considered by my father to be as good a fixed-spool reel as any on the market (apart of course, from the top of the range 'Intrepid Deluxe'). A small plastic tackle box completed the outfit; there was nothing in this box, but I was told that I could use any birthday or Christmas money I received to stock it with floats, shot, hooks etc. You might think I was desperate to use this straight away, but the reality was that we just didn't fish in the winter. Although I never specifically asked either of them why not, I think it's because for them, the joy of fishing the pond was associated with summer days; the big beds of iris, the pond weed nearly covering the surface of the water, the trees being in full leaf, especially the willow trees by the pond which they'd planted themselves in their first years at the house. As I've got older, I can totally relate to this. You will see in the following chapters that I also display a silo mentality to much of my fishing: each species or venue has its own time and place, which is essential for me to derive any significant enjoyment from my fishing. I haven't decided yet whether this is 'sad' or 'inspired'...

For myself, I think I decided that the fish hibernated during the cold weather and therefore it wasn't worthwhile fishing for them.

The pond did, however, provide winter entertainment in other ways. When it froze over, which it did every winter in my childhood, and the ice was considered to be of sufficient thickness, I and assorted neighbours and friends were allowed to go sliding out across the pond. Interestingly, I can't remember how the ice was tested. Anyway, great fun could be had for weeks at a time, until the ice started to melt.

The first time I used my new fishing tackle was, I think, late spring or early summer (there was no 'closed season' on our pond). I don't recall who loaded my reel with line or attached float and hook to it, but I do recall that I was using maggots, so this must have been a 'planned' trip. Another development was that, having learnt to swim, I was allowed down to the pond unsupervised. From today's viewpoint that might seem a little misguided, but in those days, I think it was the norm for me and my friends to be kicked out of the house at a relatively early age with an instruction to go and amuse ourselves but be back in time for lunch or tea.

My memories of what I believe to be my first 'solo' session are not very clear, but the sun was definitely shining and fishing with maggots about a foot below the float I had bites instantly; in fact I caught three tiny rudd in my first three casts, all of which were carefully unhooked and placed in my fathers keep-net. In those days, my father cycled home from work every day for his lunch, arriving between twelve-twelve and twelve-sixteen, depending on whether or not the level crossing at Navigation Road railway station was closed. On this day, I was waiting for him on our drive to drag him down to the pond to show him what I'd caught. He was indeed impressed with my net of tiny rudd, and I think his pleasure was as much to do with the fact that he could now start to plan some fishing trips further afield on the basis that I wouldn't need quite so much babysitting. Trips further afield were now possible due to my father having passed his driving test – my mother passed a couple of months before he did – and our family now being the proud owner of a red Ford Anglia. The rest of my summer days, especially the long summer break from Primary School, were spent doing many things: football, cricket, general messing around, but increasingly they were spent down by the pond catching rudd along with roach and perch. As long as I was getting bites, life was good and I was happy.

Fishing trips to the pond now tended, for whatever reason, to be more with my father. The potamogeton grew rapidly in the warmer months and we frequently had to clear out the swims in front of us. This was done with an old rake head attached to an old washing line with the weed being piled up at the water's edge, giving my father a chance to lecture me on the various bugs found within it. 'That's a dragonfly nymph, those are snail eggs,' he'd explain. The weed would be left there for a few days 'so that all the bugs can crawl back into the water' before it would be removed to his compost heap. Not surprisingly, the fishing after raking the swims could be rather good.

After clearing the swims one Sunday afternoon, we both settled down for an evening's fishing. My father had few idiosyncrasies, but one was that it was bad luck to wet your landing net before catching your first fish. The landing net was therefore laid in the grass behind us as my father mashed up the bread mix that was to serve as our groundbait. A few small handfuls were placed in each swim and we sat back – him on his creel and me on my mother's fold-away chair – to await the arrival of the carp.

One of the beautiful things about fishing for crucian carp is the way they announce their arrival in your swim by 'bubbling' – dense patches of tiny bubbles, and occasionally, a little tail-flicking splash on the surface. It had been a warm day, and although the temperature remained high enough for us both to be in our shirt sleeves, the sun had disappeared behind a thick band of cloud, giving an oppressive feel to the evening with the possibility of thunder later.

Sure enough, given these almost perfect conditions for crucian fishing, patches of bubbles started to appear. I had the first bite, which I missed quite spectacularly, and there followed a short interlude as my father retrieved my float and hook from the upper reaches of the nearest willow tree. 'Try not to strike quite as hard next time' was all he said.

A strange silence descended on our fishing – I was rarely quiet for long when fishing with my dad - but there was an expectation of something momentous about to happen. (An aside here: other anglers have talked about being certain that something special was about to happen and although this has only happened to me a few times in my angling life I have to agree with them that sometimes you just know that you're on the brink of something momentous.

My father's yellow-tipped quill slowly slid away and a short strike put a healthy bend in his rod, only for everything to go solid as the fish dived into the remaining weed at the far end of my father's swim. For nearly five minutes nothing happened, despite my father trying different angles of attack. I asked him, 'is he still there Dad, or has he gone?'

My father held his rod up high and let the tension on the rod tip ease off. 'No, he's still there, I can just feel him.'

On tightening back down to the fish again, both fish and a large clump of weed started to move slowly towards the bank. 'Quick, get the landing net, you'll have to do the honours,' he said. With trembling hands I held the net out as the biggest crucian carp – no, the biggest fish of any description that I'd ever seen – was brought across the net cord and into the landing net. It was a battered old warrior of a carp, but one worthy of accurate weighing. My mother and her kitchen scales were summoned and lead weights added till the pan was in balance; a one-pound weight; an eight-ounce weight; a two-ounce weight – a bit too much – a one-ounce weight; perfect. At one pound and nine ounces it was the biggest crucian carp I ever saw from our little pond. Nothing else was caught, which was hardly surprising after the disturbances on both bank and water, so I went to bed and dreamt of carp.

Fish and fishing were starting to dominate my young life to the extent that when we had a family day trip to Chester Zoo I spent most of my time watching the fish in the various moats and waterways that surrounded the animal enclosures. Much to my parents' amusement, I was excitedly pointing out to them the large roach, rudd and occasional carp in these patches of water, whereas all the other children were in similar fits of ecstasy over monkeys and elephants. Of course, best of all was the aquarium, which contained one very large tank with a collection of mirror carp, some of which were enormous to a child whose carp were usually measured only in ounces.

Not all of my memories of the pond are happy ones, however. I arrived home from school one Tuesday to find a number of police cars in our road and my mother waiting at our front door for me. She ushered me inside and explained to me that two young children from a house further up the road, not one with a garden that backed down to the pond, had got to the water's edge through a neighbour's garden. Once there, they'd decided to retrieve some apples from the water but unfortunately for them the water in this particular spot shelved quickly down to about six feet deep, whereas the margins around the rest of the pond had much gentler gradients. They'd quickly got out of their depth and started screaming, which alerted our next-door neighbour; she shot round to where she could see them and managed to drag a small boy out of the water, but by then the little girl was nowhere to be seen. The police were called and eventually, a body was retrieved.

I didn't really know either of the two children, but I have a very clear memory of the dead girl's father, ashen-faced, coming round later that evening to thank my mother for helping to calm his hysterical wife and also to ask if he could go down to the pond to see where the drowning had occurred (the actual spot of the drowning was still 'out of bounds'). I realised at the time that this was a very serious occurrence, but it's only when you have, or have had, young kids of your own that you look back and think... well you just think, don't you?

I also remember walking down to the pond before breakfast one school morning to see virtually all the fish in the pond gasping for air on the surface. A period of hot and still weather had dangerously reduced the oxygen levels, according to my father, who had been rapidly summoned from his tea and cornflakes. It was one of the worst days I ever had at primary school... would the fish still be alive when I got home? Thankfully they were, and not long after I'd raced back at the end of the school day the Fire Brigade arrived to re-oxygenate the water. They did this by pumping water out and firing it back into the air through their hoses so that it landed back from a great height, with this extra agitation allowing more oxygen to be absorbed. This did the trick, and disaster was averted.

Certainly by the age of nine or ten, the pond dominated my life, at least during the spring and summer months. Most weekends, the two-week Whit holiday and the six-week summer holiday would see me down there fishing almost every day – I was truly obsessed, even at that tender age. The obsession was not just with catching fish, but one fish, not surprisingly, the crucian carp. It may have been the first fish I caught, but I hadn't replicated its capture since then despite hour upon hour of trying. The reasons for these failures wasn't too hard to find: I was using large hooks – size 10s – and six-pound breaking strain 'Fog' line. Anglers of sufficiently advanced years will remember 'Fog' line. It was cheap – it was the only line that my pocket money would stretch to – and came on a green plastic spool, but was so thick it was actually quite difficult to thread through the eye of those size 10 hooks. Add to this a big lump of rock-hard bread paste and it was no surprise that I wasn't catching much. Of course, I didn't have the patience either and often resorted to 'tiddler bashing' after thirty minutes or so of biteless action. Fishing lumps of bread paste in the upper layers of water guaranteed instant bites, but the inability of these fish to swallow lumps of bread paste on a size 10 meant that few were ever actually hooked.

This time, it was my mother to the rescue. For some reason, I wasn't fishing the pond much with my parents in those days – my father often worked seven days per week and my mother had gone back to nursing, this time in an old people's home at the end of our road. When we did fish together, we tended to drive out to waters belonging to Altrincham and District Angling Club. Anyway, one summer's morning, my mother decided that she would come fishing with me. Groundbait was prepared, bread paste was made – a much softer paste than I was used to making – and, most importantly, she declared that she wasn't interested in catching anything other than a carp.

Bubbles soon appeared and I quickly had my first bite – a roach, but a slightly bigger roach than those I normally caught, so I was happy enough. I should point out that by this time I was using my first 'proper' fishing rod, my last birthday having provided me with a beautiful ten-foot split cane rod, complete with cork handle and a hollow glass fibre tip. It really was a thing of beauty; my father had held it lovingly and explained to me that 'split cane makes the best fishing rods'. I still have it in my garage, and although I am not wedded to old fishing tackle (having said that, my tench fishing is still done with a forty-year-old Mitchell 810 reel), I have to admit that it is still a beautiful rod. To this rod had been added a second-hand Intrepid Deluxe reel – the top of the range Intrepid, replacing my Intrepid Elite, which had started to make strange grinding noises, having obviously failed to cope with the severe misuse that it had been given.

I had no premonitions that this morning was going to be any different from the other carpless mornings, and although I'd caught a roach, I wasn't now getting any more bites and was starting to get restless. I was considering moving the float down the line and seeking bites further up in the water, but my mother assured me that there were crucians down there and I should be a little more patient. More than an hour had passed, an eternity in the life of a young angler, before I got another bite. This produced a fish that was pulling back in a manner that indicated it wasn't a roach. I held my breath until I saw a flash of gold and very shortly after that – there was no giving of line in those days – I swung a four-ounce carp to hand. Fantastic! So that's how it's done. A little bit of patience was all that was required to crack the secret code, and after this I started catching crucians on a reasonably regular basis, although never usually more than one or two a morning.

The more crucians I caught, the more obsessed I was, and now comes the tricky bit: why was I so fanatical about them? After all, these were not big fish and I was catching them often enough to mean that such captures weren't 'red letter days'. Looking back in time and relating how I feel now about my fishing obsessions to the way I felt then, there are two parallels that I can draw. Firstly, I took great comfort in the familiarity of my settings, in other words, the place where I was fishing, even down to the position of my float in the water, and secondly, I craved the adrenaline rush that the hooking of a crucian of any size gave me. I don't suppose in my early years I had a great deal else that would have given me such a buzz, The 'familiarity' thing is something which runs through a lot of my fishing and, at times, it has doubtless held me back in terms of trying new venues and ultimately from catching bigger fish.

I didn't have many friends who were that bothered about fishing in those days, although there was a lad a year younger than me from just up the road – our families were quite close and we often went out together – and he became a semi-regular fishing partner. Another angling friend was the grandson of the old lady who lived next door to us (the opposite side to the woman who had the unfortunate task of trying to rescue the drowning children). His grandmother's garden also backed on to the pond, but fishing from her garden was almost impossible due to a large overhanging ash tree whose branches actually touched the water and the willow trees in the corner of our garden. He used to spend at least one week of the Whit holiday with his grandmother, and we would spend every morning down by the pond fishing together.

One morning remains fixed in my memory. It was hot and still, as per a lot of my childhood memories. Surely the weather can't always have been so good? I suspect that I didn't go fishing quite so much in wet weather, as we didn't possess a fishing umbrella and sitting there holding one of my mother's umbrellas in one hand while trying to fish with the other was problematic to say the least.

On the morning in question, the first Monday of the Whit holidays, I'd already caught a small crucian of about six ounces, so the day could already be marked down as a success. Then the float lifted slightly before sliding away. My strike was met with a lot more resistance than I was expecting with the rod adopting an impressive – and hitherto previously unseen – curve. Eventually, well, maybe after about fifteen seconds, a significant expanse of gold appeared; a crucian carp of at least a pound, maybe even one and a half pounds. There was no swinging this fish to hand and my friend grabbed the landing net as I dragged the still kicking fish towards him… only for my float to suddenly ping back into the willows behind me. Disaster!

I was heartbroken, devastated, my little world collapsed around me. To make matters worse, when I retrieved my line I realised that I'd lost this fish because my hook knot had come undone. You would have thought that being able to fish from the age of four would have meant that I had been taught to tie numerous fishing knots, but for reasons which will always remain unknown, neither of my parents ever sat me down and showed me how to tie a single knot. As a result of this, my knots only ever consisted of multiple over-hand loops (granny knots) and by tying about five or six of these I ended up with a knot that was often almost as big as the hook itself, which would hold reasonably firm, until of course, it was put under any significant strain. So, did I learn my lesson and learn to tie a proper know? No, of course I didn't, I just put it all down to bad luck.

The loss of this fish ruined my entire holiday, despite catching more carp over the next two weeks and over the course of my angling life this is one thing that has changed; losing a big fish can be a disaster, but you get to learn that there are far worse things that can happen in life.

CHAPTER TWO

CLUB WATERS, AND
SOWING THE SEEDS

Smells are great evokers of memories. Whenever I smell damp compost, it takes me back to a little farm pond called 'Doublewoods,' the fishing rights to which were controlled by Altrincham and District Angling Club (henceforth to be known as ADAC, as I can't be bothered to keep typing it in full). I don't know exactly when I was enrolled as a Junior Member of ADAC but I would guess that it coincided with the purchase of our car and both parents passing their driving tests. This enabled my father to revisit many of his old haunts on a regular basis, which he was particularly pleased about since his brothers-in-law were no longer in positions to provide regular lifts. Dennis had long since moved up to Cumberland to run a pub on the banks of the River Derwent, and John's job and increased family responsibilities had significantly reduced his fishing time.

These ADAC waters provided me with a whole new fishing

experience, not that I altered my approach at all; same float and same tactics prevailed wherever I fished. I can't say that any of these new waters grabbed me in the same way as our little pond did, but they did lay the foundation stones for some mighty obsessions in the future.

Doublewoods was one of my favourite pools to fish, possibly because it was small, like 'our' pond, and I could use my usual float fishing set-up here and still catch fish. It was not much more than an acre in size, set amongst mature trees and shaped a bit like a figure of eight, although the top circle of the eight was bigger than the bottom one and the pinch point in the middle was still about twenty yards wide. The margins and shallower water were covered in a mixture of potamogeton and water lilies, and the centre parts of each 'circle' were about eight feet deep, with the margins starting at about three feet deep. Although a busy road ran quite close to one bank, the presence of the trees reduced a lot of the road noise and also meant that the surface of the water was always very still apart from those days when an absolute gale was blowing.

Doublewoods also had two features that marked it out to me as being very special: firstly, it had a cattle drink at the top end of the pool, a proper one with barbed wire which stopped the cattle from coming right into the pond but still allowed them enough access to drink their fill of water. Secondly, early in the morning and in the evening the air would be filled with the sound of fish – I always presumed carp – 'kissing' the undersides of the potamogeton leaves. The importance of the cattle drink and these strange kissing noises grew as I got older and cannot be overstated. I had started to discover angling literature – more of this later, as my parents' bookcase contained a healthy number of angling books –

and a number of the stories therein referenced both cattle drinks and kissing carp. This provided me with an absolute link between the written word and the reality of my own fishing. Stories about Redmire Pool and the like were exciting, yes, but I had no reference point to them. I could, however, relate to stories about pools with cattle drinks and kissing carp, and since these pools contained monster carp – which could be hooked, but more often than not lost after a valiant battle – it was nothing but a small jump for my imagination to transpose these fish into Doublewoods.

This little pond did indeed contain some large carp, although it would be me many more years before I started to catch them. In the meantime, I was always just happy to be there and to catch a few perch, roach or rudd, although I do recall watching my father hook something which charged straight into, and through, the dense weedbeds before snapping his line. I'm not sure how I would have reacted, but my father was quite philosophical about it: he just retackled and carried on fishing.

Doublewoods also provided me with my first-ever bream, a silver bream. I'm not sure if these fish were true silver bream (my father called them 'Pomeranian bream') or immature bronze bream, but I did have a rather good catch of them one morning. I can't quite remember how old I was, I'm guessing about twelve or maybe thirteen, and it was a weekday. My father had offered to take me to Doublewoods on his way to work. He had started to regularly use the car by then, as a recent promotion meant that he was no longer 'on the tools' and had to wear a collar and tie, and arriving in work hot and sweaty was fine when you were doing manual work but less so when sat at a desk.

The deal was that he'd drop me off about seven o'clock in the morning and collect me about half five. It was a heavily overcast morning, warm and drizzly, and I arrived to find the place deserted; this was fine by me, as I was already preferring to be by myself when I was fishing (my parents and the odd fishing friend excepted). I chose a pitch on the far side of the pool where there was a small square of clear water amongst the weeds, and the canopy of a large beech tree provided some shelter from the fine rain. Baitwise, I was well equipped; maggots, bread paste and some 'proper' groundbait that had recently been purchased from the tackle shop in nearby Altrincham. A few handfuls of this were thrown into the swim along with a handful of maggots, and I sat down on my basket – another birthday or Christmas present – and started to fish. Float fish, of course, although since I was using maggots I did downgrade my hook size from a ten to a fourteen.

It didn't take long to get my first bite, but instead of a perch or roach I found myself connected to something a little bigger than expected, although it wasn't fighting particularly well. I soon realised that it was a silver bream of about half a pound, and never having seen one of these before I was pleasantly chuffed with the capture and even more so when I went on to catch a dozen or so more bream throughout the morning, with the biggest one going to just over the pound mark.

The other noteworthy event was that for some reason I'd taken my mother's rod with me and on to her rod and reel I attached a small self-cocking float and a size ten hook, onto which I put a large ball of bread paste, which was then dropped in right amongst the weeds themselves. I'm not exactly sure what I expected to achieve with this, but twice I glanced across to see that the float had disappeared and the line was straining further into the weeds. Each time the culprit was a small crucian carp of about an ounce – if the fish had been any bigger then I would never have got it out.

This capped a perfect morning's fishing. The sun broke through the clouds early in the afternoon, the fishing tailed off completely and another angler arrived. He walked past me and I showed him my net of bream and carp, to which he was most complimentary; what was he going to fish for, I asked? 'Carp,' he replied and I was almost tempted to say that he should have arrived earlier, as they were unlikely to feed during the afternoon, especially with the sun now being out and the 'kissing' having stopped. Thank goodness I didn't say anything.

He set himself up by the lily pads to my left, but the bankside vegetation meant that I couldn't see exactly what he was doing; he was obviously legering, but I couldn't see what bait he was using. At about four o'clock there was a tremendous commotion by these lily pads and I looked across to see his rod bent over and after a short battle, a huge – at least six pounds – common carp was slid into his landing net. This was the first 'big' carp I'd ever seen, and although I'm certain that the seed of a carp fishing obsession had already been implanted within my brain, this capture certainly helped it to grow.

One of our first days out was to Astle Mere, still a beautiful piece of water despite the felling of the mature trees which surrounded it. On one bank, the fishing was from wooden jetties that stretched out through dense beds of rushes into the mere and we – my father, mother and I – chose three adjacent jetties to fish from. We all started catching small perch. I'd been given a small tobacco tin in which were placed a handful of maggots (we were a one bait-tin family) and I was quite happy catching perch – until disaster struck. I must have been standing right on the end of the jetty and I slipped, and for the first, and strangely enough, given the amount of time I've spent by the waterside, the only time, I fell in. The bottom of the Mere consisted of extremely soft mud, and I sank in up to my stomach. Fortunately, I was able to haul myself out and wander rather tearfully round to my mother; the tears were partly due to the frustration of knowing the trip would surely be at an end and also because I wasn't sure how my father would react as he'd been so looking forward to his return to Astle. As it was, he thought it rather funny but, sure enough, the session was brought to a premature close.

Astle now disappears from my life for over twenty years before returning as a full-blown, if extremely short-lived, obsession.

Booths Mere, an old man-made roughly square estate lake of some fifteen acres in the grounds of Booths Hall, was another favourite venue. It could be fished from an old wooden punt or from the bank, but in those days we just fished from its banks, usually what was known as the 'Knutsford Bank,' where trees lined the shore as opposed to the far bank, which consisted of grass-covered concrete banking and was known as 'The Wall'. The other two sides of the square were lined with reeds which grew in soft, deep mud and were therefore almost impossible to fish.

In one of my early trips there, an evening visit, two significant things happened. Firstly, I was quite happily sitting there, fishing away with the same float, line and hook that I always used and catching a steady stream of small perch when another bite saw me attached to something that that just wouldn't stop. There was no fuss, no explosion in the water, just a fish trundling away from me until my line eventually snapped. The power of the fish was something I'd never experienced before and, of course, it never occurred to me to give it some line. The surprising thing is that the line snapped before the knot unravelled.

I explained to my father what had happened and he said that it was most likely a tench –

wow, a real tench! I'd never seen one in the flesh before, I'd only ever seen drawings of them in angling books or photographs in the *Angling Times*, which my father sometimes brought home from work. Strangely enough, since I hadn't seen the fish, I wasn't too bothered about losing it. I think if I had actually seen it I would have been just as devastated as when I lost the 'big carp' in our pond, but having never seen a real-life tench I couldn't visualise what I'd lost.

There were no more encounters with unstoppable fish for either myself or my parents, although I think we all caught a steady stream of perch. Just as it was getting dark we packed up and began the long walk back around the mere to the car. We passed a fellow angler, only to find him playing a powerful fish, and he asked my father if he would stay and net the fish for him. I remember that he had a bright flashlight and my father had to hold the net in one hand and the light in the other as the fish approached the net. I saw a commotion in the water and my father lifting the net, complete with the fish, onto the bank. And there, lying in the net was a beautiful, sublime... tench. The angler and my father agreed that it was 'about three and a half pounds' and it was soon slid back into the water. The contrast between that tench, not just the size, and the fish that I was used to catching was immense: I was genuinely astonished at how beautiful it was. I said to my father, I'm going to fish for tench from now on. Fair enough, he said, with a smile. A tiny seed had been planted which was to grow into a glorious lifelong obsession.

One morning, a couple of weeks later – it must have been during the school holidays – I got up with my parents and announced that I was going 'tench fishing' down to the pond. They didn't really respond as they continued with the daily bustle of getting my father fed and watered (filled with tea, which had to be passed from one cup to another until it was cool enough for him to drink) and out of the door by seven fifteen exactly. By half past seven, I'd had my breakfast and was sat fishing down at the pond. One recent innovation was that I'd stopped using the little fold-away chair and had replaced it with a plank of wood supported at each end by a column of bricks, a much more stable fishing platform.

Groundbait was lobbed out and a piece of bread paste dropped into the middle of the baited area. Bubbles soon started to appear, and my excitement grew as I anticipated the first bite. Three gardens away from me, another angler turned up, a priest from one of the local churches, and his rod was soon bent into a nice fish which turned out to be a crucian of about half a pound. I was ever so slightly jealous. I watched him return the fish only to find when looking back to my float that I couldn't find it. This wasn't too unusual, as I didn't sink my line in those days and sometimes there was enough surface drift to drag the float under as the bread paste was significantly heavier than the float. I struck anyway, just to be on the safe side... and all hell broke loose as a fish charged around my swim. Whereas the crucian carp tended to give dogged, 'jag, jag, jag' fights this one tore around like a fish possessed, but steady pressure (i.e. heaving) soon brought it to the edge and as I slid it up onto the mud at the edge of the water – I didn't have the presence of mind to grab my landing net – I realised that I had caught my very first tench. It was the first I'd ever seen from our little pond, although I'd heard rumours of other people catching them and at one and a half pounds exactly – kitchen scales having been utilised once again – it was my first one-pound fish and therefore my biggest fish too. It was placed into the keepnet for inspection by my father when he returned home for his dinner. I think I caught a crucian carp later that morning but I can't be sure, as the memory is dominated by my first tench, but I do recall my father watching as I showed him the contents of his keepnet and, yet again, him being almost as happy as I was.

Two more obsessional seeds were planted during an autumnal day on Tabley Mere. This was another old estate lake, irregularly shaped and only fishable from a boat. The banks were either heavily overgrown with trees and shrubs or covered in dense beds of bulrushes. Trees that had fallen into the margins had been left there to rot, providing perches for large numbers of herons. I must have been seven or eight, as I was still using my white solid fibre glass rod and the three of us were to be joined by my Uncle John. Tabley Mere was his favourite fishing spot; I have a very distant memory of my father deciding to fish there as opposed to Booths Mere specifically at my uncle's request. I was really looking forward to the day's fishing, as I'd never fished from a boat before, never spun for pike, or even seen a real live pike. Best of all, my parents said that the mere was full of jack pike and I was certain to see at least one caught, and had a very good chance of catching one myself.

The day of the trip dawned dull, and by nine o'clock we were all – apart from my Uncle John, whom I presume must have been working overnight and didn't therefore join us till mid-morning – sitting in the boat spinning away. At dusk, some eight or nine hours later, we were still in the boat fishing, having covered every square inch of the mere without so much as a sniff of a pike. To be fair to my parents, they hadn't fished there since I was born and I'm guessing that in the intervening years the number of pike had reduced, unknown to them, quite dramatically. Not that the lack of fish affected my enjoyment too much; just being in with a chance of a pike and being in a boat was good enough for me. There was something special about being away from the bank, drifting around amongst the fallen leaves, at times being almost close enough to the wildfowl to touch them. Boats and pike – both stored away at the back of my mind for future reference.

Another little aside: you'll get used to these by the end of the book. I came across my old ADAC Club Card from my pre-teenage years while doing a little research for this book and looked at the 'Club Record Fish List' on the back inside page. This would be in the early 1970s and makes for interesting reading, because it shows how different the fishing was back then as well as how much lower my expectations were in general, and I'm guessing for other anglers too. Here are a few excerpts:

–   Barbel – unclaimed (the club only had two rivers, the Bollin and Dane and in those days neither contained barbel).

- Carp 15lb 6oz
- Crucian Carp 2lb 6oz
- Pike 15lb 9oz
- Tench 6lb 13oz 8dr

These days, none of the above fish would raise an eyebrow, except possibly the crucian carp, and even then, I'm not sure there are that many hardened crucian carp fanatics out there any more.

One of the other joys of fishing ADAC waters was talking to other anglers when the fishing was slow, ie when I'd gone thirty minutes without a bite. I don't think any of them were unfriendly, but two were always willing to chat with me. Arthur Lea was the holder of the club carp record, the 15-pounder, and he had me enthralled as he described its capture in fine detail. Keith Crowther, hair always perfectly Brylcreemed back in place and pipe always lit, was another helpful soul - someone H T Sheringham would have described as a 'contemplative angler' – and I bumped into the pair of them regularly on ADAC waters well into my twenties. They never hesitated to offer advice and answer my questions and didn't take exception to my sometimes-over-enthusiastic approach to my fishing, so I just assumed all anglers were like that. They weren't, as I would find out later.

You might think that with a positive smorgasbord of fish available at these waters, most of them considerably bigger than anything I had available back home, I would lose interest in fishing in 'my' own little pond. Not at all. The more I fished, the more I wanted to go fishing, and the pond was the easiest way to satisfy this craving. And it *was* a craving, at times a complete addiction even in my pre-teenage years, although the obsession had distinct parameters that had to be met in terms of time (it had to be morning, preferably starting at dawn), species (crucian carp, of course), and methods (float-fishing, and by now, the float had to be red).

Every now and again, I would bend one of these parameters just a little; for instance, the first time I fished at night. I was eleven or maybe twelve and it must have been during the Whit holiday, because I was fishing every morning with the boy next door, the one staying with his grandmother. I wish I could remember his name, but I can't. I can recall minute details about some of our fishing sessions together, but I can't recall his name. I know he had a very attractive sister called Juliet and lived in Sunderland, so that narrows it down a little. If he ever reads this book and recognises himself, then do please get in touch.

The second week of the holiday was very warm and for some reason I thought it would make a change to fish at night; whether this was due to having a tent pitched at the bottom of the garden or reading about Dick Walker catching his record carp at night, I'm not sure. Maybe it was due to the fact that Mr Walker pitched his tent before catching his carp and this association of ideas produced the desire to fish at night? Night fishing presented a problem though – how would we see our floats? A trip to the local fishing tackle shop, Joe Dyson's in Altrincham, was therefore required to see if such a thing as a luminous float existed.

Dyson's was one of two tackle shops in Altrincham, the other being Bailey's, and with two other hardware shops (we called them 'Ironmongers' in those days) in the area also selling bait and a limited amount of tackle we were well served on that front. Going to Dysons was always a big deal: the smell of the maggots combined with the smoke from Mr Dyson's pipe made for a unique fug or 'atmosphere'. Then there were the rows of floats under a pane of glass on the counter, the lines of small cardboard boxes behind him which contained either spool after spool of line of differing quality and strength with brand and breaking strain written on the front ('6lb BS Fog') or packets of hooks ('Eyed size 10'). Above these boxes, and requiring the use of a small ladder, were boxes containing reels, including Mitchell reels, which were way out of the range of our family's budget despite my father saying 'Mitchell make the best fixed spool reels in the world'. There was also a board on to which were pinned photographs of big, for those days, fish, or newspaper cuttings from local papers. One which always caught my eye was a picture of a teenage boy under the headline of 'local boy catches huge pike'. The narrative told the tale of how he'd caught the fish, I think it weighed just under 15lb, which for years had terrorised both fish and waterfowl alike in the brickworks pool at Mobberley. This was another ADAC water that I had occasionally fished with my parents and again caught only roach and perch. That combination of 'brickworks pool' and 'pike' was lodged in my mind though, for future reference.

Having caught the bus into Altrincham, I and the boy-without-a-name went into Dyson's and asked Mr Dyson (always Mister, never Joe) if he had such a thing as a luminous float. After all, our watch faces were luminous and glowed in the dark, so it should be feasible to have a luminous float too, shouldn't it? Mr Dyson was a short, thin man with a grey moustache and a pipe permanently placed between his teeth. Add to this a brown shopkeeper's coat with a multitude of pockets and he presented quite a stern persona, although in reality, he was always very helpful. 'A luminous float, eh?,' a deep draw on the pipe. 'Let me see'. The ladders were summoned and from a box on top of the reels another smaller box was produced from which two items were placed on the counter. The first was a small plastic bag containing white plastic floats about five inches long with the last quarter inch being made of what looked very much like the same material that you'd see on your watch face. Another deep draw on the pipe and a pause. 'These are quite good, but you need to charge them up first, you know, with a torch'.

The second item he produced was a small tin – the same size I used to buy to paint my Airfix airplanes and ships – of Humbrol luminous paint. He explained that it was the same material but you could use it to coat an existing float to make a bigger surface area. By pooling our money, we were able to buy two floats and a tin of paint and on returning home we set about painting two large peacock quills with said paint. A quick test drive of both sets of floats – under the blankets of my bed – seemed to show good results, but, just in case, we also borrowed a couple of torches and a supply of batteries.

Neither my parents nor the grandmother next door had any qualms about us fishing at night by ourselves, and by about nine o'clock we were ready to take up our positions on the wooden bench-supported-by-bricks at the bottom of our garden. The tent contained provisions: sandwiches, biscuits, cakes and pop; suitable reading matter if we ever got bored (The Fisherman's Bedside Book and Confessions of a Carp Fisher) and a large supply of batteries. Since we were to be fishing all night, an extra-large portion of groundbait – the good stuff from Dyson's, as opposed to the home-made variety, as this was a special occasion – was thrown out into our respective swims, which were, of course, only a couple of feet apart. This went totally against what we'd normally do as my father's mantra on groundbaiting was 'little and often,' but we weren't sure we'd be able to see where we were throwing the stuff in the middle of the night.

Even though it had clouded over, it must have been nearly eleven o'clock before it was completely dark, this being the end of May or early June, and we soon realised the limitations of our various floats. A charge with the torch only produced a couple of minutes of 'glow,' and even then, it was a glow we could hardly see. In the end, we decided to use our torches, and by angling the beam of light from a point to our left we found we could use one torch to see both of our floats and thus conserve batteries. I don't recall us getting any bites to begin with, but this didn't matter – the stillness, silence and the darkness had added an extra dimension to our fishing and provided enough excitement. I knew every feature of our garden and the pond intimately, but at night everything seemed *different*: the too-wit-to-woo of owls; rustles in the undergrowth could have been anything (cats, more than likely) and every now and again the splash of a fish out in the black water, to be followed eventually by our torch beam picking up the ripples.

At some point in the night I had the first bite. The float was there one minute and gone the next. Strangely enough, it took me a couple of seconds to realise what had happened and my strike met no resistance. The next bite produced a much better-timed strike and I was instantly connected to a decent fish which charged around the swim – how I didn't tangle up with the adjacent float, I'll never know – and a few seconds later (my creed was still 'thou shalt not let any fish take line') my second-ever tench, about the same size as my first (every chance that it was the same fish), was dragged into the landing net. What a result, I thought, this night fishing lark is absolutely brilliant!

I don't remember either of us getting any more bites till dawn, when we both missed a couple of sail-a-way bites that you would describe as unmissable. I do remember that the morning was extremely warm and oppressive, perfect fishing conditions, but that my friend decided that he was too tired and disappeared to his bed at breakfast time. Much to my annoyance, my parents decided it was too dangerous for me to carry on by myself, as I might doze off and fall into the water, so I too had to pack up and head for my bed. Night fishing is great, I thought, as I drifted off to sleep, and yet another little seed was planted, although it would be many years before I started night fishing regularly.

The summer before I started secondary school produced another first for me from our little pond. I'll come on to this shortly, but first, another little aside. One of the great joys of angling is 'firsts'. Whether it be your first fish of any species, ie first carp, tench, pike, bass or ray or your first 1lb fish, then 5lb and ultimately your first 10lb and joy of joys, 20lb fish, you remember these captures intimately. Every feature of the capture becomes imprinted on your brain in the same way that, for example, you can remember the birth of a child or your wedding day. Or is it just me? I look at today's angling generation and I have some sympathy for them. It took me years to accomplish the above feats, each one a cherished adrenaline-fuelled memory, but today a teenage coarse angler could quite conceivably accomplish all but the magic '20lb fish' in his first few 'sessions'; it's not inconceivable that he might even achieve the magic twenty too. I can't believe that the satisfaction, the sheer buzz, of achieving these milestones could be anywhere near as great when you *expect* to do this so quickly.

Anyway, back to my next 'first'. My first mirror carp. The number of hours I had fished in this little pond without even seeing a mirror carp makes the following captures all the stranger.

The morning was much the same as many mornings I fished there and started well enough with a small crucian carp on my first cast.

I put the early success down to the fact that I was using a new float, one of a pair of free ones that came with the *Angling Times* which I now received weekly instead of the *Beano* or *Hornet*. It was black with a wide red tip; very important, that red tip, as it sat perfectly in the water and was easily visible even in the low light conditions at dawn. When fishing in my pond I used to cast to the same spot. You have to understand that this was very important to me; the float had to be in _exactly_ the same spot each time, and deviation by no more than a couple of inches was not acceptable! It was a spot in the middle of a green patch of water, the 'green' resulting from the reflection of a small tree on the far bank. The float, when viewed against this green backdrop, would appear as a red tip, then a gap (the black bit), with another red tip – the reflection of the tip on the water – below it. When you got a bite, the two red tips would merge before disappearing. Even to this day, if I have the opportunity to fish 'into the green,' I'll take it, even if it isn't quite the best spot to be fishing in.

My next fish was 'the' large goldfish known to us – it was often seen near the surface, floating around like an overgrown carrot – and it weighed just over a pound. I wasn't really pleased to catch it, as goldfish weren't 'proper' fish, were they? And since my swim was a mass of bubbles, I was hoping for some more crucians or maybe even another tench. It didn't take long for me to get another bite and this time it was a proper fish. My rod hooped over as it had never done before – God only knows how my hook knot didn't come undone – as a large fish charged around my swim. I could normally subdue even the biggest crucian in seconds, but this continued to charge around for almost half a minute before I even saw it. When I did see it, I realised it was a mirror carp of sorts: dark green with golden scales, but most definitely a mirror carp. It weighed two and a half pounds and left me absolutely astonished. Why had I never seen this fish before? I'd never even heard of other anglers catching such a fish. Fifteen minutes later I caught another identical 'mirror carp,' albeit a pound smaller. Stranger still, but what the hell, they were mirror carp and the biggest fish I'd ever caught from the pond.

Curiously, I never saw those carp again or heard of them being caught. Had someone recently 'stocked' them into the pond? Did they not survive capture? I don't recall hearing of anyone seeing their dead bodies, and I have no explanation for either their appearance or disappearance.

At this point in my life, I would have been quite happy if someone had told me that I would have to spend the rest of my life float fishing for carp and tench in this little pond. Yes, I enjoyed fishing other waters, but I looked forward to the familiarity and the security I derived from fishing 'my' pond. Thankfully, although these feelings would also manifest themselves myriad times in later years, I did become a little bit more adventurous in my obsessions.

My father in the punt on Booths Mere in the 50s with a fine net of roach

Booths Mere in the 50s again, and my father with a 4lb tench

My mother with a small pike from Tabley Mere, again sometime in the 50s

Skating on the pond circa 1969

The Fire Brigade to the rescue, circa 1972!

The author with a small tench

A fine net of crucians

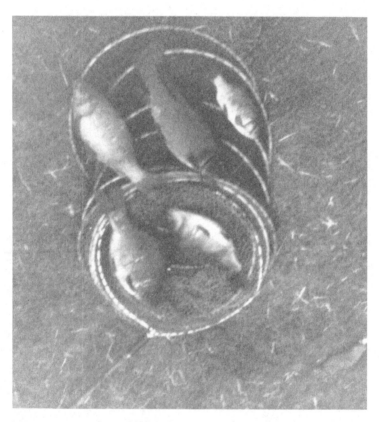

Crucian carp, a tench, a goldfish and two mirror carp that were never seen again!

CHAPTER THREE

DISCOVERING ANGLING LITERATURE, AND CATCHING MY FIRST PIKE

As I approached my teenage years, a new school beckoned, a grammar school no less, having passed my 'Eleven Plus' exam, and for the first time in my young life, matters other than my fishing started to get serious. Neither of my parents came from wealthy backgrounds, especially my mother, and it was impressed upon me in no uncertain terms that good qualifications were essential to getting a good job. Sciences were to provide the key to my future, whether it be in engineering, like my father, or medicine, like my mother; not a nurse, but a doctor would do very nicely thank you as a career.

Academic performance was pushed very hard at this school and it was made clear to me by my parents when the summer's exams loomed large that revision came before fishing. Fishing wasn't banned as such, but it was frowned upon in a sideways manner with comments such as 'you can go fishing as long as you think you've done enough revision to get good marks'. But what was 'enough revision' and what were 'good marks'?

School did have some plus points though. It had a library, and in that library was a whole range of magazines. Whereas most boys headed directly for *Paris Match*, which held the potential for a hint of naked female flesh, I headed straight for *Angling* magazine. I cannot overstate just how important this magazine was in both providing and developing the obsessional seeds of my angling life. The writing was brilliant, and each issue eagerly awaited. Some articles have stayed with me to this day: an article on tench fishing from wooden punts on Blenheim Lake in Oxfordshire complete with photo of two anglers sitting back in their punt waiting for a bite stirred something in the back of my mind (Booths Mere, Tabley Mere... punt... tench...) These were the first shoots of an obsession which has endured to this day, as you will find out.

Another article was entitled 'Not all cod live at Dungie' and written by either Ian Gillespie or Jim Gibbinson. It was about catching cod from the beach at Aldeburgh at night. Not only was it well written, but it featured a black and white photo of an angler, complete with headtorch, walking out of the surf – visible only as white lines in the background – and carrying a large cod. What a picture! To use modern parlance, because I didn't have a word in my vocabulary then to describe it, it was quite literally the coolest picture I'd ever seen and it made a huge impression on me.

All articles written by Clive Gammon and John Darling were also consumed ravenously. I'd never been bass fishing, never been to Ireland - I'd never been abroad with the exception of Wales, which didn't really count - but their description of bass fishing in Ireland, and in particular on the Dingle Peninsula, had me transported there to the extent that I swear I could almost smell the surf. Along with time in the dining hall – chips with everything – some of my happiest school times were spent in that library.

Another aside now follows: I've always wondered if my memory exaggerated the quality of the writing, so I decided to track down, if I could, some back copies of the magazine. A trawl of the internet produced four copies of the old *Angling* magazine, including the one with the Blenheim tench article, but alas, not the article with my beloved cod photograph. Had the quality of the writing stood the test of time? Yes, it certainly had!

By this time I was also reading, and re-reading, my father's angling books. Particular favourites were two masterpieces by the great 'BB' (Denys Watkins-Pitchford): *The Fisherman's Bedside Book* and *Confessions of a Carp Fisher,* along with *Coarse Fishing with the Experts* and Clive Gammon's *Salt Water Fishing in Ireland.* The latter book was unusual in as much as sea fishing was restricted to our two-week holiday in Anglesey every year – more of this to come – and I never remember my father ever expressing any wishes to go to Ireland. Maybe he just liked the quality of the writing, or more likely, someone at work had given him the book to read and never asked for it back.

Grammar school also put me into contact with a lad of my own age who turned out to be just as obsessed with his fishing as I was. We still fish together to this day, and our angling interests have often run in tandem for years, whilst at other times, we have followed different directions. His name was John Woodhouse. We shared obsessions with carp, tench, pike and rays, but my interest in bass and barbel never quite matched his.

The trauma of the long summer holidays finishing and new school year starting never disappeared throughout my academic life, but just before the start of my second year at grammar school, my father, in an effort to relieve this depression, suggested that we should have a day's fishing in the punt on Booths Mere. This was a first for me, as although we'd fished a few times from the bank, we had never availed ourselves of the old and somewhat leaky wooden punt.

The other trauma, albeit one with an upside, that I'd recently encountered was discovering that I needed glasses. I'd increasingly noticed that I was having difficulty seeing my float, my friend would be saying 'you've got a bite' and I'd be squinting and saying 'huh?'

I'd also started to creep closer and closer to the television to see the football results come in on the 'teleprinter' on the BBC's Saturday afternoon sports programme Grandstand. For younger readers, this was a device that resembled a small dog with flapping ears which ran across the bottom of the screen, printing the results as it moved. Well, that's what it looked like to me. In those days, unless you had money to burn, which we didn't, you were lumbered with thick, square, brown NHS glasses which gave all your schoolmates licence to take the mickey out of you, which they duly did in my case. The upside was that I could see my float with total clarity again, which did somewhat compensate for the mickey-taking.

My father collected maggots and 'boat keys' from Dyson's on the Friday tea time and Saturday morning – he'd given up his Saturday morning overtime to take me fishing, a grand gesture indeed as money must have been tight, not that I ever realised that – saw us both rowing out into what was known as the 'deep hole' in the middle of the mere, where there were two permanent posts for us to tie up against. It was just me and my father, as my mother had stayed at home to look after my little brother, who had appeared a couple of years previously. Apologies to my little bro, but his appearance obviously created less of an impact in my life than a tench or mirror carp! No no, not quite true!

Our intention was to simply sit there and catch whatever came along; almost certainly perch, a good chance of roach and maybe some small bream as well. We had with us our float rods and one of my sea fishing rods, an eight-foot-long, solid yellow fibre glass beast of a rod, and a reel of unknown make which contained 18lb line. I've no idea why I'd taken that outfit with me, but fate was going to be very kind to me on this day. On starting to tackle up, my father dropped his float, which ended up under the seat of the boat; this was retrieved easily enough but was found to have become tangled with someone's old pike trace. The trace and hooks were in good condition and my father put them into his basket. The trace was soon forgotten about as we both started to catch perch, roach and small bream; not quite a fish a cast, but enough bites to keep us entertained.

The 'deep hole' itself was roughly circular and about thirty yards wide in diameter. Outside it the water was about three feet in depth, but the hole itself was eight feet deep with quite steep sides and around the edge of it could be seen shoals of small roach flicking and splashing on the surface.

As the morning progressed into a still and warm afternoon, the fishing slowed, and having gone nearly fifteen minutes without a bite, I was contemplating reducing the depth at which I was fishing and having a cast across towards the shallower water where the roach were playing. And then it happened. Without any warning or fanfare, all the roach threw themselves out of the water and up into the air, to be followed a second later by dark torpedo which launched itself after the fleeing fish. 'Pike!' my father and I said in perfect stereo, and to be honest, regardless of what else happened, the day could now be called a success – this was the first pike I'd ever actually seen.

But the day was about to get even better. My father dug deep into his basket and produced a bright orange pike bung, almost as big as a tennis ball, and this was combined with the pike trace from the bottom of the boat to convert my sea rod into a (very) heavy-duty pike outfit. A roach was sacrificed from our keepnet and I was told to swing the float out towards where we'd last seen the pike strike. Surely it wouldn't take more than a few seconds for it to find a poor roach which was fighting for its freedom? Well, thirty minutes passed and even the roach was getting bored.

My recall of angling events varies; I look at some photos from years ago and remember nothing except a vague feeling of how I *felt,* but the memory of a lot of the key angling milestones in my life is usually very sharp, more so than other milestones. For instance, I couldn't tell you what we ate at our wedding reception dinner but I could tell you what I had in my sandwiches when I caught my first 20lb fish (luncheon meat with plenty of tomato sauce, if you must know).

The exception to the above is that, unfortunately, I can't remember if I then had a 'run' or if I started to wind in and the pike grabbed the roach, but what I can remember is suddenly being attached to a small pike which leapt clear of the water before compliantly being allowed to be dragged into our relatively small landing net. The whole episode can't have lasted more than ten seconds. Thankfully, as we had no pliers – forceps hadn't been invented then, at least not in our angling universe – or 'pike gag,' it was very lightly hooked in the top lip which tends to suggest that it had indeed grabbed the roach as I was retrieving it. Whatever the manner of its capture, it weighed 3lb exactly according to our Salter spring balance and was much admired before being returned to the water. This was indeed a special day: first pike seen, first pike caught and biggest ever fish caught. And just to top everything off completely, my father, bless him, decided that we should have a Chinese takeaway for tea to celebrate, a once-a-year treat in our house, and he also suggested that we return to Booths Mere the following weekend. If, of course, I wanted to…

The next week passed interminably slowly but with a mounting tension as my father said that they had 'a rush on at work' and there was a possibility that he'd have to work all day Saturday. He wouldn't know about the work situation for certain until Friday afternoon. In addition to this, he would not therefore be able to 'book' the boat until the Friday teatime and there was always the possibility that someone else might book it first. Friday teatime found me stood by the door waiting for him; the smile on his face and the tin of maggots in his hand told me all I needed to know. He'd also bought some more pike traces, three much smaller pike bungs and some swan shot to help 'cock' these new floats.

The following morning saw us back on Booths Mere in the identical spot to the previous weekend. The weather was near identical too, but the fishing was much slower and it took us more than an hour to start catching our live baits. This time it was my father's turn to get the first run and after an extremely short fight – on his own sea rod and reel – a pike of similar size to the one I'd caught was soon in the net. A pike 'gag' was used to secure the unfortunate fish's jaws (and yes, I am cringing when writing this, but it was the early seventies) and a pair of pliers soon had the hooks removed.

Nothing came initially to my pike bait, so my father suggested that I recast every fifteen minutes or so, starting out at two o'clock (imagine twelve o'clock being directly in front of you) and then gradually working round to six o'clock. He'd do likewise, but obviously in the opposite direction.

I got to about four o'clock before I saw my float sliding across the surface. 'Wait,' my father said, 'until the float stops, and then strike as soon as it starts moving again'. I'm cringing again, but this was accepted wisdom in those days, certainly as far as my father understood it.

Not surprisingly, having done what my father suggested, my strike met with some resistance. Some, but not much, and a pike of maybe 1½ lb was soon in the net, although with the tackle I was using I could quite easily have swung it in to hand in the same way I was doing with the roach and perch on my float rod. Thankfully, being so small, it hadn't been able to completely turn the roach livebait and was only lightly hooked in the scissors of its jaws.

By late afternoon, we'd had no more runs and the flow of perch and roach had dried up. My father looked at his watch and said that we'd give it one more hour, and I guessed he was 'developing quite a thirst' again. He also suggested we move across to the far side of the deep hole where we'd seen a small shoal of roach disturbing the surface. Our last bit of groundbait and a handful of maggots were deposited into this new swim and our live baits positioned at two o'clock (mine) and nine o'clock (his) respectively.

After about ten minutes my pike bung started to behave strangely: it didn't slide away or move far across the water but it did start moving in a slow circle in front of me. Pike, or over active livebait? My father said he thought it was a pike and that I should give it a 'gentle but firm strike'.

I did as I was told and instantly found myself connected to something that was much bigger than anything I'd hooked before. A few weeks earlier I'd watched an angler play a large fish on a television programme – it must have either been 'Out of Town' with Jack Hargreaves or 'Angling Today' with Terry Thomas – and he used a revolutionary (to me!) technique called 'backwinding' when playing this fish. I decided that this was what I'd do with the next big fish – or should that have been first? – that I hooked.

Unusually for me, this was good self-advice and my newly adopted tactic of backwinding coped admirably with the slow but powerful lunges that the fish was making. The fish swam in gradually decreasing circles in front of me until at last, in reality maybe five minutes later, a large pike rolled on the surface next to the boat. To my young eyes, 'large' was an understatement; it was huge!

Now this presented us with a slight problem: how on earth were we going to get this into our little landing net? I needn't have worried. My father manoeuvred the net under the back end of the pike while 'chinning' the fish with his other hand and in one movement lifted it into the boat. It can only have been very lightly hooked, as by the time it had been removed from the net, the hooks had fallen out.

I reached for the spring balance to weigh it. 'I wouldn't bother with that' said my father, 'it only goes up to 8lb and that fish is nearer 12lb than eight'. I ignored his advice, tried to weigh the pike and promptly broke the scales. I then decided to do something which shames me still to this day. I had to know the weight of this fish, and I also needed photographic evidence of its capture, so I left it to slowly expire on the bottom of the boat...

On returning home we ascertained that it's weight was 11lb 3oz. Photographs were taken and the fish buried in the back garden, a terrible end for such a beautiful fish. That was the first and last time that I knowingly killed a pike.

I was now obsessed: I had a serious pike addiction. I'm sure one of the reasons behind this was the fact that I had so little opportunity to actually do any pike fishing. There were no pike-containing local waters that I could get to under my own steam (there was one, as you will find out later, but I didn't realise it at the time) so I was totally reliant on my father to take me with him. Interestingly, this particular obsession was wholly species orientated – I needed to catch pike but didn't mind where or how. Some of my other fixations, as you will discover, were not just species related but place, time, method and even swim related as well, up to the point that it just didn't feel right unless, for example, my float was in exactly the right spot. A psychiatrist would have had a field day with me, most likely still could!

Despite needing to maximise his overtime, my father took me pike fishing whenever he could over the next few years, and the months from September to March often saw us either in the punt or, if he had to work the Saturday mornings, on the banks of Booths Mere. In those days, I was convinced that live baits were the only way to consistently catch pike. Of course, I'd read articles in *Angling* Magazine about catching pike on deadbaits such as mackerel, sardines and sprats, but I gave these up as a bad job after using sprats for all of one day on a pool in nearby Altrincham, King George's Pool, a pool which may not have actually contained any pike, but in those days a *possibility* of containing pike was good enough for me.

The best place I knew for catching small roach and rudd was my only little pond, so I started to fish it into the winter months for the first time. Providing I scaled down to small hooks – size 18s, which were classed as small in my world – attached to finer lengths of nylon, and used maggots for bait, I was able to catch a steady stream of small fish. A few trips come back to me quite readily: there was a trip out in the punt which produced my second double-figure pike of exactly ten pounds, according to my father, whose guesswork I now trusted implicitly, and another trip out in the punt with both parents, my little brother having been despatched to one of his friends for the day, that produced an eleven-pound fish for me right at the end of the trip. I seem to recall being on the verge of a major strop as both parents had caught pike that day and I'd remained runless until every rod apart from my pike rod had been packed away.

Under the terms of the angling club's agreement with the owners of Booths Mere, juniors were not allowed to fish unless accompanied by an adult member, so I had no opportunity to fish there by myself. I needed a club water that contained pike and where Junior members could fish without adult supervision... and then I remembered the photograph in Joe Dyson's tackle shop, the young lad with the pike that had 'terrorised the local waterfowl'. Mobberley brickworks pool was only a couple of acres in size, deep, with heavily wooded banks and as the name suggests had been dug for its clay, which was used in some nearby brickworks that had long since disappeared. The water was gin clear and on a still day you could see the old iron rails of a tramway on a clay bank which ran downwards through the middle of the pool. It wasn't too far away; maybe my parents could be persuaded to drop me off there occasionally?

Indeed they could. And so it was that one very mild, still February day during the spring half-term break from school, my father found himself cycling to work so that my mother could have the car in order to drop me off at the brickworks pool. I was dropped off at the side of the road, complete with a small bucket containing six little roach, and told to be back there waiting to be collected by no later than five-thirty that afternoon.

I picked a swim about three or four yards wide on the bank nearest the road with overhanging branches to both my left and right that trailed into the water. The same trees formed a canopy above my head, but by kneeling I could cast a bait out without catching the foliage. I soon had a float rod, complete with little red float and maggot hook bait, set up by the left-hand branches and a small red pike bung, complete with livebait, set up just beyond the right-hand branches. It gently bounced away, giving the impression that at any second it could slide away and leave me attached to a pike, and a pike of any size would have been welcome and would make the day a complete success.

My initial enthusiasm soon gave way to restlessness. The restlessness manifested itself in me wandering around the pool looking for what might prove to be better swims. I came to a small clump of reeds, which oddly enough for a completely still day, were waving around in the air. The water around the reeds was also very murky and I could see leaves and bits of weed vortexing up to the surface. Most odd. And then a huge tail broke the surface and slowly waved at me. A carp's tail, and a massive one too!

I stood there completely transfixed until the reeds stopped waving and the water started to clear; for some reason, it never occurred to me to get my float tackle and drop a hookful of maggots into the dirty water. In hindsight, I think that I just didn't associate maggots with catching big carp, or maybe I realised that hooking such a beast on light float tackle in the middle of a red bed would have produced nothing but a broken line. I think the former rather than the latter, because I was not averse to trying to hook fish in impossible situations.

It was early afternoon before either float stirred and after a couple of slow bobs the little red float with the maggots slowly disappeared. I struck, missed and wondered where my float had gone. I followed my line from my rod tip up, up and further up until I saw my float sitting high up in the overhead branches. Even by standing on my creel – yes yes, another Christmas or birthday present – I couldn't reach the float, and eventually I had to pull for the break which duly occurred. It was my favourite float, red of course, although the shade of red had varied as it had required repainting on a number of occasions.

Its loss punctured my upbeat mood, until I looked round to see my pike float sliding away from me. A run! My first ever solo pike run! OK, I thought, don't strike too soon, let it turn the bait first, but the float just kept on going. I waited for ages, or more than likely about thirty seconds, but when you're thirteen or fourteen years old and your hands are trembling with the excitement that comes from such a huge adrenaline rush time does appear to stand still. A gentle but firm strike met with... nothing. I'd missed it.

I stood there, mouth open, for a good minute before winding in the slightly dazed, but still alive, little roach and depositing it as close as possible to where it had been when I'd had the run. Of course, I should have put it out closer to where it had been when I struck. This was a disaster of major proportions, and sadly for me there was to be no reprieve that day, no second run or bite of any other description on either maggot or livebait. Still, I knew now that there were definitely pike to be caught there, and I thought I knew, purely on the basis of that one run, how to catch them.

A return trip was negotiated for a Sunday shortly after, but it had to be postponed as the country was gripped by a sudden drop in temperature which left the brickworks pool frozen for nearly three weeks and for reasons I can't remember, I wasn't able to return there in the short time between the ice disappearing and the end of the season. The addiction was therefore quite literally put on ice until the following autumn. I had no inclination to pike-fish in the summer – it wouldn't have felt right. Like so many of my angling obsessions, it was limited to a specific period of the year.

It was just before Christmas in that year – on my birthday no less – that I finally broke my brickworks pool pike duck. Birthdays were always special in our house; there might not have been extravagant presents, but the whole day was made to be special and 'indulgences' were often granted. Having finished school the day previously, I pleaded with my parents to be taken to the brickworks pool for a day's piking, knowing full well that they would find it difficult to say no. Of course, they agreed, and I was doubly excited: birthday presents, a day's piking and doubtless an opportunity to try out the box of spinners that I'd asked for as a present.

The evening before, I waited nervously for the weather forecast... thick cloud and cold at 3°C, but no frost. I was so excited that sleep only came fitfully to me that night and at some point, I looked out of the bedroom window to check that the sky wasn't clearing; a cloudless sky would have meant a sharp frost, ice, and no fishing trip. But what I saw was – snow! This was potentially disastrous, and I spent the rest of the night repeatedly getting out of bed to check on the depth of snow. Although by present-opening time it had stopped snowing, there must have been at least three inches of the stuff on the ground.

I shuffled down to the pond at the bottom of our garden; it wasn't frozen but it was covered in what my father called 'snow broth,' a layer of snow over an inch thick. I found a stone that I thought to be about the same weight as one of my live baits and lobbed it out – it just about sank through the snowy upper layer. My father said it wasn't worth going as nothing would feed in these temperatures, but my mother, very reluctantly, offered to take us (my angling buddy, John, from school was coming as well) if we wanted to go. I faltered a little, partly because the scenario I'd created in my head certainly didn't include a snow-covered pool, but my buddy turned up all ready to go fishing, so I decided, what the hell, let's go for it.

We slipped and slid through the snow-covered country lanes until at last we arrived at the pool. My mother has recounted many times since then just how terrified she was on that drive, but, bless her, she never considered turning back and disappointing me on my birthday. We parked ourselves at the 'top end' of the pool, which was narrower and where the overhanging trees pushed further out into the water, meaning that there was less 'snow broth' there than in the previous spot I'd fished.

We divvied up the live baits and started fishing. I cast my bait out towards where I knew there to be a weedbed, the roach landing with an audible 'plop' before slowly sinking through the snow. My little red pike bung wobbled every now and again to indicate that there was still some life in the poor fish. My friend fished just across a little inlet from me, and we could see each other's bungs.

It didn't take long for the cold to start seeping through into our fingers and toes – there was no thermal underwear in those days (actually, there was: a rather large guy called Don Bridgewood advertised 'Damart thermals' on the back of the *Angling Times*, but we couldn't afford such luxuries) However, I had taken special precautions to guard against the cold and had sneaked away some of my father's whisky to add to our coffee. I had to top the bottle up with water or it would have been obvious that some had been removed, and I had to look away when my father poured himself a large one on Christmas Day and announced with some astonishment that the whisky was 'off'.

Despite the whisky, sitting still proved a toe-numbing experience, so I soon proceeded to set up my float rod and attach one of my new spinners, my parents having not disappointed me on the presents front. I had to attach a quite large 'drilled bullet' lead to the spinner just to get it through the snow on the water before wandering down to the far end of the lake where I spun away for twenty minutes without, unsurprisingly, any sign of action.

My father was usually right about most things angling-wise and I'd resigned myself to another pikeless day when I spotted my friend running along the bank. I assumed he was doing this to keep warm, but he wasn't. He came up to me and uttered the magical words: 'you've got a run!'.

I dropped my spinning outfit in the snow and raced back to my swim at breakneck speed to find that my bung had vanished and line was slowly falling off the open spool of my reel. This time I waited a good minute or two before striking. I had no idea if the pike had stopped and turned the bait, as once the float was underneath the snow it couldn't break back through. I struck, and, joy of joys, there was resistance. I carefully played the fish back towards me – after all, I didn't want it to snap my eighteen-pound line or put undue strain on my heavy-duty sea rod – and eventually the pike appeared underneath my rod tip. We both had a good view of it, about the three-pound mark... and we both saw it drop the roach with my hooks still attached.

Time stood still for a few seconds and a deep despair welled up inside me, but the birthday gods were on my side, as the pike decided that a roach that couldn't escape was an early Christmas present that just couldn't be ignored, so it picked the roach up again and slowly moved away. This time, I waited even longer before striking and, having hooked the fish, kept a steady pressure on her as I drew her into the waiting net with the minimum of fuss. The elation that this fish brought me was no less than that which came with pike of over twenty pounds in later life. It was lightly hooked, weighed three pounds and four ounces and was photographed before being returned. Unfortunately I was using a 'disposable' camera that had come free with tokens from a cereal packet, and when I returned it to have the photos developed, nothing ever came back.

It was John's turn to have the next piece of action. He suddenly stood up and started peering at his keepnet – we'd put the fish into our respective keepnets to keep them 'fresh' – and then moved his livebait right in to the side of the net. I made the short walk round to see what was happening. Apparently, a small pike had started to attack the roach in his keepnet and he'd dropped his bait straight in front of it. We could both clearly see the pike and watched it pick up the little roach and slowly move away. My friend gave the fish plenty of time but, alas, his strike met with no resistance and despite his best efforts, he had no more action.

On the other hand, a couple of hours later I had another run. There was less drama this time and a slightly smaller pike was soon drawn into the net, weighed, photographed and returned. It was soon time to pack up, as my mother did not want to be driving back through the lanes in darkness.

Of all the memories of this day, the one that is most vivid is of me waiting in our front room, our lounge, no lights on save for the ones on our Christmas tree, waiting for my mother to return with my father, it being far too snowy for him to cycle to work. I couldn't wait to tell him about my pike, my friend's missed fish and, well, everything.

It's been over twelve years since he died and the power of this memory takes me by surprise, bringing a lump to my throat.

CHAPTER FOUR

'PROPER' CARP AND TENCH FISHING, AND THE JOYS OF DOUGH BOBBINS

So as I ambled through my teenage years I'd found a winter obsession that provided me with angling fulfilment. What I needed now was a summer angling obsession; yes, I still fished in my own little pond but I had started to dream of catching some bigger carp now that I could be reasonably assured of catching small crucian carp on virtually every trip. How could I go about making the dream a reality? By this time, courtesy of more Christmas/birthday presents, I'd 'upgraded' my float-fishing rod to a new-fangled glass fibre one (I think it was a 'Milbro Blue Maestro') and acquired the pride and joy of my fishing tackle collection: a Mitchell 810 fixed spool reel. This was top of the range stuff with a 'six-to-one' gear ratio to help match fishermen retrieve their end gear back a few precious seconds earlier than their non-Mitchell-810-using neighbours. Why on earth

I considered this a virtue, I've no idea, but it was certainly the nicest looking reel I ever owned (and I'm still using it today!)

I mulled over all the possibilities while fishing in 'my' pond one morning; it had to be somewhere reasonably local, preferably somewhere I could get to under my own steam, it would help if it was picturesque and it had to contain big carp; well, carp of at least five pounds in weight with the possibility of a double-figure one. I think most of my angling obsessions have started in this way. I just sit and mull over all of the possibilities in a completely random way before finally distilling everything down to a couple of options. I then further refine these options into specific scenarios which will incorporate time of day, weather, a particular swim, a method – even to the point of visualising my float in the water, or, in later years, other forms of bite indication – and finally, a strike resulting in the hooking and landing of my intended quarry. Which would of course be huge. I have always found that one of these scenarios would produce a strange buzz in the pit of my stomach – doubtless, a small release of adrenaline or other endorphin – which would form the obsessional seed.

In later years, when my job would cause me to spend inordinately large amounts of time driving across the UK, I could while away whole journeys creating and discarding or refining such scenarios. Whether or not the seed germinated into a full-blown obsession would then depend on how the reality matched the fantasy, or, just every now and again, exceed it.

I distilled everything down to two options: the local Bridgewater Canal and Mobberley 'New Pool'. They both produced the required buzz, so I decided to try them both.

The canal had one main benefit in that it was close enough for me, and my angling school friend, to walk to, but it wasn't at all like any of the other places we fished, being a concrete jungle with barely a tree in sight. It did, however, contain some quite large carp, as we knew from reading the match reports in the *Angling Times* every week; they showed that the winner was invariably the person who had caught a solitary carp to go along with an assortment of small silver fish.

We made our first experimental foray to the canal on a wet and cold July morning and proceeded to try and copy what we assumed the matchmen's tactics would have been: heap in large quantities of groundbait – made from loaves of mashed white bread, not dried crumb which we couldn't afford to buy in the sort of quantities we were using – and then fish maggots over the top. The experiment didn't last long. My normal float fishing set-up just didn't work on the canal, which had a significant 'flow' to it which continually dragged my float out of position. After three of hours of catching nothing but a couple of 'jacksharps' (sticklebacks) I stormed off back home, the reality being nothing like the fantasy, although in this instance it was my own total inability to adapt to an alien fishing environment that was to blame.

Thoughts then transferred to Mobberley New Pool. As you may have guessed, this was a man-made pool adjacent to the Brickworks Pool (henceforth called 'Mobberley Old Pool' in an act of appalling lack of imagination by the angling club). Irregularly shaped with an island in the middle, it was the brainchild of the aforementioned Keith Crowther, and I suppose it was the seventies equivalent of a 'commercial' fishery but thankfully without the barbel, ide, ghost carp or other monstrosities usually associated with such venues. The 'New Pool' had just been stocked with normal coarse fish including mirror carp, common carp, tench, roach, rudd and perch; I also seem to recall the odd dace too, which was about as exotic as it got. If I was going to fish there on a regular basis, I'd need to be able to get there under my own power, pedal power, no less. I'd usually cycled to school, some three miles from where we lived, on a very basic bike complete with its three Sturmey Archer gears – although second gear never worked properly – and a flat pannier-type attachment behind the seat on to which could be attached briefcase and sports bag by means of bungee ropes. Surely, being a resourceful youth, I could find a way of getting my basket balanced onto my bike whilst carrying rods, rod rests, landing net etc in my newly acquired 'rod holdall'? (No, not a Christmas or birthday present this time but bought with my own pocket-money).

Of course I could. Rooting around in our garage I found a piece of quarter-inch thick plywood into which I drilled four holes which would enable my basket to sit securely thereon. Wire was then used to attach this plywood to the rear pannier with bungee ropes then securing said basket to the bike frame itself. The whole ensemble was not especially stable, but it passed parental inspection on the condition that I didn't ride my bike through the country lanes at night, where the extra wide load might not be picked up by unsuspecting drivers returning home from one of the many pubs that lay between Mobberley and our house.

My first trip to Mobberley New Pool, a cycle ride of some nine miles, was made on a lovely warm summer's day during the school holidays, arriving at the waterside at about ten o'clock. I would have liked to set off earlier, but my parents didn't want the 'wide load' out and about in the rush hour traffic. Of course, I hadn't a clue where to fish, but I could see a small patch of bubbles in the first swim by the car park so I deposited myself there; in fact, there were bubbles everywhere and it took me some time to realise that these weren't all fish related. Although the water was only three to four feet deep, its clarity was the polar opposite of the brickworks pool, sorry, Mobberley Old Pool, being the colour of milky hot chocolate. I utilised the same float set-up as I'd use in my own pond, which was, of course, the same one which had failed so miserably on the Bridgewater Canal. Groundbait was made and placed carefully around my float and hook bait was bread paste (for a change!)

Six biteless hours later I moved to a swim in the corner of the pool, a much better-looking location with reeds to both sides of me. The highlight of the day so far had been winning a toss of the coin with my angling buddy, John. By early afternoon we'd both demolished our considerable stack of sandwiches, biscuits and cakes and faced with the prospect of starvation by close of play - nine o'clock - we decided that one of us should go back home, a round trip of some eighteen miles, to replenish supplies. He went, I stayed, although I did wonder if fate, of which I was already somewhat cognizant, would reward him with a big fish.

When my friend reappeared, I went over to his swim (I thought I would be pushing my luck to wait for him to bring the food over to me) to retrieve my food, my mother having made another huge pile of sandwiches while he waited, and to report on the non-events of the afternoon. On returning to my own swim, I found that my float had moved a considerable distance to the edge of the reeds, and concluded that this missed opportunity was indeed fate paying me back for winning the toss. It was the only proper bite I was to have that day.

Early evening saw an influx of anglers arriving after work, and two caught my eye immediately. They set up two rods between them – obviously carp rods – with only a single hook on each line and then proceeded to tear chunks of breadcrust out of a large unsliced loaf. Some of these were catapulted out towards the centre of the pool and also towards the island; other pieces were impaled onto their hooks, dipped into the water to give some weight for casting and gently cast out.

A couple of hours later I heard and then saw a large commotion by the island – they'd hooked a carp! A few minutes later I saw them bring a lovely pale mirror carp to the net. They weighed it and someone shouted across, 'how big is it, five?' 'No, it's a good one, seven and a half' was the reply. I'd read about catching carp on floating crust in *Angling* Magazine; the author had called them 'clooping carp,' presumably after the sound they made while sucking down the breadcrusts, and I thought this was a particularly thrilling way of catching carp. To see someone transfer the written word into reality was, once again, quite mind-blowing, and in that instant, another obsession was born. Not that I stopped float fishing there and then, of course, and I finished the day completely fishless.

For reasons that I simply can't recall, it was the following summer before we returned to Mobberley. It must have either been very near the end of the summer break or we Butchers had decamped to Anglesey for our two-week summer holiday after that first trip. Anyway, I had to wait till after I'd finished my exams for my first foray into surface carp fishing.

Now this *is* a trip that stands out in the memory. The evening before my last exam I prepared all of my tackle and left it in the garage waiting for me, and my mother was under instruction to prepare sandwiches and to purchase an uncut white loaf. The exam finished late afternoon and I hurtled home as fast as I could to affect a quick 'turnaround'; I really wanted to fish the same spot from which I'd seen the carp caught and the best chance of doing this was to arrive before the majority of other anglers. It was the quickest of quick turnarounds – I was into the house, school uniform replaced by my fishing clothes (not 'cammo' ones, they hadn't been invented then), food, drink and bait collected and back out in less than five minutes. It would have been four, but for my mother insisting on interrogating me about my last exam. I lied and said it went well; it didn't, it was a German exam and I failed it, although to be honest, I couldn't have cared less because school was all but finished and a long summer of fishing was about to begin.

I arrived at Mobberley drenched in sweat and anxiously looked across the pool to where I wanted to fish – it was free! I couldn't have asked for a better evening; still, sunny, very warm and the water appeared to have an oily film to it which appeared to crease up in certain areas in which small insects were trapped. The air was filled with the sound of woodpigeons cooing to each other from opposite sides of the pool and even to this day, when I hear woodpigeons, it always takes me back to that evening.

I set up my usual float rod, but attached just a single size eight hook to the line. Small pieces of crust were torn off the loaf and thrown out; they didn't go very far, so I threw slightly larger pieces out towards the middle of the pool. I then attached a small piece of crust to my hook, but instead of wetting it, I made some bread paste with the soft white middle of the loaf and moulded some of this to the bottom of the crust. This meant that I could fish a relatively small piece of crust but still cast the required distance. Then, with a bait in the water, I lay back against the grassy bank behind me and enjoyed a moment of supreme happiness.

Yet another aside. There have been a few moments in my life when I can say I've been supremely happy, moments when you think 'I wouldn't change a thing,' and this was one of them. Most of these moments have involved angling, which could be regarded as really quite sad, but personally I think it's because angling gives you the opportunity to sit there doing very little and to contemplate life, the universe and whatever else takes your fancy.

So, there I was, watching the little roach attack the free offerings when, out of the corner of my eye, I noticed that my own bait had suddenly vanished. There had been no great commotion, just a hole in the surface film where my crust had been and into which my line was now snaking across the surface and disappearing. Just when you think life is perfect, it gets even better.

I felt a surge of adrenaline as I picked up the rod and tightened up to the fish, not a strike as such, just a gentle connection, and the rod bent over as the fish was hooked. The fish stayed deep and moved slowly around the middle of the pool, which was just as well because I was only using four-pound line (the six-pound breaking-strain Fog kite string had been ditched in favour of better quality line). There were no great dramas, and after about five minutes a lovely pale mirror carp of five pounds was drawn into my net. Now this was a proper carp, my first five-pounder and a genuinely beautiful fish. I could have spent the rest of the evening just staring at it, but thought it should really be returned to the water.

I had just gone back to contemplating how perfect life was when the same thing happened again, this time with a slightly smaller fish of three and a half pounds. Mindful of not pushing my luck too far with my parents and heeding their warnings of cycling through the lanes at night, I packed up just before dark – when the pool looked at its most enticing – and cycled home to regale them with tales of clooping carp.

For the rest of the summer I cycled to Mobberley several times each week, usually leaving before breakfast and staying there all day. Carp weren't always caught, but enough were taken to keep enthusiasm levels high, and eventually I took a seven-and-a-half-pound mirror carp which took pride of place as my best ever. I also had my first encounter with a 'younger generation' of carp fishermen (still older than me though, in their twenties). During a slow afternoon during which I was doing little more than kill time before the hoped-for evening feed, I saw two anglers emerge from the car park. They unloaded an enormous quantity of tackle and headed round towards the 'Old Pool,' which contained much bigger carp than the New Pool, but these were almost impossible to catch. I had briefly tried for them, but they treated my pieces of breadcrust with utter contempt and I soon returned to where the carp were more appreciative of my offerings.

With nothing better to do and with a sense of curiosity, I wandered across to the Old Pool to see what they were up to. The first angler was setting up in the swim in which I'd had my first pike fishing trip, and I started to chat with him. Maybe 'chat' is a bit of an overstatement: I asked questions and tried to make conversation. He just grunted before asking me, 'How long have you been carp fishing?' 'From the age of four,' I truthfully replied. 'Well,' he said, 'you should know by now not to ask so many questions, so eff off!' Although it's true that I could doubtless be both a little over-enthusiastic and borderline annoying, I was taken aback by the force of this response.

By chance, Keith Crowther turned up later that evening and I recounted this little tale to him. He told me, with long pauses as he drew on his pipe, that I shouldn't worry, they'd been extremely rude to both himself and Arthur Lea (holder of the club carp record at that time) too, and they were typical of the modern carp fisherman; secretive and rude.

At one point I thought I might spend the rest of my life happily fishing the summers away at Mobberley and catching carp 'on the crust,' but two things happened that changed that. Firstly, the carp started to wise up to the fact that pieces of crust had a nasty habit of containing hooks, and secondly, and more importantly, John, my angling buddy, had turned his attention away from carp to catching tench from a place called Cicely Mill Pool. His tales of legering for tench and catching them up to nearly four pounds in weight were suddenly quite attractive.

I'd only ever tried legering once before, when I had accompanied my friend, his brother and his father to Budworth Mere in Cheshire during the autumn half term to try for the bream. The day was wet and windy and the fishing almost totally uneventful. Casting a large drilled bullet as a leger weight as far as I could, I caught nothing. For bite detection, I was using a 'dough bobbin'. I'd read about this in one of my father's old angling books. It seemed quite straightforward enough; you just pinched a large piece of bread onto the line and waited for it to pull up to the rod when you had a bite. The reality was completely different; dough bobbins didn't sit properly on the line, they became soggy and fell off when it rained or jammed in your rod rings when they dried out. This was a major disappointment, not least because I'd always taken everything I had read as angling gospel.

The only interesting thing that happened during the day was the arrival of some 'proper' bream fishermen, who mixed up a huge amount of groundbait in a large blue washing up bowl and then proceeded to catapult it all out. They both used swimfeeders and quiver tip rods, both new to me, although of course I'd read about them. I knew they were bream fishermen because I'd asked them what they were after – bream, they'd replied in a very knowledgeable way, and explained that it wasn't a question of 'if' the bream arrived over their groundbait, but 'when'. They caught one tiny perch between them, although to be fair, this was one more fish than the three of us managed and I was sort of impressed with the idea of putting out a large bed of bait and waiting for a humungous shoal of bream to arrive.

I had another schoolfriend who had an interest in fishing, though not quite so obsessive as either myself or John, my other angling buddy, and he suggested I join Warrington Angling Association in order to benefit from a whole variety of other waters, including the aforementioned Cicely Mill pool. This was an L- shaped pool, very shallow and weedy with about twenty-five fishing platforms, which were needed to get through the reedbeds at the top end of the pool and to broach the mud around the rest of the pool. Fishing was only allowed on the 'outside' of the L, the inside being a nature reserve. My friend had enjoyed some good days spinning there, catching mainly perch of up to half a pound, although he assured me that the pool did contain pike too. I have some recollections of going there in August the previous summer and catching plenty of perch on spinners, but I don't think any of them were bigger than four ounces at most.

However, it was a dull but mild day in September that saw me hook and land my first pike on a lure; a fish of maybe three pounds (I can only look at the photograph as I have no recollection of weighing it) which, on the last cast of the day, took my spinner within seconds of it hitting the water and me starting the retrieve. In truth, you only got about five seconds of realistic fishing time each cast before the spinner was engulfed in weed. The brevity of this 'first' is a reflection of my ambivalence towards lure fishing. I know some anglers are more fanatical and obsessive about their lure fishing than I've ever been about any of my own little (!) obsessions but, try as I might, I just cannot get addicted to it. And I've tried. Initially with pike and then with bass, I've acquired decent lures and flung them into areas that should have produced fish, but my patience soon runs thin and I switch to bait fishing. Maybe I'm just too lazy to be a lure fisherman!

My first tench trip to Cicely Mill occurred at the beginning of September the following year, on a morning that felt more suited to pike than tench. It was cold, and I was cold when the glow from the cycle ride had worn off. Only one thing of note happened. I'd ditched the dough bobbins and moved on to the plastic tops of washing-up bottles, these hung nicely on the line and had the advantage that by filling the little recess with plasticine you could vary their weight. My friend had also experimented with having the rod butt a good two to three feet from the ground so that the plastic had a good distance to move, giving you plenty of time to strike. Having only caught a few small perch on my legered lobworm, I had a much better bite – the little piece of red plastic moved confidently up to the rod – and connected with something a little larger, although it didn't feel strong enough to be a tench. It turned out to be a big roach and pulled my new Salter Spring balance down to two pounds and four ounces. A two-pound roach was a special fish. I would have preferred a three-pound tench but what the hell!

On returning home later that day I went to the trouble of validating the weight by taking the lead weights from my mother's kitchen scales, putting them into a plastic bag and weighing them on the spring balance. I eventually settled on a weight of two-pounds and one ounce, and it remains my biggest roach. (I did catch a bigger 'roach' from Budworth Mere in later years, but there were so many roach/bream hybrids in there that I could never be sure it was a pure roach.)

What was more pleasing about the day was how much I liked the 'feel' of my legering set-up. The movement of the bite indicator and the plastic top from the washing-up liquid bottle gave me the same feeling, the same 'buzz,' as seeing a float move. During that winter's pike trips I would imagine myself sitting at Cicely Mill on a still, warm, misty summer's morning, waiting for this new bobbin to rise up to the rod, upon which event I would strike into a beautiful green tench which would give me the run-around before being skilfully drawn into my waiting net.

This was the summer that saw me finally turning my back on the little pond at the bottom of our garden. The fish therein now seemed small and inconsequential, its familiarity now being a negative, an over-familiarity if you will, as opposed to a comfort. The pond itself had changed too. Someone had introduced a pair of white Aylesbury ducks to the pond when the swans failed to turn up one year. These ducks were a nuisance, and as soon as they realised that you had groundbait they would sit on the water in front of you waiting for it to be thrown in, at which point they would grab as much as they could before it disappeared out of reach.

I also blamed them for the disappearance of the surface pond weed. The weed started to appear as usual in late April, but I noticed that the ducks seemed to be nibbling away at the fresh tips of weed until nothing remained. With hindsight, they may or may not have been responsible for the weed vanishing, as it could have been due to a change in the water quality. Then, one stormy autumn night, the little island of flag iris was uprooted from the shallows and blown into a far corner of the pond, so that the pond that I knew and loved was replaced by a distinctly inferior version.

My birthday and Christmas of that year saw three new rods arrive in the Butcher household. For myself I received two carp rods in kit form; a glass fibre rod classed as a 'heavy Avon rod' and even better, a genuine Bruce and Walker Mk IV split cane carp rod. My father received a two-piece glass fibre float rod from my mother, green in colour and with a lovely through action, although for the life of me I can't remember why he wanted a new rod. I also purchased another Mitchell 810 with the money I received from various relatives for birthday and Christmas.

The following summer saw me sit my 'O' levels, and all fishing was strictly off limits until they were finished. My last exam paper was yet again a German one and in a carbon copy of the previous year I was out of the exam, back home and out again in next to no time, although this time I didn't have to lie as the exam had gone quite well. The weather was, strangely enough, exactly the same as the previous year, but I suspected that the carp might not be quite so accommodating in taking floating crust. They weren't and I resorted to legering large balls of bread paste with which I caught small tench – less than half a pound in weight – but no carp. Although I returned to Mobberley a few times that summer, and still caught a few carp on floating crust, a new twin obsession was growing inside me... legering and tench.

Why did legering creep up on me and replace float fishing in my affections? I'm not sure; maybe I saw it as a natural progression and associated the method with the catching of bigger fish. Whatever the reasoning, the following week saw me up before dawn and off on my bike to Cicely Mill. In the far corner of our garage I'd found my father's old rucksack from his scouting days; it wasn't as wide as my basket and this, along with the fact that there would be no inebriated drivers on the lanes at three or four o'clock in the morning, meant that I was free to depart in darkness. I arrived just as a smoky dawn was breaking on what was going to be a lovely warm summer's day.

Another little aside. Was the weather in my childhood really so much better than in recent years? Or was it that with having more time to choose when to go, as opposed to only having the weekends, I naturally went when the weather was at its best? I'll settle for it being a bit of both.

I'd made my groundbait the night before – no, I've no idea either why I did this – and also brought with me a bag of sweetcorn. I'd read about a certain Mr Chris Yates obtaining instant results with corn at Redmire and had decided to try it out during one of my increasingly rare trips to my own pond at the bottom of our garden. Sure enough, I caught carp and tench almost immediately and was instantly converted, although I couldn't afford to buy the tinned stuff and had to buy the big bags of frozen corn, which were distinctly inferior as well as having to be cooked prior to use.

The groundbait contained a less than generous helping of sweetcorn and was thrown out as far as I could manage. I then threaded four or five pieces of corn onto a size eight hook, and with an Arlesey bomb link-leger, cast out a good ten to fifteen yards beyond my groundbait, which I deemed to be near enough. I didn't need anything to sit on as I could perch myself on the end of the wooden platforms which jutted out from the muddy margins and dangle my wellington boot-clad feet into the water.

I was using two rods, having borrowed my father's new float rod. They were positioned parallel to each other and directly in front of me, butts well up from the platform with matching red plastic-washing-up-liquid- bottle-top bite indicators. So far so good; the reality of the morning was matching the scenario that had been playing in my head all winter. All I needed now was a bite, and it materialised just as I was about to take a bite of my own from my peanut butter sandwiches. Once again, the bite was just as I had imagined it; the indicator rising smoothly up to the rod, with me lifting into the fish in a gentle but firm strike. The fish was on and judging by the weight, it had to be a tench.

It slowly circled around for thirty seconds or more before I caught my first glimpse of it. A large humped bronze back popped up onto the surface and a large dorsal fin waved in the air – a bream? I didn't even know there were any bream in Cicely Mill, let alone one of this size, but thankfully for me it did what bream do best and decided to lie on its side to allow me to drag it through the very shallow water and into my net. A neighbouring angler came to inspect the fish and helped me weigh it: just under seven and a half pounds. Not a tench, but not to be sneezed at either and I was delighted when he asked me if I minded if he took a photograph. I posed with the fish and he took two photos, one of which he promised to leave at Dyson's for me. Nearly forty years later, I'm still waiting for that photo…

The morning was a success and soon got better when my second bite provided me with a much better fight and a tench of three pounds and nine ounces. I packed up just after eleven o'clock so that I could get home in time to tell my father what I'd caught. I had no inclination to carry on fishing anyway, as by then more than half of the pool's twenty-five 'pegs' were occupied by other anglers and I was starting to become quite intolerant of fishing in a crowd. Having a car park right by the water made for easy fishing and meant that by nine o'clock in the morning other anglers would be appearing in their droves. This also precluded the prospect of fishing there in the evening, as you risked only being able to fish some of the 'duff' pegs where the water was only inches deep.

Another aside. The older I get, the more intolerant I get. It's not that I'm anti-social, I just don't like fishing in a crowd, although my wife (don't worry, you'll get to meet her soon enough) will disagree with me and tell you that, yes, I am indeed increasingly anti-social.

The rest of that summer was spent carp fishing at Mobberley and tench fishing at Cicely Mill. But if I was ever going to fish Booths Mere or other waters by myself I would need a different form of transport from my bicycle, as Mobberley and Cicely Mill pool were the only places I could realistically cycle to. I'd already taken on a part-time job on Friday evenings collecting 'potato money' – a bloke in a van would drop pre-ordered bags of potatoes off at your house during the week and I'd collect the money on a Friday. The round would take a couple of hours, for which I was paid a sum of money, the exact amount of which I can't recall. It was enough, however, to furnish me with life's essentials such as rod rests, bait, and a proper green fishing umbrella as well as enabling me to save a little money too.

An opportunity then arose to work full time for four weeks at a local seed merchant's. This would dramatically reduce my fishing time that summer, but provide me with much needed additional funds. I worked forty-five hours per week, including a Saturday morning at 'time and a half,' and got paid twenty-five pounds; daylight robbery on their part, and my father shook his head in disbelief when he saw my payslip. It didn't stop him charging me 'keep' from that money though!

Eventually, I had enough money for a second-hand motorbike, an MZ 150. Both my parents desperately wanted me not to get a motor bike; my mother had worked in a hospital long enough to have seen too many young lads being admitted with life-changing injuries. I promised I would be careful and enlisted the help of an older relative who had also been a big bike fan in his youth. Eventually I got reluctant permission to proceed with the purchase. I knew nothing about motorbikes; had I done so, I would not have bought this one. It was big for a small-engined bike, with a box on the back that was large enough to put my fishing creel in. The engine was an old fashioned two-stroke, requiring a slug of oil to be added to the petrol when refuelling, and was difficult to start; if it didn't fire up after three hits on the kick-start you had to remove the spark plug, clean it and replace it before trying again. It also had a nasty habit of 'kicking back' when you were trying to start it, resulting in a crippling whack on the ankle. Within a couple of years, I'd replaced the bike with a bigger four-stroke Honda version, which, having an electric start, was a much more civilised bike to ride.

By the way, would I have allowed my own kids to have a motorbike? Absolutely not!

The following summer was notable for a day spent fishing with my father in the punt on Booths Mere. He'd taken a few days off work and this coincided with me finishing my mock 'A' levels – I'd done sufficiently well in my 'O' levels to be invited back to the Sixth Form – so he suggested that we try for the tench at Booths. I'd never fished from the punt in the summer before but I dusted off my float fishing tackle, boiled up some sweetcorn and contemplated a morning in the punt. I pictured the old article in *Angling* Magazine, the one about tench fishing from the punts on the lake at Blenheim Palace, and created some little vignettes in my mind: a misty morning, tench bubbling, tench rolling, a float sliding away to be followed by the rod hooping over as a big tench powered away from the boat. Yes,

I could get, indeed was getting, quite excited over this, especially as the tench in Booths Mere were generally bigger than those at Cicely Mill pool. I'd caught quite a few there but nothing much bigger than the first one I'd had at just over three and a half pounds.

It was a lovely morning, still, cloudless and hot – honestly, it was – but by mid-morning we'd seen no tench rolling, no 'needle bubbles' or anything which could in any way be construed as a sign of a tench. My father suggested that we move to the far corner of the mere, where there was a small bed of lily pads about thirty yards from the bank. I readily agreed, for no other reasons that my father knew what he was doing, and more importantly, the picture in *Angling* magazine showed the anglers fishing from their punt next to a bed of lilies. I fished my now usual four pieces of corn on a size eight hook, and since we were fishing in little more than three feet of water, I put on a larger float to cast a bit further away from the boat. But I didn't like the way the new float sat in the water and this, combined with the increasing temperature and lack of fish, was irritating me. This reality was some distance away from what I'd imagined, and I was getting seriously annoyed.

My father, on the other hand just put on a large ball – think small ping-pong ball – of bread paste and used this as sufficient casting weight to fish a reasonable distance away from our mooring. My increasingly dark teenage thoughts – stupid and selfish, as could there really be a better place to be on such a lovely morning? – were suddenly interrupted by the sound of his centre-pin reel screaming as he hooked into a decent fish, the first run ripping more than twenty yards of line off his spool. His new rod behaved impeccably and after a fight in which the tench obligingly decided not to rush into the adjacent lily bed, I netted a fine tench for him of just over four and a half pounds. Was I delighted for him? No, I'm ashamed to say that the fact that he'd caught the fish, and not me, left me with steam coming out of my ears. What an ungrateful sod I was!

No more bites were forthcoming and we packed up at dinnertime with my father consoling me by saying that we could stop for a pint on the way back – after all I was nearly seventeen. Yes, a beer or two would improve my mood, and I also made a mental note of where he'd hooked the fish, comfortably within legering distance of the bank. A bank I'd be able to fish on my own soon when I would no longer be a Junior member of ADAC.

Going for a beer with my father was not a totally alien concept to me by then. He had first sneaked me into his 'local' when I was not quite sixteen – in fairness, I always looked older than I was (and still do!) – to celebrate Manchester United beating Liverpool in the FA Cup Final. Sport of many hues was big in our house: football, cricket, rugby (League more than Union, due to my mother's roots in Barrow) as well as the major sporting occasions such as the Grand National were avidly consumed by both parents. I was born to be a Manchester United fan – my mother gave birth to me in what was then Park Hospital, the nearest hospital to Old Trafford – but I could just have easily been a City fan. My father was one of the very few men in Manchester to support both clubs. This was due to the fact that in his pre-marriage days he would work Saturday mornings and then hurtle home on his bike to meet up with his brother-in-law and other friends at the Snooker Club in Sale. A few games of snooker were played, along with a few pints of beer, before the group departed to either Old Trafford or Maine Road, depending on who was playing at home that day. Of course, in those days, all games kicked off at three o'clock!

When I was young, he was more red than blue and I can remember being allowed to stay up late to watch the European Cup Final. In those days, children's bedtimes seemed to be more strictly governed than in my own kids' era, so it was a big treat; I have many memories of that evening, not the first goal or Benfica's equaliser, but Stepney's save from Eusebio (my mother had screamed 'noooooo!' as he broke through) right at the end of normal time, the injury time goals and the lap of honour with the trophy.

My little brother decided he was going to support the other team in Manchester and on derby day, I think my father's allegiances were slightly more blue than red in support of the younger sibling. Having said that, he was on the phone to me within seconds of the final whistle going in United's dramatic 1999 Champions League triumph over Bayern Munich to share in the post-match euphoria.

Incidentally, this was the last time we used that old wooden punt on Booths Mere; vandals broke into the boat house and smashed it up. It wasn't the first time this had happened, so the club decided not to repair or renew the boat.

A consequence of having my own transport was that fishing trips with my parents, and particularly my father, diminished significantly. I think with all teenage boys there comes a time when you want to strike out and do your own thing. Having been though that experience from the other side, as a parent, I know that it can be difficult to let go and the teenage me must have been more than a little insensitive in not wanting to fish at weekends as well as being much more intense – obsessive and therefore irritating – about my fishing than my father was. He was a much more laid-back type of angler, happy to be by the water and catching fish on the basis that a bad day's fishing was better than a good day at work. A feeling that I was yet to learn.

My parents were a little worried about just how much time I spent going fishing, although I think it was my friend's father who summed it up best when on collecting us late one evening from a fishing trip somewhere in Cheshire and seeing a group of young boys and girls at a bus stop, remarked, 'wouldn't you have preferred to spend your evening snogging girls in a bus shelter?' Possibly, but having gone to an all-boys' school, fish were easier to catch than girls...

My first double figure fish, all of 11lb 3oz, which died in order for me to
have this third-rate photo!

First pike on a spinner from Cicely Mill pool.
Note the NHS glasses and the mountain of hair.

Six chub from the River Dane to 2½ lb in December 1978

CHAPTER FIVE

River fishing

I was sixteen before I fished my first river. For some reason, my father, who had often spoken fondly of fishing the River Dane, never took me river fishing; not in my childhood nor in my youth. It was in accompanying my friend and his father to the River Dane one frozen Christmas that I had my first taste of river fishing. The River Dane is a small river that twists and turns through the Cheshire countryside. A mixture of fast, shallow water and slower, deeper glides, it provides the mobile angler with a different challenge at every bend. I was not remotely prepared for these challenges. I wasn't mobile, having a heavy creel and rod holdall with me, hadn't read too much about river fishing, didn't have any scenarios in my mind to try and reality-match and, consequently, approached the whole venture with less enthusiasm than I would have summoned for a midwinter pike trip, for example. However, it was a fishing trip and I'd never caught a chub before, so much better than sitting at home revising for the post-Christmas exams.

It was bitterly cold with snow on the ground, and I spent from early morning to mid-afternoon moving from swim to swim with no success. I was using my usual float rod set-up, the only concession to fishing a river a change of float: I'd found a 'fluted Avon' in my tackle box that had been bought the previous summer while on holiday in Wales and had been intended to be used in the pursuit of small wrasse.

My friend managed to catch a chub of about a pound by float fishing a worm almost beneath his rod tip, where he'd managed to find about four feet of water. I tried to find an identical looking spot to give myself what I perceived to be the best chance of catching a fish, and eventually settled into a swim in the middle of a long straight run overhung with trees. Although the water was reasonably clear, I couldn't quite see the bottom, but on plumbing the depth, I was disappointed to find that that I'd parked myself in a swim that was shallower than expected. Rather than move yet again, I decided to cast across the current and let the float drift down, carrying my double maggot hookbait with it. I had to be careful to retrieve the cast before it reached a single trailing branch in the water, otherwise I'd be in danger of losing my float, the one and only float I possessed that was in any way, shape or form suitable for this type of fishing.

With each cast, I let the float edge closer to the branch, until the inevitable happened and it caught round it. I gave it a tentative flick to try and free it and instantly found myself attached to a fish. The fish freed itself from the branch and moved slowly upstream; the fight was dogged and unspectacular, and soon a chub of a similar size to my friends was in my net. The most difficult part of the fight was getting it out of the water, as my landing net had frozen solid and was reluctant to open up until it had been immersed in the water, which was a couple of degrees warmer than the air. My first chub; most acceptable. After that I deliberately allowed the line to catch on the branch and hold the bait back, and the fish was soon joined in my keepnet by six other chub to over two pounds in weight. I had accidentally found a winning method that allowed me to completely override my total incompetence in fishing the river.

Over the next few years I fished the River Dane quite a lot, although it would be wrong to say that I was obsessed with the place. Yes, I liked it, I enjoyed the challenge and the fact that you could fish it in the close season provided you didn't use maggots, but I wouldn't have been heartbroken if I'd been suddenly told that I could never fish it again. I soon moved away from float fishing to legering, initially using the same plastic bottle tops that I'd been using for my carp and tench fishing, and then quiver-tipping. Not that I had a quiver-tip rod, I just used my float rod and waited for the tip to pull round, these chub not being noted for their lightness of touch when it came to taking maggots, worms or breadflake (a new bait for me). I never caught as many chub as I did on that first visit. I usually managed to catch at least a couple, but the biggest barely nudged the three-pound mark.

There were two other rivers that I fished, but only briefly. The first was the River Bollin, a river that had been badly polluted and fishless for many years, although I do recall going swimming in it with friends when I was five or six. Maybe it wasn't quite as badly polluted as everyone made out, or my mother thought that swimming in detergent-contaminated water would do me some good, after all, a bit of Fairy Liquid never did anyone any harm, did it? The Bridgewater Canal crossed the River Bollin on a large aqueduct near Dunham Park and a couple of years previously this aqueduct had suffered a catastrophic failure which completely drained a large section of the canal and, allegedly, infused the river with a host of coarse fish. This appeared to have been borne out when, on a family walk close to the river, I saw a fisherman remove his keepnet and return a large number of sizeable fish that I took to be chub and roach.

Another angler had told me tales of large carp and a twenty-pound pike coming from this same stretch; I'm not sure if I was completely gullible in my youth or if I just wanted so badly to believe that such fish existed, because if they did, fishing there would be tinged with an added frisson of excitement. In hindsight, always a wonderful thing, I not only enjoyed tales of unfeasibly large fish from any of the waters where I wet a line, I *needed* them to provide that little bit of the unknown. As I get older, I am so much more cynical and my first thought is to always dismiss fisherman's tales as either over-excitement or the product of the rather sad and delusional mind of an attention-seeking angler. The real sadness is that in not believing such tales, my own enjoyment has been much reduced.

The length of river from where I'd seen the fish caught belonged to a club to which I didn't belong, but immediately below that was a 'free stretch' which was actually closer to where the canal had breached. Despite the alleged infusion and the presence of fish no more than a hundred yards away, my friend and I fished it several times and we never had a bite or even saw a fish.

The other river we, my usual friend and I, fished was the Ribble, a much bigger river than the Dane. Our first trip to the river, again a 'free section' and not far from the M6, provided us both with chub to about the two-pound mark. I caught them by float fishing – the fluted Avon again – with cubes of luncheon meat, another new bait for us and one which was to be soon used exclusively, and my friend caught his fish by legering the same cubes. We went back a couple of times to the same stretch, but the river was higher and dirtier and we blanked. Once again, I had no great empathy for this river, and to this day I've never fished it again despite it now producing some huge barbel.

Looking back, most of my recollections of river fishing in this part of my life are what I'd class again as incidental memories; their recollection not bringing back any great emotion. The fishing was pleasant, enjoyable, but not exceptional. I think that one of the reasons for this is that the river I mainly fished, the Dane, had no record of producing big chub. A three-pound chub was regarded as a special fish, and it didn't at that time contain any barbel. There was therefore nothing for me to fantasise about; no scenario that I could develop that would provide a real buzz. The shortness of this chapter is an accurate reflection of my ambivalence, at this point in my life, to river fishing, although this would change slightly in later years.

CHAPTER SIX

UNIVERSITY CHALLENGES

Having worked diligently and obtained a decent, if not exceptional, set of A level results, I accepted an offer to study Biochemistry at Manchester University. Why Biochemistry? I'd long since decided that I didn't want to be a doctor, besides which my grades were nowhere near good enough for medical school, but, having studied biology, chemistry and physics for A level, there was a certain logic in continuing along the same path to get a good solid science degree which would lead me into a good job. The whole purpose of going to university for me, and I suppose other working-class kids, was to get a qualification that would get me a job; no pretence of going there for the fun of it (although, believe me, I did have fun, but the course itself was never 'fun') or to do something I wanted to do.

Going to university, and living away from home, would reduce my fishing time at certain points in the year – term-time – but leave me with the whole summer from the middle of June to late September to fish as much as I wanted, provided I could find myself a flexible part-time job. Which was what I did, finding work as a barman and 'waiter' at a local pub. The Gardeners Arms in Timperley had a reputation for serving the best pint of Boddingtons in south Manchester and was the 'local' for my father and his friends. Having accompanied them there a few times, it seemed fairly natural to ask the landlord for a job; he readily agreed and I found myself 'waiting on' on some Friday and Saturday evenings, when I wasn't going to join the masses in going fishing anyway, and working a few lunchtime shifts behind the bar during the week. Incidentally, 'waiting on' involved going around the pub asking people if they required more drinks, going to the bar, collecting the drinks, handing them out, collecting the money, hopefully with tips, before cashing up at the end of the evening. The reason that this practice continued was that the Gardeners only had a relatively small bar and the landlord felt that people would drink more if they didn't have to queue there. In reality, it was a pretty small pub with the 'front room' being little bigger than the sort of lounge you would expect to find in a detached house.

This left me free to pursue twin obsessions. Carp from the canal and tench from Booths Mere. During the summer prior to my departure for University I had made a return to the canal in Timperley and using sweetcorn for bait and legering tactics I'd managed to start regularly catching carp up to about five pounds in weight. There were common carp, possibly 'wildies' given their classical torpedo-like shape, but I had caught my first double figure carp there. Given my previous heralding of 'firsts,' it's surprising just how little emotion this memory brings back to me. I think it's because it was without doubt the ugliest fish I've ever caught: think large grey football covered in red blotches and with stubby fins and you'll have a pretty good picture of what this fish looked like. I think it weighed twelve pounds or thereabouts. Although such fish are quite common these days, I'm fairly certain that its shape was due to it being spawn-bound, as boilies were never used there to my knowledge and I don't think 'pellets' had been invented back then. The surroundings were also pretty grim, with an office block behind me, a bridge to my left and an underpass in front. The only green in sight was the broken glass of the beer bottles which drunks returning home would hurl at me from the bridge along with rolled up balls of chip-newspaper and anything else that was to hand. While I soldiered on in this grim environment, my friend did the sensible thing and found a much more pleasant stretch of canal to fish in the local countryside.

It was around this time that I bought my first electronic bite alarm, a very cheap one which worked on the basis of the line moving a thin metal wire to close two contacts (I think it was called a 'BJ Bite Alarm'). I was perpetually frustrated with it and one evening in a fit of rage, after my line jammed, causing me to miss a run, I kicked it into the canal. I didn't mean to do that, I meant to kick it along the towpath, but my soccer skills were never up to much and I wasn't too distraught to see it sink into the canal's murky depths. I also made one myself out of some aluminium sheeting, provided by my father from his work, and from something called a 'GPO Circuit,' a combination of capacitors and resistors which I soldered onto a circuit board following instructions from a friend's electronics magazine. This was more sensitive than the 'BJ' but wasn't waterproof, which was a slight drawback, and this too was soon ditched.

By this time, I'd used some of my hard-earned cash to buy a pair of Avon dial scales which would have enabled me to weigh a fish of up to 32lb in weight. We had heard many rumours of twenty and maybe even thirty-pound carp being caught. We were sceptical of these tales but not totally so, as we felt there was just an outside chance that some of them may have been true, and this made every bite we had that little bit more special.

My last exam in my first year of university was on the afternoon of the 15th June. Absolute perfection. So, while my fellow students were planning to go out and get completely out-of-their-heads drunk, I was heading to the Cheshire countryside to fish a swim on the Bridgewater Canal that I'd just spent a week pre-baiting.

I arrived at my swim at about nine o'clock, it was mild, not hot, with enough cloud cover to ensure a warm night ahead. There were now a number of major refinements to my carp fishing. I'd purchased, well all right, I'd *borrowed* one of my parents' fold-away plastic chairs, which was kinder on my back as my fishing sessions were getting longer and longer. There were too many smaller fish around to make sweetcorn a viable bait here, so I had moved on to using luncheon meat. Although it could eventually be whittled away by the large roach-bream hybrids that inhabited the canal here, it did generally last long enough for the carp to find, if they were about. Only one rod was used, my heavy Avon rod as opposed to the Mk IV split cane rod, because its lighter action was more suited to this type of fishing. My end tackle was a simple link leger with a size eight hook.

The greatest progress had been made in the bite indicator department. White plastic from an old ice cream tub had been cut into oblongs, roughly two to three inches long by one-inch wide, and then folded in half. A knitting needle minus the blob on the end was then placed into the ground at a forty-five-degree angle underneath the rod; once the bait had been cast across to the far side of the canal the little piece of plastic would be placed over the line and onto the bottom of the knitting needle. The bail arm of the reel would be left open and a bite signalled by the plastic flying up the knitting needle and falling off the line, upon which one hand would immediately go to the rod whilst the other would feel for the line, hopefully finding it pouring off the spool, at which point the bale arm would be closed and a gentle strike made.

Well, gentle in my case, but not always in my friend's. Many was the night when the following sequence was heard... clop (bale arm closing) ... pause ... swish (rod being hauled savagely back) ... crack (the line snapping) ... f***, b******, b******* (my friend swearing). It was quite understandable really; he was working, so he had much less fishing time than me. He'd wait for hours for a bite, the tension building all of the time, and then suddenly find it being released all in one uncontrollable strike. 'Did you miss it?' I'd ask with as much innocence as I could muster. 'Eff off!' would come back the reply.

Even on the darkest night you could still clearly see those little bits of white plastic and the knitting needle held the plastic in place in all but the windiest of conditions, although I don't recall it ever being really windy; wet, yes, but windy, no. The downside of these little bits of folded plastic was their tendency to fly off into the darkness when you had a really savage run, or to be catapulted off the line when you struck a slower run. For some strange reason, although you would have four or five identical pieces of plastic in your tackle box, you had to try and find the one piece of plastic you'd just lost! Maybe we thought that one little piece of plastic was especially lucky, or, more likely, we were both suffering from a little bit of OCD.

We only ever fished at night now, which was slightly risky as night fishing wasn't allowed under the rules of the club which had the fishing rights. This transition from day to night fishing for carp seemed to just suddenly happen. It was quite understandable at Timperley, where the semi-darkness – there were plenty of street lights around there – hid some of the urban backdrop, but maybe less so in the picturesque Cheshire countryside. The reasons for the transition, I think, were partly related to the very first times I went night fishing in my own little pond and realised just how different the world looked at night and, of course, very much related to the angling literature I'd read with tales of carp caught after dark. We also found that, with a few notable exceptions, most of the carp we caught came between dusk and dawn.

Back to the night of the 15th June. I had a little radio with me which I turned on a couple of minutes before midnight so that on the last 'beep' of midnight I could cast my ready-baited line into the canal. There was no one about, so I could quite easily have fished from ten o'clock onwards if I'd wanted to, but that would have felt completely the wrong thing to do. Fishing at night was a completely acceptable breach of the rules; fishing before the 16th June was most definitely not. Besides, the wait allowed the excitement, which had been growing since the middle of May, to build to an almost mind-blowing crescendo.

A quick aside. Remember how I talked previously about moments of supreme happiness? This was another one: spending the last few hours of the close season sitting by the canal, a long summer of fishing ahead of me, exams finished (and I was fairly sure I'd passed them too), a stack of luncheon meat and tomato sauce sandwiches and a packet of custard creams; what more could a man ask for?

On the dot of midnight, I swung my bait across to the far side of the canal, tightened my line up to the bait and started to place my lucky piece of folded plastic onto the line, only for it to be pulled from my grasp. It took me a couple of seconds to realise what was happening, but a quick feel of the line told me that something had instantly picked up my bait and was heading at some speed along the canal. A firm strike and my rod hooped over as a fish powered away from me. One of the joys of fishing the canal in this area was that there were very few snags, so you could fish relatively light line and just let the fish run. This made for great sport with medium-sized fish, although this particular leather carp turned out to weigh 9lb 12oz, which moved it into the 'larger' category of fish by our standards.

There were no head torches in those days, so when landing fish we used small torches that we stuffed into our mouths and then used our heads to direct the beam to the requisite place while drooling uncontrollably down our jumpers. Instant success when first fishing pre-baited areas would become a common occurrence, although the night fizzled into a bit of damp squib as rain moved in and I caught only one more carp, a little smaller than the first, and a roach-bream hybrid of about two pounds.

Looking back at the photographs I took of the fish we caught in those days, I'm struck by two things; firstly, my total lack of ability in using a camera, and secondly, how beautifully proportioned these carp were. No boilie or pellet induced pot-bellied fish, just good solid, muscular carp, mainly mirrors with the odd common or leather.

Just when I'd imagined fishing this little stretch of canal heaven for the rest of the summer, disaster struck. John Woodhouse, who couldn't get the day off work to fish the opening night of the season, decided to fish most weekends, and since my stint at the Gardeners didn't start until early July, I joined him. It was either late June or early July, and just after five o'clock on a lovely Sunday morning;

we were about to pack up after a fruitful night's carping – my friend had not long since grassed a beautiful thirteen-pound leather carp – when a figure loomed up out of the early morning mist. Another angler, but not just any other angler, the bailiff. It was pointless trying to deny that we'd fished through the night; the empty sandwich boxes and bait containers were a too-obvious sign of our guilt. He let us off with a warning, but said we'd be reported to the committee if he found us again. A fate worse than death... possible expulsion from the club!

Did we stop night fishing? No, we just looked for a spot which was further away from any parking areas, a spot from which we could see anyone approaching us on the basis that if we were caught during the night, we'd be able to wind our baits in and claim that we were waiting for dawn, as there was no rule to stop us actually being on the canal bank during the night. We also kept our sandwich boxes hidden and took a spare tin of meat with us in case we were caught at dawn – 'look, we've only just arrived and we haven't even sorted our bait out yet'.

I found what I considered to be the perfect spot, invisible from any bridge or other vantage point and a decent walk from the nearest car park. The walk was irrelevant to us as we rode our motorbikes along the towpath anyway, only stopping to walk when we came across another angler. For reasons I can't remember, I was on my own when I first fished this new area, having once again spent a week pre-baiting, and yes, it produced instant results with a catch of more than a dozen carp including a beautiful looking twelve-pound mirror. This stretch of canal became my second home as I fished there at least twice, and often three times per week, until the end of August, and although the number of carp I caught gradually declined, I wasn't too bothered as I found the place to be familiar and comforting in the same way that my own little pond had once been.

If the canal was my second home, then Booths Mere became my third, and I wasted no time in putting that mental note I'd made on the boat trip with my father into practice. My first solo trip to Booths as a fully-fledged senior member was made early in the season. I arrived just before first light on what promised to be yet another lovely summer day (yep, the weather must have been better in my youth) and made my way across the fields, past the cattle which were busily chewing the cud, trying and failing to avoid the cow-pats before getting to the water's edge.

Mist was rising steadily from the water as I walked around the mere, along the 'Wall,' past the old boat house and then through the woods of the Knutsford bank to the very far corner, where the lily beds were. I chose the swim nearest to the exact spot where my father had hooked his tench – coincidentally the same swim where I'd lost my big fish many years earlier – although I was slightly nervous about the proximity of a large tree which jutted a good ten yards out into the water where it had fallen.

Sweetcorn-laced groundbait was fired out using my newly acquired 'Whopper Dropper' – what a fantastic name for a catapult! – and I was soon sitting behind my rods, technically my rod and my father's, waiting for the red plastic washing-up-liquid-bottle-top indicators to rise up from the ground. Why not the white plastic? I was fishing with closed bale arms and, far more importantly, all of my tench from Cicely Mill pool had been caught with this set-up and thus, it just felt the right way to tench-fish.

By half-past five I was poised in anticipation of an imminent bite, and by eight o'clock I was starting to wonder what I was doing wrong. It was mid-morning before I had my first bite. For months I'd pictured myself sitting there, in exactly that spot, watching as the little red indicator rose steadily up to the rod, which is precisely what happened. I also pictured in my mind's eye a gentle strike upon which the rod would adopt a lovely curve as a tench powered away, which is also what happened. The tench would then be slowly worked towards me, each surge taking increasingly smaller amounts of line from my reel until it would glide over the rim of my landing net...

Which is exactly what didn't happen. The tench simply kited in to my right and went straight into the tree. It soon became clear that it had cunningly transferred the hook into something woody and after some steady pressure I eventually saw a large branch glide into my waiting net. To say I was frustrated would be an understatement; frustrated for losing the fish, yes, but more frustrated by my own stupidity in fishing somewhere that made landing any tench hooked such a lottery. I had no more bites, but found another swim to fish, which, although requiring a slightly further cast, would give me a better angle to stop any fish from getting into that tree.

I returned to Booths a couple of days later: same weather, same bait, different swim. This time I made no mistake with the two bites I had, landing both tench, which weighed between three and a half and four pounds. For the next month, I proceeded to fish that same swim once or twice per week, catching one, two or occasionally three tench, including my biggest ever at 4lb 13oz. I knew exactly how to fish this swim, loved the familiarity – you might have spotted a little trend here – and expected to spend the rest of the summer fishing there, until one morning I was joined by a pair of anglers, Graeme and his mate Ray, who I'd seen and talked to before. Good anglers, friendly and helpful, they parked themselves a good hundred yards or more along the bank from me and due to the thick bankside undergrowth, we couldn't see or hear each other. By eleven o'clock, I was in the process of packing up, quite pleased with a two-tench catch, when they returned, having already packed up, it being yet another hot and still summers day (!).

'Caught anything?' they asked me. 'Yes,' I replied, and told them about my impressive catch of tench. 'Did you catch anything?'

'Yes, we had nine tench between us, float fishing, by that little patch of surface weed just along the way there.'

I was gobsmacked. I didn't think it was very deep there, I said. I wasn't fishing in much more than four feet of water and it must have been less than three feet deep where they'd been. They said it was deep enough there, and, being the wonderfully helpful sort of anglers they were, they explained to me exactly how they'd caught the tench: 'You'll only be fishing a few rod lengths out so just use a little bit of groundbait, loose feed with plenty of maggots and you'll know when the tench have arrived because you'll see the bubbles and the fish rolling.' Their parting words to me were, 'Don't worry about the weedbed, the tench always seem to run away from it'.

That evening, I lay in bed and thought about float fishing for tench at Booths. I pictured a little red float sitting close to the weedbed, saw it surrounded by a fine patch of pin-prick bubbles and then disappear, and almost felt the rod buck in my hands as the fish shot away from the weedbed. I decided that this was indeed a most agreeable little scenario, and one that should be pursued at the earliest opportunity.

The next opportunity was, unusually for me at that time, a Saturday morning. And for once the weather wasn't hot and sunny, it was better than that as far as tench fishing went; warm, yes, but heavily overcast and humid. I headed for 'their' swim. All the swims on the Knutsford bank were beautiful, being little gaps in the bankside vegetation that included rhododendrons, willows, oak, beech and birch, but I had to admit that this swim with its little bed of potamogeton was especially nice. I did exactly what I'd been told and, joy of joys, I soon had a swim that was fizzing with bubbles (a sight that still excites me as much today as it did then). If you've spent your life fishing overstocked commercial fisheries using a baggin' waggler or some other monstrosity of a float, you will have no idea just how I was feeling at that moment. My heart was pounding, time stood still and I was completely focused on a little red piece of float no more than twenty-odd feet away from me.

Twenty minutes passed. Reality matched the dream scenario, and the float vanished. I struck and the rod bucked in my hands as the fish shot... straight into the weedbed. Crap. (Apologies for the bad language, but sometimes only a swear word will suffice.) Trust me to hook the only tench in the whole mere that hadn't read the script; it was stuck solid, and although I could almost see it, I couldn't move it and had to pull for a break, the line parting at the lowest split-shot.

I quickly attached another hook and split-shot and was soon fishing again. No more than ten minutes later I had another bite, but managed to miss it – not a good idea when you're surrounded by trees and assorted other float-,grabbing vegetation. Thankfully, it didn't take too long to get a bait back into the water and sure enough, with the water still fizzing away, another bite wasn't long in coming. Another strike, another tench hooked; this one shot straight out… before turning right and heading back into the weedbed. Same result. Bugger.

I hooked *five* more tench and lost them all. I could describe each loss but I'd run out of swear words, or at least the printable ones.

I don't know why Graeme and his mate had been able to hook and land their fish – they weren't lying, I'm sure of that – when it was patently clear to me that I could have hooked another hundred tench and lost every single one of them unless I'd stepped up my tackle to pike-fishing proportions. Losing fish was one thing, but losing them with hooks and line still attached gave me a real sense of guilt, so I figured out a Plan B, although this would now have to wait until my next trip.

Plan B was to fish much further to the left and use a 'float-leger' arrangement; basically, a self-cocking float on a very short link leger. This worked perfectly and on my next trip I landed fourteen tench and a bream. The tench weren't huge and according to one of my old fishing diaries the biggest was only 3lb 15oz with the bream being the biggest fish of the day at 6lb 3oz.

For the rest of the summer I exclusively used the float leger set-up on Booths Mere and quite enjoyed watching a float again. Of course, on a float-leger rig you didn't get any knocks, just sail-away bites which were reasonably easy to hit and best of all, I didn't lose a single tench in that weedbed. And I caught plenty too, although nothing bigger than the 4lb 13oz one that I'd caught earlier in the summer.

The 29th July 1981 is memorable to most people as the date of Charles and Diana's wedding. For me, it's the date of my last coarse fishing trip with my father. We were to share more than a few sea fishing trips in future years, but I don't recall another coarse trip.

Having regaled him with tales of my successful tench trips to Booths, I wanted to 'show-off' to him, I wanted *him* to see *me* catching tench. Maybe this was some sort of validation exercise on my part to show him that the boy-fisherman had become a man. The more I think about this, the more I think it's true: my father was never one for saying 'well done,' and like many fathers of that era he would never have dreamt of saying that he loved me, although I'm certain this was the case. Affection was expressed in different ways: sometimes in pithy one-line putdowns delivered with a slightly suppressed grin. For example: if I struck hard and missed a bite, he'd say something like 'you might want to strike a little harder next time,' or if I was skint – being a student, I was perpetually skint, despite working in the pub –

and it was my turn to get a round in, he'd slip me a fiver and forget to ask for the change. Of course, the biggest way he showed his affection for me was in the time he spent taking me fishing, initially with him, and then in my teenage years by dropping me off before work and then collecting me later in the evening, no mean sacrifice when he was often working seven days per week.

On the Wednesday in question, a Bank Holiday, which meant a day off for my father, I decided that we'd need to get to Booths just before first light as there would doubtless be a lot of anglers similarly eager to do anything to avoid watching a royal wedding. I was keen that we should be fishing adjacent swims, but my father said there was no way he'd be getting out of bed at three-thirty in the morning as this was the first day off he'd had in the last four weeks. It was therefore decided that I'd borrow my mother's car (we were a two-car family by then as my mother had gone back to working almost full time) and transport both sets of fishing tackle to the waterside. I would then bait up both swims and start fishing before my father arrived at about six o'clock.

The walk round to the far side of Booths Mere was a reasonably long one when carrying one set of fishing tackle. When carrying two, on another hot and sunny morning, albeit at first light, it was a gargantuan effort which left me drenched in sweat by the time I arrived at my chosen swims. At least they were empty. I was yet to catch anything by the time my father arrived, flask in hand – he'd graciously agreed to carry that one item – and he responded to me showing him his (pre-baited!) swim by asking me why I hadn't set his rod up. Muttering away to himself, he soon had a bait in the water, and within two minutes he had hooked into a tench. At about three and a half pounds it was an average fish for Booths and I was quite pleased that he'd caught something, although the purpose of the trip was for him to watch me catch some fish. He almost immediately caught another tench, by which I was slightly less pleased. Then I had my first bite and connected with something that just wouldn't stop; twenty yards of line slowly disappeared from reel, then thirty, fifty, eighty until I was getting to the point where I knew I'd have to clamp down on the spool. I was using a 'correctly set' spool by then, having dispensed with the back winding, mainly because I loved the sound the spool made when yielding line.

Whatever was on the end of my line was big, no *huge*, and very powerful. As soon as I saw the bare plastic of the spool I put my thumb onto it and hoped the fish would stop; surprisingly, it did. I turned it and gradually over the course of the next fifteen minutes I was ever so slowly able to inch it back towards me. Whatever it was, it didn't feel quite so huge by now.

Eventually, I saw what had happened. I'd hooked a tench right in the root of its tail, and quite a small tench too, smaller than either of my father's fish. It was dragged into my landing net, much to the amusement of my father, who pointed out that it was much smaller than his and had taken me ten times longer to land!

My father went on to catch yet another tench of average size, but still bigger than mine, whereas I had one of those rare mornings when I couldn't buy a bite. So much for the pupil teaching the master.

I've often wondered why he never came fishing with me again. Was I too enthusiastic, just a little too intense about my fishing? My father always had a more pragmatic approach to his fishing, something borne out by the fact that if he ever lost a good fish he just shrugged and carried on whereas, as you've already seen, I would be inconsolable and sulk for hours unless I caught another fish comparable to the one I'd lost. I think maybe the intensity of my approach to fishing intimidated him a little and showed him a side of my character that he found a little alien, maybe even didn't like, and this simply took away his enjoyment. In addition to this, he also had to cater to the needs of my little brother, who had interests other than matters piscatorial, so had less spare time anyway.

The remainder of my university years, the summers that is, were spent on the canal and at Booths Mere. Two carp fishing sessions stand out in my memory. The first concerns my capture of my biggest-ever canal carp.

It was a Friday evening early in the season and I was only fishing because my friend, John, who worked during the week wanted to go. We fished from about six o'clock Friday evening through till first light, by which time he'd caught four carp, including a lovely twelve-pound mirror, while was yet to have a run. It was one of those summer mornings when first light seems to drag on for hours; a grey, cool morning, which meant that we ended up staying longer than we normally would have done. If it was a bright day then we'd be packing up well before six o'clock in the morning, as we knew we'd had the best of the fishing by then.

I was thinking of packing up and feeling distinctly disgruntled; I didn't often blank at this point of the season and my friend had caught carp too. I didn't mind him catching but in these situations, it would have been fairer if maybe he'd only caught three carp and I'd caught one. Or better still, two each. And then, without warning, which was always the case, the little piece of plastic jumped off the line, which then poured off the spool. A surprisingly gentle strike then connected with a fish that shot off down the canal towards where my friend was fishing. He was fifty or sixty yards away from me, and I had to call out to him to bring his line in – we always fished the far side of the canal – but the fish continued past him and just kept on going. I'd never had to 'follow' a carp before, so I knew this was a special fish. It went another sixty or seventy yards beyond my friend and he came with me, bringing his landing net with him. I should point out that I was only using six-pound breaking strain line and was quite happy to let the fish run, much to the annoyance of my friend, who adopted a much more aggressive attitude to his fish-fighting. I can see his point of view in this case, as I was using up the last of his valuable fishing time.

The carp's long runs soon became shorter ones and after maybe twenty minutes or so I had it circling beneath my rod tip. It took a further ten minutes – having seen it in the water, I knew it was a big fish and I was therefore reluctant to bully it too much – before it rolled into my friend's landing net. A sling was wetted, the scales zeroed and the fish weighed – 16lb 4oz. My best ever carp. Photographs were taken, and if you look at the photograph you would be forgiven for thinking it was caught in the middle of the night – it wasn't, the morning was so dark that the flash went off, making it appear more nocturnal than it really was.

The second session stands out for other reasons. It was a weekday evening – my friend must have been on holiday, as he was with me yet again – and we were both set up in our usual spots. It had been another warm day (told you!) and as night began to fall I noticed an ominous bank of dark cloud on the horizon. Now this stretch of canal was set in flat open countryside with nothing in the way of tree cover. I mention this because when we stood up, we would have been one of the tallest things for a couple of miles in either direction, which made us both slightly nervous about fishing in thunderstorms. Of course, the rational part of your brain tells you that the odds of being struck by lightning, even in those situations, are extremely long, but when you're in the middle of a storm the rational part of your brain gets beaten up by the irrational side, which is driven by a primeval fear of the lightning. Well, that's what happens with me.

Darkness fell, an unusually black darkness as the clouds came across, the wind dropped and it got warmer. Nothing moved on the surface of the canal; it was almost as if everything was holding its breath. And then there were a few flickers of lightning on the horizon… I wandered over to my mate. 'What do you reckon?'

'If it looks like it's coming this way, we'll pack up,' was his reply.

'Fine by me,' I said.

We stood next to each other making small talk for a further five minutes or so, during which time the flickering on the horizon ceased. Maybe the storm had slid away from us? Then a much closer flash of lightning was followed not many seconds later by a large clap of thunder. I think we both said 'time to go' simultaneously.

I was in the middle of de-tackling when it happened. A huge flash of light, a blast of heat with an instantaneous bang of thunder – quite the brightest light and the loudest noise I'd ever heard. Sparks seemed to jump off the barbed wire fence on the far side of the canal.

Not even the mechanics who change the tyres during a Formula One pit-stop could have beaten me in getting my tackle onto my motorbike that evening. Within seconds we were both tearing along the towpath in increasingly heavy rain, and we didn't stop until we reached the shelter of a road bridge. By the time we got there, the rain was that heavy, the thunder and lightning so frequent, that safe biking was impossible. We therefore turned off our bikes, removed our crash helmets and considered what had just happened.

'That was pretty intense,' I said, still exhilarated by what had just happened.

'Hell, yes,' he replied.

'That lightning struck not too far away to my left,' said I.

'No, it was to my right.'

'Left.'

'Right.'

Then it dawned on us that the lightning must have struck somewhere on the far side of the canal, but between us. At least in those days we didn't have carbon fibre rods.

I never did catch anything bigger than that sixteen-pound carp, and my obsession with the canal, and carp fishing too, started to wane. I loved fishing at night – for years, carp fishing only felt right if it was carried out during the hours of darkness – but as the years progressed, proper employment started and children arrived, I guess night fishing became less practical. Maybe the waning of the obsession was a defence mechanism on my mind's part, a sort of 'if you can't have it then you'd better not want it' attitude. If it was, then this was the only time it happened, as I've never been able to reconcile other obsessions in that way. I think, in reality, that it was just the beginning of a long and slow decline in my love of carp fishing, a creeping malaise which would take nearly a decade to reach its peak. New waters, some of which you'll read about later, almost, but not quite, reinvigorated the obsession. I also couldn't reconcile everything that I loved about carp fishing – the seclusion, the feeling of isolation (we never saw another carp fisherman on our stretch of canal), the emotion of catching a big carp, the fact that a double-figure carp *was* a big fish – with modern carp fishing. Chris

Yates summed it all up perfectly when he referenced modern carping as the business of putting carp on the bank as quickly, and with as little emotion, as possible. Doubtless there was also a little bit of jealousy on my part as the modern cammo-clad carp warrior could catch more, and bigger, carp in a couple of bivvied-up days sitting by an overstocked carp puddle than I could in a whole summer. Although it shouldn't have done, this somehow made my own captures seem just that little bit inferior.

Having said all that, there's a part of me that thinks I still have unfinished business on that canal. Neither my friend or I ever caught a twenty-pound carp, and I've recently been thinking what it would be like to turn the clock back, pre-bait a swim and fish it in the old-fashioned way. I've thought about it a lot, but I have yet to summon sufficient enthusiasm to do it.

I eventually graduated with an upper second-class honours degree to my name and had to decide what I was going to do next. I didn't have a clue what I wanted to do. I wondered, very briefly, about becoming a teacher, but in a rare moment of common sense, I decided that I had no vocation whatsoever towards the teaching profession and the only real attraction was the long summer holiday. Besides which, most years I would have to work on June 16th and to me, this day, the start of the coarse fishing season in England in those days, was the most important day in my year. When my university tutor told me that I should stay on to do a PhD, insisting that an upper second was a waste of a degree if I didn't continue my studies, I agreed, simply because there was nothing better on offer.

My parents were absolutely thrilled; not only did they believe – wrongly – that a doctorate would provide me with an even better job, they would also have a son with the moniker 'Dr Butcher'.

I was living with university friends in Fallowfield, Manchester, by then and my doctorate was to be split between Manchester University and the Freshwater Biological Association based on the banks of Lake Windermere, during which time I would share a house with other students in Bowness. I wasn't certain how often I'd be commuting between the two places, so I traded in my motorbike and bought an old Mk II Cortina from a man in the pub (the Gardeners Arms, of course).

There was some attraction to living in the Lake District; I thought I might be able to do some fishing there, maybe even get to the coast for a bit of sea fishing too. The PhD itself was concerned with the study of humic acids, their chemical categorisation and possible link to the removal of pesticides from aquatic systems. A tenuous link to my hobby, but enough to almost grab my interest.

I soon realised that I wasn't going to be making dramatic eco-changing discoveries at any point in the near future. I won't bore you any more than I have to with the fine details, but my work at the FBA consisted of washing little plastic beads with solvents in a device called a 'Soxhlet Extractor'. These beads had to be completely pure in order to adsorb the minute traces of humic acids that they would later encounter. There were a lot of beads needing a lot of solvent washing, and the Soxhlet Extractor was quite small. I was bored witless and during the day, to the slight annoyance of my supervisor, who was actually a really nice guy, I would slope off into other departments which were doing much more interesting stuff. In particular, they were at that time conducting experiments which involved netting pike and arctic char: I saw some huge pike being brought in, some well over twenty pounds, although it always saddened me that they were dead. At least *they* had died for a better cause than just having their photo taken. Morning and afternoon coffee breaks and lunch were the highlights of the day, formal affairs when everyone stopped what they were doing and gathered in the dining room to talk, drink and eat. Amongst the male staff, the primary topics of conversation were fishing and football, in that order, and I enjoyed listening to tales of sea trout, salmon, occasionally bream and tench, or cod and flatfish.

The evenings were almost as tedious as the days. I'd been used to living just outside the centre of Manchester with friends who were ready to go out whenever the fancy took us. In Bowness, you had one option: the pub, which was usually empty save for the same faces drinking their beer and staring into slowly emptying glasses. Actually, that's not completely true; Bowness did have a large, old-fashioned cinema which must have been capable of seating around five hundred people. I went there with a girl from the FBA once; the woman who sold us our tickets was the same one who offered us our ice creams at half-time and doubtless was the one who ran the film too. So for that evening there was a sum total of three people in that cinema.

After six months, I'd had enough and told everyone I was leaving. My parents were less upset than I expected and said that if I was unhappy then I was doing the right thing. I started looking for a job, easier said than done in those days, but necessary, as I had no money and therefore no ability to go fishing.

A leather carp of 9lb 12oz caught just after midnight on the 16th June 1980

A mirror carp of 16lb 4oz caught in June 1981

A 4lb 13oz tench from Booths Mere.

CHAPTER SEVEN

A REAL JOB, SOME REAL SEA FISHING, AND LOVE IS IN THE AIR

Eventually I found gainful employment, strangely enough only a few hundred yards from where I was living at a place I never even realised existed. I was to be an 'Occupational Hygienist'. Most people immediately think 'toilets' when they see or hear this, but it actually entails workplace monitoring of hazards such as solvents, asbestos and other deadly dusts or vapours. The beauty of this job was that it wasn't based in one place but entailed travel to all parts of the north-west of England, and occasionally beyond. I and seven other guys of a similar age would troop into our manager's office first thing in the morning and be given one or two jobs to be done, after which we'd collect our equipment and head out. Most of the work was asbestos-in-air monitoring, either precautionary or post-

95

asbestos removal, to check that the air was clear of the deadly fibres. We'd set up our equipment, which then ran by itself for two hours, leaving us free to do, well, whatever we wanted to really.

The work was varied and interesting: you could be in a power station one day, a hospital the next, then a factory or school. Quite by accident, I'd been incredibly lucky with my first proper job. Whereas my friends were coming home from banks, supermarkets and warehouses numb from yet another boring day at work, I would be irritatingly full of what I'd seen and done that day. Although the basic wage was a pittance, a mere five thousand pounds per annum, I was also being paid a healthy mileage rate and had the opportunity to work overtime if I wanted to. I'd traded in my old Cortina for a 'Mini Metro Sports' – low mileage, good fuel consumption, hatchback, but lime green in colour with an interior that smelt of sick (a smell I could never get rid of) – so my motoring overheads were pretty low. I was only paying nine pounds and sixty pence per week in rent, so I quickly started to accumulate some spare cash and decided to splash out on some new fishing tackle: sea fishing tackle.

Sea fishing had played a major part in my life for two weeks every year from the age of four, when we first started going to Benllech in Anglesey. These two weeks were spent in a caravan on the 'Golden Sunset' caravan park, a short walk from both the beach, and more importantly, the flat rocks where we went fishing. They say that childhood memories, good or bad, can stay with you for the rest of your life, and thanks to my parents, most of mine are happy ones, with this summer holiday being the major highlight of the year, bigger even than Christmas and birthdays. The build-up to these holidays began about a month before we were due to go: holiday clothes and other items, including sea fishing tackle, would start to accumulate on the spare bed in the back bedroom and a four-week hand-drawn calendar would appear at the bottom of my bed. Each evening we would go through the ritual of crossing off a day with a consequential ratcheting up of the excitement level until the Friday before we departed, I was almost too excited to sleep. It was, in my younger years, a big deal for my father too, as he only got two weeks' paid holiday per annum.

If I needed any more reason to be hyper, then our holiday always seemed to start the day after school had finished for the summer – and we got to travel there by train, and if we were very lucky, a steam train too! Travel by train did present one or two logistical problems though: for example, if you wanted to dig bait – lugworms – you needed a spade. Since we all, me included, were weighed down by cases and fishing rods there was no possibility of taking the house spade with us. Cheap 'bucket and spade' type spades wouldn't last more than a few minutes, so my father made two spades at work, one for him and one for my mother – we didn't do misogyny when it came to the important task of digging lugworm – which could be split into three pieces and assembled when we got the caravan. The shaft, the 'T' bar and the aluminium shovel piece were all connected together by a series of nuts and bolts, and being in three pieces, it would all fit into a normal suitcase. I had the important job of carrying two shoulder bags, one with the leads and assorted end tackle, the other with the reels.

I fell in love with Benllech from the very first time I saw it. It was a scorchingly hot day (definitely true – my mother confirmed this). We'd taken the train to Bangor, then the bus from just outside the station to Benllech itself. The bus was packed; my mother tells me that the bus conductor was determined that no one was to be left behind, to the extent that I sat on her lap and she sat on my father's lap. Other seats were similarly occupied!

We got off the bus outside the caravan park, picked up our keys and walked down towards our home for the next two weeks. That was when I saw the sea and beach for the first time. The sea was a perfect blue, marked with parallel white lines of surf which cascaded down onto a golden sandy beach. Our caravan was right down by the coastal path, with a glorious view of the sea and beach.

I have only two other memories from that first holiday. The first, not surprisingly, is angling related: my father went out fishing one evening on an amphibious DUKW, a sort of military vehicle suited for both land and sea (look, just Google it if you want to know more) and I awoke the following morning to see a variety of fish – I can't remember what sort – which we filleted and fed the offcuts to the seagulls. Apparently, I wasn't very happy at not being allowed to go!

The second memory from that summer of '66 is brief but pertinent. I was on the beach with my mother on the middle Saturday of our holiday. Yet again, it was hot and sunny, my father wasn't with us for some strange reason and I was busy trying to make sandcastles. My mother was listening to the radio, again not unusual, when she suddenly swore. Proper swearing. And then turned the radio off and threw it onto the sand. I'd never heard her swear before (and I've never heard her swear since). Most odd. I thought I'd better say something but couldn't think of anything to say other than 'what's wrong?'

'Those... (she just managed to avoid swearing again) Germans have just equalised with the last kick of the game!'

England's one and only World Cup win therefore passed me completely by. My father was in the pub that afternoon, along with every other Englishman in Benllech, but I have no recollection of him coming back to the caravan in high spirits, nor do I recall my mother mentioning the result. They must have talked about it, but obviously, I didn't warrant it to be of sufficient importance to store it away as a 'major memory'.

As soon as we acquired our first car, we drove to Anglesey for our summer holiday, which deprived me of a precious train trip. In those days the journey, which would start by six am, would take up to three hours and had to include a stop for breakfast and possibly a toilet break too. We always stopped in the Little Chef car park at Penmaenmawr; we didn't go into the café itself but sat outside in the car park overlooking the sea and ate our sausage sandwiches and drank our flask of coffee. We'd also sneak inside to use their 'facilities' if we needed to. Having a car did enable us to move around a little more. Not that I wanted to move away from Benllech much, I was quite happy spending those two precious weeks digging bait, fishing, damming rivers on the beach and eating ice cream. We caught dabs, mackerel and whiting from the shore and every Friday hired a rowing boat so that we could get out into the bay itself, where, if we were very lucky, we might even catch a dogfish. The sun always shone and it never rained: truly idyllic. Incidentally, my mother disputed this last sentence and claimed that my brain had airbrushed out the times we spent huddled together underneath a 'Pac-a-mac' waiting for the rain to stop.

As I got older, I graduated from a hand-held crab line to my own sea fishing rod; the same rod you met earlier at Mobberley and Booths Mere and which accounted for my first pike. We always fished from the same spot, and having no tripod or other form of rod rest in those days, we leaned our rods against a large rock – my mother always called it 'our' rock – while we waited for a bite. In later years, I even persuaded my father to splash out on a primitive beachcaster which was 'on offer' - in other words, it was crap and no one else would buy it - in a local tackle shop (not Joe Dyson's, I hasten to add).

Every year that passed my fascination with sea fishing grew a little stronger, and that obsessional little seed, nourished by articles in *Angling* magazine and in the books by the likes of Gammon and Gillespie, started to flourish. We even tried some new marks, including one on the Menai Straits where we saw an angler return to his car with a very large bass. That mark would eventually become one of my favourites. The trouble was that we were complete beginners at this sea-fishing lark; we knew how to catch a few fish from the one spot near the caravan in Benllech, but this simply didn't translate to any other marks that we knew. To be honest, my father was quite happy fishing the same spot for most of the time and never developed any obsessional need to fish anywhere else being, as always, very laid back about what he caught and how he caught it.

When I got to my late teens, I started a few exploratory trips to Benllech by myself, or with my buddy John. I'd managed to find another caravan site on the outskirts of Benllech, where you could hire a caravan for eight pounds per night 'out of season'. I started to catch a few more fish from the shore – mainly dogfish and whiting – and started to fish some other marks in the Benllech area, but still felt I was missing something.

Actually, there were two things missing.

The first absentees were cod. Or codling, or even codlets. I couldn't get that picture of 'man plus cod emerging from the surf at night' out of my head. I would call it a fledgling obsession, not a full-blown one as I did not yet have a reference point – in other words, somewhere I could catch cod – to be able to dream up the relevant scenarios.

The other 'something' was decent fishing tackle. The ability to put a medium-sized bait any sort of distance requires a reasonably competent rod and reel, not necessarily an expensive one but certainly something better than anything I possessed. It was in those first few months of work that I decided to start taking my sea fishing seriously. I started to use the time I had free during the day, when my air monitors were running, to start reading up on how exactly I should be fishing. I re-read some of my old fishing books, concentrating on rigs and baits, as opposed to the descriptions of beach and fish, and I bought a book on *Long Distance Casting* by John Holden. A trip to the tackle shop in Urmston, where a much better choice of sea fishing tackle was available, saw me purchase a large fixed-spool reel designed solely for sea fishing, a 'Paul Kerry Supercast' thirteen-foot fibre glass beachcaster, assorted leads, line and rigs and an 'Anchor' paraffin lamp, as I intended to do a lot of night fishing. I also bought some proper wet weather gear – a one-piece waxed cotton affair, think of a cross between a pair of overalls and a Barbour Jacket – and a head lamp.

My new sea fishing reel, a Mitchell 498, was nicknamed 'the mangle', being as heavy and ungainly a fishing reel as can ever have been invented. It was effective though, and after weeks of practice on a local sports field I could perform a very loose approximation of a 'pendulum cast' and a respectable 'off the ground' cast.

In October of that same year I booked three days off work, which in addition to the weekend would give me five days of bait digging and fishing time. I couldn't wait, and felt the same giddy excitement that I'd felt as a kid. By sheer coincidence, two days before I was due to finish work we got a job in for the following morning for some air tests to be carried out on the old Army Camp at Ty Croes on Anglesey. My boss said that I could have this job and simply stay on in Anglesey, provided I could get the equipment back to the office via the Red Star parcel office at Holyhead train station. What a result! An extra evening's fishing, and the company would pay my mileage rate to and from the job, which would effectively pay for the whole trip.

The job took a little longer than expected, but one of the Army Guards at Ty Croes was a keen fisherman and directed me to a house in Holyhead where I could buy some worms. It was almost dark when I arrived at the caravan site and after throwing my clothes and rations for the week into the caravan I immediately headed out to fish. I went to a mark at the point of St David's Bay, really just an extension of Benllech Bay, but someone had assured me that the fishing was better there than off my usual mark. It was my most successful session as a sea fisherman and I caught whiting, dogfish and best of all, two decent sized plaice of maybe a pound each. I didn't catch what I most wanted, which was a codling, but I did see another group of anglers turn up who claimed they were after bass (a fish I could only ever dream of catching at that stage).

After some persistent interrogation by yours truly, one of the anglers was willing to give me a little advice – well, a lot really. 'If you want to catch a codling, try the Straits,' he said. 'You can fish anywhere at low water but Port Dinorwic would be a nice easy place to start.'

Low water? I never fished low water. Surely you could only catch fish in the hours leading up to high water and, obviously, never on the ebb. I had so much to learn. He also suggested a mark beyond Beaumaris, and said that Dinas Dinlle, the other side of Caernarvon, was a great beach to fish; whiting were plentiful, but it would also offer the possibility of bass and codling.

The following morning, I was up early to catch the low water and dig some proper worms: big black lugworms. The only facet of sea angling that I could claim any expertise in was bait digging, both blow lug and black lug. Black lug required a particular technique if you were to get the whole worm and not just severed bits. Firstly, you looked for a black wormcast that looked like nothing more than a few concentric circles of black sand; you then skimmed the top of the sand off until you could see a definite hole and the tail of the worm itself, which would promptly vanish. You then dug like crazy until you could see the worm again, at which point you would drop to your knees and plunge your hand in after the worm until you felt it. A slow extraction while gently wriggling the worm ensured that the black lugworm came out intact and ready for use. You then had to bury it back in the sand in your bait bucket before it decided to quite literally turn itself inside out. The difference between black and blow lug was that black lug would last for ages on the hook, especially in the vicious currents of the Menai Straits, whereas blow lug would be washed out in minutes.

That afternoon I headed off to Port Dinorwic and drove down to the front of the harbour. The harbour had been built in the 1800s to serve the Welsh slate industry, and at one point boasted both full size and narrow-gauge railway lines. By the 80s these had long since gone, and you could drive across compacted cinders and stone right to the front of the harbour wall. The harbour itself was around two hundred yards long by forty yards wide and was starting to be filled with yachts, a sign of things to come. Behind you, lines of grey terraced houses rose up from harbour level in parallel rows along the hill side. The whole feel of the place was one of dark, dank, post-industrial desolation. It was low water, dusk, heavily overcast, incredibly quiet and very still; I can still distinctly remember the smoke from the terraced houses behind me rising ramrod straight up into the evening sky, where it seamlessly joined the low grey cloud.

A one-hook clipped-down paternoster rig was loaded with two very juicy black lugworms and then launched about 60 or 70 yards into the Straits. After no more than about five minutes something strange happened; instead of the tap-tap-tapping I normally associated with a bite, the whole rod started bouncing up and down. Stranger still, when I picked the rod up and started winding in, something was pulling back quite hard, until at the bottom of the harbour wall I saw my first cod, or more accurately, codling. It was unceremoniously hauled up the wall, unhooked, weighed (all of 2½ lb) before being gazed upon adoringly. Such a beautiful fish; I couldn't bring myself to kill it, so I threw it back into the water. Or tried to throw it back into the water. Unfortunately, there was a short gap between the harbour wall and the water and the fish landed just at this interface, upon which a horde of seagulls appeared out of nowhere to dismember it.

I fished on right up to high water but only remember catching a dogfish, which was disappointing in the extreme, because on striking I was convinced I had latched onto another codling. I also noted that not more than two hours after low water the Straits ripped through at quite a pace, the surface becoming a mass of fast moving boils and ripples meaning that effective fishing was difficult unless you were fishing inside this current. I didn't think there would be many codling in this slower moving, shallow water.

On the way back to the caravan, I stopped at the 'chippy' and treated myself to fish and chips – a rare treat, as I was very much in the grip of a full-blown health and fitness regime –

or should that be obsession?

Whilst sitting in my caravan eating this little treat, I experienced another moment of supreme happiness. I had a job I enjoyed; I was fit and felt good about myself; I had some spare money; I had caught a codling; I could even try and catch another codling tomorrow *and* go to Dinas Dinlle, where there was just a possibility that I could recreate that photo I had imprinted on my brain.

There was another reason why I was happy. A few weeks prior to this little break I'd gone down with some friends to the Cellar Bar Disco in the Manchester University Student Union building. While there, I'd got talking to a strikingly attractive blonde girl, asked her to dance and then asked her out. She'd accepted this invitation and forgiven me when I cancelled the date in favour of some overtime. We had been out together several times since then and shared our first kiss. *(I really enjoyed writing those last few lines: they make me sound very cool, as if I was in the habit of successfully chatting girls up at discos...)* Anyway, her name was Lorraine, she was doing a PhD in History at Manchester University and she was my new girlfriend.

The following day I drove down to Dinas Dinlle for a quick recce. I liked what I saw; a long flat beach which ended with a short bank of shingle upon which you could park your car. So, later that afternoon I headed back to Port Dinorwic, but I wasn't able to replicate my success of the previous day. Instead of staying there until high water, I packed up after a couple of hours and headed down to the beach at Dinas, arriving there just as the water was in sight of the shingle. It didn't take me long to realise that I'd found a spiritual home: not necessarily Dinas in general, but the beach. For a start, you could hear the waves breaking onto the shore, the rod tip moved with the waves, and the place felt much more alive than the flat waters of the Straits. I didn't catch a codling, but did manage some large whiting, much bigger ones than I'd ever caught in the Benllech area. It was at this point that my fledgling obsession with codling burst into a fully formed one. And all because of a single photo in an angling magazine.

I soon discovered that North Wales was not the best place to have such an obsession. The north-facing beaches around Abergele, which in those pre A55 dual carriageway days were the only places I could realistically get there and back to in an evening, were not generally known for their run of codling. This meant that I had to use every possible opportunity to get back to Anglesey for three or four-day breaks.

The following Easter I asked Lorraine if she fancied coming to Anglesey with me on holiday. I was totally honest with her and said that there would be at least one bait digging session and one fishing trip every day. No problem, she said, she'd love to come both bait digging and fishing with me. We drove there through heavy pre-Easter traffic while singing along to Lloyd Cole and the Commotions which was the tape (note: tape, not CD or iPod) which I'd been listening to on the previous autumn's trip. I don't remember much about that little Easter break apart from a feeling of happiness. We dug bait together – well, I dug, but Lorraine found the worm casts for me – and went fishing together. I can't even remember what we caught.

A few months after Easter I had an opportunity to go back to Anglesey with work again for a couple of days: same place as before, the Ty Croes Army Camp. Lorraine came with me and the tides just happened to be perfect; I could get my work done by mid to late afternoon, rush back and dig bait, then head out to Dinas for an evening's fishing. Just a few words on bait digging: as you will have gathered, when I was young this was a family ritual in which we all took part and was often as enjoyable as the fishing itself. Worms were dug, then streams were dammed and finally, ice creams were eaten. I still found bait digging rewarding in my twenties, even more so when I was told how to dig 'king ragworm,' a beast of a worm with large pincers. The larger specimens, which can be over two feet long, can deliver a hefty nip.

The day in question was one of those rare days when everything goes better than planned, and I found myself digging for ragworm on the Menai Straits by mid-afternoon, having managed to get my work completed far earlier than expected. The ragworm was also obtained without any dramas and so off to Dinas we headed.

It was a lovely late May evening; still, warm, bright with hardly any movement in the water, not exactly ideal bass conditions. I'd already decided that we were going to try and catch a bass; I'd never caught one before but had been told that Dinas Dinlle was as good a beach as any to catch them from, indeed, it had been regarded as possibly Wales's premier bass beach back in the sixties. With absolutely no surf I thought the chances of catching a bass were virtually non-existent and that any fish that were about would be a long way out. Pendulum casting time; I swung the lead and let rip for the horizon... well, maybe some of the casts were over the 100-yard mark. And some were nearly straight too. I attached a small fixed-spool reel onto my father's old beachcaster, added trace and bait and passed it over to Lorraine, who had decided that she would 'have a cast or two'. I thought better of trying to teach her to pendulum cast and just showed her the basic mechanics of a gentle overhead cast. She coped with this well enough to be able to drop a bait a good... well, about 15 yards out. Five minutes later her rod doubled over and such was my surprise it took me a few seconds to realise that this might well be a bite. What else could it be? Yet her bait was so close to the shore that you could almost see it in the gin-clear water. She picked the rod up and it was obvious that she had indeed hooked a fish. After the shortest of battles a little bass of less than a pound was dragged up onto the shingle. Small it may have been but a bass is a bass, especially when you've never even seen a live one before, let alone caught one.

Fifteen minutes later, after she'd caught her third small bass, I finally conceded that I might be fishing a little too far out, but by the time I'd adjusted my distance the shoal had moved on and I blanked! So, there we have it: Lorraine, my girlfriend, catches a bass before I do. (And she never stops reminding me of it!)

I made a few other half-hearted attempts to catch a bass. Although I was impressed by both their appearance – they are the epitome of a bristly, aggressive hunter-fish – and if those little bass were anything to go by, their fighting qualities, I never felt compelled to try and catch one. Why not? Well, I thought of bass fishing as essentially a summer occupation, and I already had other angling obsessions which were much stronger for this time of year.

Lorraine and I went back to Benllech every autumn for the next few years. I caught codling from the Straits on a regular basis, but struggled to catch one from any of the beaches. It didn't matter as we always enjoyed ourselves there and found plenty of other things to do as we explored the island; visiting places that I'd been to in my childhood and discovering new places of our own.

I knew that any girl who was willing to come fishing with me in all weathers just had to be a 'keeper', and I wondered how to approach the subject of us possibly getting engaged.

We'd made the long walk from the car to the Old Lifeboat Station, just south of Beaumaris on the Menai Straits; technically, it's called 'Friars Bay'. It was a misty evening in late October and with a bucketful of black lugworm and low water approaching on a big tide I was confident of catching a few codling. 'Let's make this a little more interesting,' I said half-jokingly, 'if we catch more than two codling tonight we should get engaged.' She just laughed and said 'OK'. I caught the first codling just after low water, a nice fish of nearly three pounds and followed it shortly after with a smaller one of a pound and a half. And just before we packed up, I brought in a codlet of maybe six ounces, small but still technically a codling. Nothing was said.

We moved on to a high-water mark, the point at St David's at the far end of Benllech Bay. There's a little patch of grass there, just before you climb down onto the rocks. It's the patch of grass where I went down on one knee and asked my girlfriend to marry me. She said yes.

My mother fishing on the rocks at Benllech in the late seventies.

Me plus dab outside our caravan in the late sixties or early seventies.

Dinas Dinlle, May 1987

CHAPTER EIGHT

THREE FIRSTS

Having got engaged, we decided to buy a house together. It was the logical thing to do as we'd effectively been living together for some years anyway. We looked at a few properties before deciding on one in Chorlton, a suburb of south Manchester. It was a three-bedroomed semi-detached house which was almost a carbon copy of the one I grew up in, but without the pond at the bottom of the garden. It was a short bus ride into the university for Lorraine and a ten-minute car ride for me to get back to my office in Fallowfield.

Although I'd had a pay rise, money was still tight and Lorraine had to take a part-time job in a supermarket in order for us to make ends meet. I'm going to sound like a real old fogey now, but here goes anyway. We would never have dreamt of asking my parents or Lorraine's father for money; it just wasn't the done thing and would have been pointless anyway as they didn't have spare cash. We simply lived within our means. We didn't regard foreign holidays as an essential; a takeaway or a bottle of wine was a once-per-month treat and all our furniture was second-hand, either bought or cast-offs from relatives. As long as we had enough money to feed and clothe ourselves and to pay for my angling subs and bait, we were happy. Well, I was happy, and I think this made Lorraine happy too!

We loved our first house. We gradually redecorated it from top to bottom and made the overgrown garden presentable.

Another first came as a result of my growing obsession with tench; not any old tench, but tench caught from the boat on Tabley Mere. I'd had a few exploratory trips there in my student days but failed to catch anything. Although not a large expanse of water, Tabley Mere has depths varying from little more than a couple of feet to in excess of twenty feet. I struggled to float fish in the deeper areas and had no confidence in fishing the shallower ones.

Two things happened which set me on the road to success. The first was a chance meeting with Keith Crowther, during which I explained my total lack of success at Tabley; he had one piece of advice – look to fish in water between five and eight feet in depth. The second was that one spring, the managers of the estate had to lower the water levels in order to repair the outfall sluice. This gave me the opportunity to see the contours of the Mere in all but the deepest areas, which still held enough water to safely contain all of the fish. The bottom dried out sufficiently for us to walk around the mere, a surreal experience if ever there was one. You could still see the remains of the stumps of the trees which had been originally felled to make the mere in the first place, and apparently a rusted 'man trap' had been recovered from the lake-bed. Early gamekeepers had used these vicious foot-trapping devices to deter poachers.

I was also mindful of a comment by Chris Yates regarding Redmire Pool, possibly the world's most famous carp water. During the long hot summer of 1976, the water level in Redmire dropped and left much of the bottom to dry out. When the rains came and the water level returned to normal, he thought that the water seemed 'sweeter' and the carp more invigorated than had been the case for many a year. It occurred to me that there might be a similar effect with Tabley Mere.

Some of my angling obsessions result from one defining moment, for example, *that* photograph in *Angling* magazine which was the origin of my cod and sea fishing obsession. Some start small and develop over time, and some result as a combination of almost random events falling into line. In this case, it started with seeing my first tench at Booths mere when I was young. Then, of course, there was the *Angling* magazine article concerning tench being caught from the punts on Blenheim Lake. And finally, my pike fishing trips – in the boat – to Booths and Tabley Mere in previous years. Add to this the fact that Tabley was known for producing big tench – a six-pound fish was possible, and who knows, the 'sweetening' effect of the water could maybe even push these six pounders into... well, suffice to say that I was determined to catch a tench from there, and with the new information I possessed I was almost confident.

I knew exactly where I was going to fish, and the boat was duly booked. Then disaster struck, in the form of a back injury sustained somehow at work. Although I could sit still and fish, there was no way I could row a boat... er, Lorraine, would you fancy taking a day off from your studies and rowing me around a Cheshire mere? Incredibly, she said yes.

The day in question dawned dull, damp and breezy and I almost felt guilty for dragging my fiancée out of bed in the knowledge that she'd be sitting there shivering for a good part of the morning. Almost, but not quite. I did feel a little guilty as I sat there in the front of the boat giving out instructions: 'a bit more on your right-hand oar there please' or 'just push that post in a little more', but eventually we were moored up to posts in about four feet of water, which meant that I could cast to the edge of a channel which I now knew to be about six to seven feet deep. I was only just able to throw in my groundbait, although catapulting the corn out wasn't too bad.

During previous failures here, I'd had great difficulty in keeping my float in the same spot. There was a tremendous undercurrent whenever there was even the slightest of breezes and my floats were just not simply up to the job. I'd therefore acquired some 'Drennan Driftbeaters', a strange float with a bulbous body, a long slender stem and a pleasing red blob on the top. When weighted down so that only the red blob was showing it looked very good against the green backdrop afforded by the bankside trees, as we were only some ten or fifteen yards from the bank. The ripple on the water made it difficult to see if there were any tench bubbling, but there was no mistaking the sight of one rolling at about six o'clock.

A few minutes later, I had my first bite and promptly missed it. I didn't feel too distraught as I was sure that there were more to come; in fact it added to the level of excitement I felt. To catch one straight away would have lessened the experience.

Eventually, at around seven-thirty, the little red blob lifted a little, then stayed upright in its new position for three or four heart-stopping seconds before disappearing completely. I struck and made contact with what could only be a tench. I let it run and run, and when I felt the initial power reduce, I slowly turned the fish and worked it back towards me. As soon as it saw the boat, it shot off again, and this cycle repeated itself on three or four more occasions, although each time the run was shorter and less convincing.

There is little to beat that feeling of elation when you look into your landing net and think... that's a good fish, it's a *really* good fish, it's just what I've been after. At 5lb 8oz, it was my first Tabley tench, my first five-pound tench and therefore my best-ever. I could get used to this, I thought, but little did I know then that over thirty years later I'd still be getting just as much pleasure from it.

Lorraine kindly took some photos for me of this fish and a slightly smaller one – 4lb 12oz – which followed about an hour later. I could quite happily have stayed there all day but decided that, in deference to Lorraine, and with the wind getting stronger by the minute, we would leave soon after the coffee and sandwiches had run out.

Having finally cracked the Tabley code I continued to catch tench, but only from that one spot. It would take years before I felt confident in a whole host of swims on this beautiful piece of water.

The arrival of this obsession led to the death of another. I simply stopped fishing the canal for its carp, although by this time my trips had become far less frequent anyway. It wasn't a conscious decision; I was working and had limited time to fish and other angling obsessions to feed. It wasn't that I could say that I'd caught the biggest carp in the canal or that I didn't enjoy fishing there, but, I didn't *need* to fish there any more. My life could be lived without twice-weekly trips to the canal, and before I knew it I'd lost any real desire to fish there. It's very difficult to put all of this into words, but quite simply, I think my Tabley Mere tench obsession superseded my canal carp obsession.

I managed to book the boat on Tabley Mere for the beginning of the following season, the morning of the 16th June. My angling buddy John Woodhouse and I arrived at 2 am and found we needed a torch, not only to set up our tackle but also to find my swim – the same swim as previously mentioned - on the far side of the mere in the darkness of a heavily wooded bank. It was a dull, grey morning interspersed with heavy rain showers, which wouldn't have bothered me in the slightest had we been catching tench, but we sat there all morning without getting a bite. This was another Tabley Mere lesson for me: the tench can be there one day and gone the next, maybe not to return for weeks or even a whole summer. Fortunately, help was at hand from another regular angler on the mere, Glynn Stockdale, who we observed catching tench from an area of the mere known as 'the Deep Hole'. It was called that because it was deep, in excess of ten feet deep in places, and roughly circular with a diameter of maybe seventy yards. You'd never have guessed that, would you?

The following weekend saw me back in the boat by myself on what can only be described as the perfect tench-fisher's morning. Maybe not perfect conditions for catching tench, but perfect conditions to *experience* tench. First light saw me moored up a few boat-lengths away from the steep shelf of the Deep Hole in around three feet of water; it was still, there wasn't a cloud in the sky and 'smoke' (ie mist) poured off the water and swirled around the boat. Every now and again the mist would form itself into pillars which would rise up from the water and drift across in front of the boat in a series of almost ghostly apparitions. 'Smoky water' is the perfect accompaniment to a morning's tench fishing; it was magical then and is no less enchanting today. Of course, the downside of this is that sometimes you have to wait for the mist to clear before you can see your float properly, especially if you're fishing at some distance, as I was.

I'd decided that to minimise any disturbance within my swim I should moor the boat as far away as possible, the actual distance being determined by how far I could cast my float. Since the Driftbeater wasn't ideal to cast, I'd found one which was similar but without the un-aerodynamic blob; I think it was called a 'zoomer'. It did have the all-important red tip though. A small amount of hemp-laced groundbait was prepared and thrown as far as I could. Small amounts of maggots and sweetcorn were catapulted out over the top of this, soon to be followed by my float and a size fourteen hook with a single grain of corn. All this was completed before five o'clock in the morning, and I sat back to enjoy the first cup of coffee of the day accompanied by a custard cream biscuit or two.

Glynn had also arrived by now and he set up a few boat lengths away from me; he had his camera with him and took a photo of me which now occupies pride of place above the television in my lounge.

At around six o'clock, I saw a dark shape emerge from the water, pause, and then slide away: the first tench roll of the morning. The pulse immediately quickens when this happens because you know you're in the right place; it doesn't by any means ensure that you're going to catch a tench, but it's always good to know that there are at least some in the vicinity. Soon after this, the first patch of bubbles appeared, a large fizzing patch that came and went as the mist moved across the water. My float was also lost from sight as the mist rolled around my swim, and then, as the mist cleared, it just wasn't there. So I struck – and missed. My hands were shaking as I put fresh corn on the hook and removed a trace of fresh tench slime from the line.

My next bite coincided with a larger gap in the mist. There came a single slow dip of the float, followed seconds later by it sinking slowly away. A strike – a little bit harder than I would have ideally liked, but I was barely containing my excitement by this time – and a tench was hooked. I played it ultra-cautiously, letting it roam wherever it wanted to go until eventually it was circling in front of me. I caught a glimpse of it in the clear waters; it was big, certainly bigger than any other tench I'd caught. With trembling hands, I guided it over the rim of the net and lifted it into the boat. The weigh sling was wetted, the scales zeroed, the tench was added to the sling and the pointer settled on 6lb 5oz. I couldn't have been happier.

I put the tench in my keepnet and cast out again. (By the way, I stopped using a keepnet soon after this and haven't used one since) Thirty minutes later, history repeated itself: a carbon copy of the bite and fight led to me weighing another beautiful tench just a couple of ounces smaller than the first one. I'd never caught a six-pound tench before, and now I'd caught two of them!

My final 'first' concerns the capture of my first twenty-pound carp. The previous spring had seen me call in on Astle Mere, the scene of my falling-in all those years ago. I'd been working in the area and wanted to see how the place had changed. The mere itself had silted up to the extent that it was less than a quarter of its original size, the feeder streams being the culprits, each bringing down copious amounts of this silt. The club had hatched a plan to divert the feeder streams, dig out the silt, and leave the larger stream permanently diverted to pick up the outgoing river without passing through the mere itself. The work had been completed a couple of years ago and the mere restocked. The bankside vegetation had started to return and the whole place had a more picturesque feel to it. More importantly, the expanse of water was back to its original size, if still not quite as deep as it used to be.

Another aside, the first for a while though: my friend and I coined a term for such places. We called them 'habitual' from the phrase in Arthur Ransome's fishing essays *Rod and Line*: 'A true record of the life of an 'habitual' carp fisher would be a book to set beside De Quincey's *Confessions of an Opium Eater*'. To be 'habitual,' a place had to comply with the following characteristics: overgrown bank-age; relatively unfished with preferably no other anglers being present; contain large carp or tench; weedy or lily-covered areas of water; and it had to be set in a secluded part of the countryside.

Back to Astle, which on this day felt decidedly 'habitual'. I wandered around the mere, ploughing through chest-high vegetation, until I came across a group of carp basking in the sun. Big carp too, bigger than anything I'd ever caught. I decided there and then that my opening day venue on the 16th June would not be the canal this year but Astle Mere.

For two weeks prior to the season I embarked on a pre-baiting campaign (sweetcorn and luncheon meat) and chose a swim on the far side of the mere from where I'd seen the carp on the basis that there was a slightly deeper channel there, about four feet in depth, caused by the need to dig out clay from the bottom of the mere to form a new bank which separated the mere itself from the diverted feeder stream. On the afternoon of the 15th June I turned up to claim 'my swim'. Of course, there was no one there, but I was paranoid that someone might have been watching me bait up and decide to get there before me. Midnight came after a long, hot afternoon and evening, and there was still no one there when I made my first casts. I fished all the way through to nine o'clock the following morning without my indicators – still the little pieces of folded plastic – moving, save for when a bat flew into the line.

I returned three times over the course of the next week but caught nothing. A friend of mine did manage to catch a couple of small carp by fishing worm on the opposite bank. I tried this too, but once again failed to catch anything.

The following year I returned to Astle Mere – not on opening day, as I was on Tabley Mere as previously described, but for a couple of evening sessions. I decided to fish on the same bank from where my friend had caught some carp, not the same spot but one much further along towards the top of the lake. There were two reasons for choosing this area to fish, the first being that I could see carp moving in this area and every now and again I could see the water 'cloud up' as they truffled for food on the bottom. The second reason for fishing there was that the bankside vegetation, a mixture of grasses and reeds, was almost head high. I therefore had to flatten a little square of bank to fish from and could sit there in my own little cocoon, invisible to the world. Not that I ever saw another angler there anyway.

On my first visit, I caught a perch and a rainbow trout, both on worm, and the trout gave an especially good bite and fight. My precious piece of white plastic was catapulted into the bankside vegetation, never to be seen again despite me spending a good hour looking for it before admitting defeat! The evening of my second visit was bright but not particularly warm and I was glad of the fact that the surrounding vegetation protected me from the breeze that that was blowing straight along the water in front of me. I catapulted out some worms and a bit of corn and sat back to watch and wait. The ripple on the water meant that it was difficult to spot if there were any carp in front of me, but after a couple of hours – I'd arrived just before six o'clock – my little plastic indicator moved slowly up to the rod and fell off the line, and I watched as line slowly left the spool. I didn't know what to expect as I struck, but the weight on the end of the line and a large commotion in the water told me that I had indeed hooked a carp.

I would like to say that it tore round the mere like a carp possessed by demons, ripping line off the spool and giving me all sorts of heart palpitations, but it didn't. It made a few slow, short runs and apart from that just wallowed and rolled as it came towards me. I brought it into my landing net without any dramas, but when I went to unhook it I realised that the hook had come out in the net. I've often wondered if I'd foul-hooked this fish. It would certainly explain the slowness of the run if the fish had just picked up my line as it drifted across it. However, in the absence of any definitive evidence, I'm claiming it as a fair catch.

I soaked my weigh-sling, zeroed the scales, slipped the carp, a mirror, into the sling and weighed it: 20lb 4oz. At the time I was ecstatic, no doubt about that, but over time the pleasure associated with this fish has faded more than, for example, my first six-pound tench, or, as you will later learn, my first ray. I'm not exactly sure why this is. I would imagine that it has to do with my gradual divorce from carp fishing and everything associated with it, which is quite sad really.

Having landed and weighed the fish, I now needed to photograph it. Although I had upgraded my camera to one which took a decent quality of photograph, I was by myself and didn't have anything as sophisticated as a remote release cable. I desperately wanted to have a photo of me holding the fish, so the only thing to be done was to leave the fish in the weigh sling and in the water while I ran up to Astle Hall and asked the owner if he would come and photograph the fish for me. The angling club had specifically asked that we stay away from the hall as the occupier, a gentleman in his seventies, had a reputation of being a 'bit difficult'.

I knocked on the door, he opened it and with more than a little trepidation I asked in my politest manner, 'I'm very sorry for bothering you but I've caught quite a large carp and as I'm by myself I was hoping that you might take a photograph of me holding this carp. I'm really sorry for disturbing you but I would be very grateful if you could help me'. He smiled at me, agreed without hesitation and accompanied me slowly back down to the waterside. I gave him the camera, showed him where the shutter-button was and posed with the fish. As he lifted the camera up to eye level, I noticed that his hands were shaking; in fact, the camera was bouncing all over the place. The poor bloke obviously had some sort of degenerative nervous disease, and that is why the only photos I have of myself and this fish are blurred, and in every shot I and the fish are at the top, bottom or side of the photo, never in the middle.

The capture of this carp was the culmination of my short-lived obsession with Astle Mere. Actually, obsession isn't the right word for my relationship with Astle: I think 'affair' is a better description, a brief dalliance that interrupted my main romance with Tabley Mere and its tench. You might think I would have spent many more evenings there, but for some reason I didn't. I can only remember fishing there a couple more times, although I did manage to catch a perfectly conditioned brown-backed mirror carp of 17lb on a floating cat biscuit. Why a cat biscuit as opposed to the usual dog biscuits (aka 'chum mixers')? Because we had cats and not dogs!

So why did the affair peter out so quickly? I think I realised that the twenty-pounder I'd caught was the biggest fish in the mere. Having therefore performed the ultimate feat with its capture, there didn't seem a great point in continuing. Interestingly, this theme would ultimately prove fundamental in my conversion to sea fishing.

My first Tabley Mere tench at 5lb 8oz, courtesy of Lorraine

Another first: two six-pound tench from Tabley Mere.

Smoky water at dawn on Tabley Mere.

The best photo I have of me and my first 20lb carp. Shame about the shaking camera.

The gentleman from Astle Hall with my 20lb carp.

CHAPTER NINE

NEW JOB, NEW HOUSE, NEW WIFE AND NEW EXPERIENCES

They say that the three most stressful things you can do are to move house, start a new job and get married. So, at the age of twenty-six, I thought I'd do all three within the space of a few months.

Although I still mainly enjoyed my job, there were some big issues looming with it. Firstly, exams: to become a qualified Occupational Hygienist you had to pass a series of them. When I walked out of my final Biochemistry exam I vowed to myself that it was the last one I'd ever do – I hated revising, hated the fact that it not only stopped me going fishing but stopped me thinking of going fishing, reading about fishing and daydreaming angling-related scenarios.

I'd tried to start revising for my first Occupational Hygiene exam, but couldn't summon up the enthusiasm for it. It was also not the highest paid profession; money had never been that important to me, I had enough to furnish my angling obsessions and to pay the mortgage on the house in Chorlton. However, one of the promises I'd made to myself was that I wanted to live in the countryside, and in particular, I wanted to be able to open my bedroom curtains in the morning and look out over fields. Thankfully, Lorraine shared this vision, but the salary of an Occupational Hygienist was unlikely to turn it into reality.

The first 'new' was thus, the new job. I moved to a waste company based mainly in the north of England and worked out of an office in St Helens. It was a commercially orientated role and I soon found that I enjoyed the buzz from winning large contracts. It was a great company to work for and within a couple of years I'd been handed the role of manager of a new unit which had been created to handle the burgeoning amount of hazardous waste that the company was beginning to handle. The unit was based in Kirkby in Merseyside and I was joined by a small group of people of similar age to myself.

I look back very fondly on these times: we knew no fear, worked hard, played hard and had total confidence in the senior management of the company. The 'work hard, play hard' thing may be a bit of a cliché, but it did represent everything that the company was about. If you were away on business you worked late, then hit the bar and stayed there until the early hours. Won a big contract? Then take your colleagues and your wives out for an expensive meal courtesy of the company. Great times, and I looked up to the directors of that company and decided that I'd quite like to be a director one day too.

One of the best things about the new job was that it came with an all-expenses-paid quality company car, meaning that all my fuel was now free, although classed as a taxable perk. I'd moved on to, or rather inherited, a company car in my first post, a second-hand Astra with nearly ninety thousand miles on the clock, cigarette burns on the seats, cigarette stubs in the ashtray, glove compartment, on the floor, under the seats and in the door trays. It was more of a mobile ash tray than a car. There were also used condoms under the passenger seat.

The big downside of the new job was that I'd be working longer hours, which meant that weekday evening fishing sessions would no longer be viable.

The second 'new' was our wedding. We got married in a church in Timperley (John Woodhouse was my best man), and had our wedding reception at a hotel near Manchester Airport. It was a scorchingly hot day in late May – I have the photos to prove it – and a good time was had by all. We had a short two-day honeymoon in the Lake District and by the Wednesday I was back in work; we'd just won a big contract and I couldn't be spared for more than a few days.

Lorraine had finished her PhD by now and had started working in local government. The third 'new' therefore involved us moving to a new house; being a dual-income family we were able to move out of suburbia in Chorlton, south Manchester to the Cheshire countryside just outside Northwich. It was still a 'semi,' in fact, it was a much smaller semi-detached house than the one we'd just left, but it did come with a view of the countryside and a big garden.

One of the first things we did was to have my father and brother across to help me dig a large pond at the bottom of this garden. Not large enough to fish in, of course, but large enough for me to stock with crucian carp (what else?), roach, perch and a single mirror carp called 'Clarence'.

I also joined the local angling club, which gave me access to a variety of waters including the local canal. The Trent and Mersey Canal was completely different from the other canals I'd fished; it was shallow and lined only with clay, which meant that the colour varied between milky tea and strong tea depending on how many boats had been through, and it contained numerous 'wides'. These 'wides', formed as a result of subsidence arising from underground salt works, were often nearly a hundred yards across. They contained a large concentration of carp and carp fishermen. My final death throes as a carp fisherman were spent on these wides.

Summer weekends generally followed the same routine: Saturday mornings on Tabley Mere and Sunday evenings on one of the wides on the Trent and Mersey Canal. I would also use the Sunday evening to catch up with job-related paperwork, I could have done this on Saturday afternoon or Sunday morning, but since Lorraine was also working hard, I felt that would have been more than a little unfair. The first few times that I tried working and fishing didn't go well; I'd be so engrossed in my work that I wouldn't see the bites and had to concede that I needed some audible bite indication. A matching pair of Optonic bite alarms were purchased. My carp rods were too soft to hit the required distances, so I purchased a pair of fast taper matching carp rods and Baitrunner reels. It was impossible to cast luncheon meat far enough on the 'wides', so I had to use boillies. Thus I became everything I despised about modern carp fishing; apart from the 'bivvy'.

I'm not saying I didn't enjoy some of this fishing, and I had some fairly epic sessions, by my standards. This included one in which I caught nearly twenty double-figure carp after becoming the first person to fish on the far bank of one of the wides when fishing was suddenly allowed there. However, despite catching carp up to fourteen pounds, being surrounded by other carp anglers doing exactly what I was doing gradually wore me down, and my new carp rods soon found themselves gathering cobwebs in the back of the garage (only to be re-invented as bass rods many years later). Carp fishing had become too serious and too technical, and I simply couldn't derive any pleasure from it any more. The fact that kids more than ten years younger than me were doing the whole thing a lot better than me and therefore catching more carp certainly didn't help either.

With us both being gainfully employed in reasonably well-paying jobs, we decided to save up for a once-in-a-lifetime trip to Australia, as Lorraine's brother had moved over there some years ago and married an Australian. Package holidays in Spain or Portugal held no attraction for me but Australia, well, that was different. It was the home of great white sharks, marlin, barracudas and a host of other sporting fish. I'd never ventured abroad or even been on an aeroplane before but thought, what the hell, I might as well make the first trip a 'biggie'.

I negotiated three weeks' holiday with my employers to cover the Christmas and New Year period and air tickets were booked with the cheapest haulier we could find, Olympic Airways. This entailed an overnight stop in Athens, meaning that we'd be spending all of Christmas Day in Athens itself. The hotel was cold and draughty and served the worst Christmas dinner since Adam was a lad: chicken giblets on rice. All the Australia-bound passengers stayed at this hotel and no one touched more than the odd mouthful, only to find it reheated and served up to us all again in the evening. Christmas 'pudding' was an apple. Before handing it over, a large Greek woman spat and rubbed it vigorously on her apron. That too remained uneaten. While walking round Athens we found a shop that was open and purchased six KitKats, which made up the bulk of our Christmas Day nourishment.

We did eventually arrive in Australia and had an unforgettable time. My brother-in-law had an old VW Campervan (known over there as a 'Combi') and the four of us travelled in this along the Pacific Highway from Sydney all the way to Cairns on the edge of the tropical rainforests. We stopped when and wherever we wanted and stayed overnight on campsites, both on and off the beaten track. I have so many fond memories of that holiday: huge cane toads in Queensland jumping against the side of our tent; swimming on deserted beaches; prawns bigger than sausages cooked on the barbecue: but most of all I remember our shark fishing trip.

I'd always wanted to go shark fishing, *proper* shark fishing on a big game boat with a fighting chair and balloon floats bobbing up and down on a clear blue sea while a deckhand ladled 'rubby dubby' (fish offal to the uninitiated) into the water to set up that oh so important scent trail. On returning from Cairns to Lorraine's brother's house on the northern outskirts of Sydney we tried to track down a suitable day's sharking, 'suitable' meaning not astronomically expensive while still maintaining the essentials as described above. We were in luck and managed to track down a boat that sailed out of Newcastle harbour, ours for the day for a paltry eleven hundred Australian dollars (about £500, but don't forget, this was 1990!) The price included hire of the shark fishing tackle, bait and 'burley'

(Australian equivalent of rubby dubby), a skipper, a deck-hand, and food, wine and beer for the four of us.

We arrived at the harbour about an hour before we were due to set sail, so we found a little café overlooking said harbour and indulged ourselves with cappuccinos – still exotic in those days – and home-made biscuits. We wondered which of the big game boats, of which there were plenty, was ours and watched a variety of people going about their business.

Two young lads caught our eye as they started loading food, rods and bait boxes on to a small water taxi – we knew it was a water taxi because it had 'WATER TAXI' written on it in large letters. John and I went to talk to them and they confirmed that, yes, they were getting things ready for the 'Butcher party'. We soon joined them on the water taxi and I asked them which of the big game boats was ours. The skipper looked at me a little quizzically before answering 'this is it'. Hmmm. Oh well, you obviously didn't get much for your thousand bucks, or more likely, I was somewhat naïve in thinking that this was a typical cost for a big game boat. To be fair, as water taxis went, it wasn't too small and a fighting chair complete with harness was produced out of the cabin and slotted into the deck near the stern. The skipper and his associate assured us that we were in with a good chance of catching a shark, having seen and caught plenty over the past couple of weeks.

An hour later, we arrived in the designated area and the engine was cut. Four rods were set up, two with balloon floats to fish baits near the surface and two with nothing but the bait, which would be allowed to drift down to a greater depth. The burley was unveiled and a goodly portion introduced into a large metal pipe attached to the stern of the boat. This pipe had holes drilled into it so that when you moved, or pounded, a large wooden plunger up and down therein, a slick of fish oil and fish bits oozed out into the water to be carried down-tide.

With the temperature well into the thirties and not a cloud in the sky, we settled down to wait for some action. The two ladies found suitable spots to sunbathe while John and I scanned the water for signs of sharks. We were well looked after by the skipper and his mate and never wanted for either food or cold beer, wine or mineral water. The boat bobbed about in the clear blue waters of the Pacific Ocean while 'Transvision Vamp' - an English band, popular at the time with a lead singer called Wendy... just Google it, ok? - played on a seemingly endless loop.

An hour passed. We took it in turns to sit in the fighting chair to get a 'feel for it'. We even took turns topping up the burley.

Several more hours passed and we gave up looking for sharks. John decided to sunbathe, while I was quite happy to be sitting there watching the world go by, or in this case, not watching the world go by but daydreaming about what a shark run might look like in real life.

What happened next bears an uncanny resemblance to a scene in 'Jaws,' but I swear it's true. I was sitting there watching the skipper's mate pounding the burley pipe with considerably less enthusiasm than he had at the beginning of the day, when he looked up at one of the rods and stopped in mid-pound. He stared at the rod for a good thirty seconds; I did too, but couldn't see any difference. Without taking his eyes of the rod tip, he silently motioned me to get into the fighting chair, which I did. My heart rate was starting to increase rapidly, although I still wasn't quite certain what exactly was happening. He took the rod out of its holder, put it into the tube which was attached to the fighting chair and put me into the harness. His first words in this whole episode were, 'just wait'.

I was suddenly aware that the line had tightened to the rod tip and that Lorraine, her brother and his wife were next to me.

Click, click, went the ratchet on the reel.

'Wait.'

Click, click, click, went the reel.

'Wait.'

Thirty seconds passed.

Click, click, click, cliiiiiiiiiiiiiiiiiiiiiicccccccccccckkkkkk went the reel as line suddenly left the spool at a steady pace.

'Put the reel into gear, tighten up to the fish and hit it!'

I put the reel into gear and did as I was told. There was a solid weight on the end of the line. I'd hooked a shark! Using the fighting chair, I pumped the fish towards me, gaining yards of line with each pump until with surprisingly little drama – disappointingly little drama – the dorsal fin of a shark appeared behind the boat. The fin disappeared as the shark tried to make a run but quickly decided that it was completely outgunned – the tackle I was using was designed for fish many times bigger than this – and it soon appeared by the side of the boat. The skipper announced that it was a blue shark, a rare capture in those waters, but ironically, a common sight in UK waters. Being the biggest fish I'd ever seen in real life it looked huge, and I wondered what the skipper was planning to do with it. If he thought it was coming on board with us then I'd have been saying the immortal line, 'skipper, we're gonna need a bigger boat'. Although in this case it would have been the size of the boat, not the shark, that was the problem. We tried to take some photos of the fish by the side of the boat and I was more than happy for the trace to be cut and this beautiful fish to be allowed to swim off relatively unharmed.

I asked the skipper how big he thought it was, and he said that it weighed about 120lb and that it was the property of the boat, meaning he'd have to ignore my request to let it go. Two things here: firstly, he was right, the fine print on the booking clearly stated that all fish caught were the property of the boat. Secondly, if you look at the photo of the shark you may dispute that it weighs 120lb; you may be right, but I couldn't care less.

This was the only run we had, despite all three of us taking turns to pound away on the burley pipe with renewed vigour. Hours passed, celebratory alcohol was drunk and eventually, around tea time, the skipper announced that it was time to return to the harbour.

I didn't want a photo of me standing next to a dead shark strung up by its tail, in fact, I didn't really want a photo of me next to a dead shark full stop. I'd always thought these photos looked pathetic in the extreme: the ultimate macho fisherman stood next to his enormous willy-extension. However, Lorraine said I'd regret not having a photo of some description of me-plus-shark, so I settled for the one you see in this book, and to be honest she was right; I would have been disappointed if I had not had a permanent reminder of this trip.

This little era of my life also gave me another new angling experience: my first, and last, fishing match. Why on earth did I, an angler who values solitude almost as much as catching the fish themselves, find myself caught up in angling's ultimate Darwinian imperative?

Let me explain. My brother-in-law Paul, the husband of my wife's sister, Jan, was also a keen coarse fisherman. When they came up to our house he always brought his tackle with him and we would have a morning or evening out fishing somewhere of my choice. We'd been to a variety of local waters, including the boat on Tabley Mere and caught tench, bream and carp together. This was my sort of fishing, not his; he was primarily a match angler and a lover of what would eventually come to be known as 'commercial fisheries', overstocked puddles containing monstrosities such as 'F1carp,' ide and barbel (a river fish which should stay in rivers). To be fair to him, he also enjoyed his river fishing too and when we went down to stay with them in the Midlands, I would accompany him on trips to the River Trent. Then on one weekend trip arranged between Lorraine and her sister, Paul told me that this coincided with a match that his club had already got booked and that he really wanted to fish. I could come too if I wanted and take part, but as I wasn't a club member, I wouldn't be eligible for any prizes when I weighed in. The alternative to fishing in the match was a shopping trip – for ladies' clothes – with Lorraine and her sister. It was a surprisingly close call, but the match won.

Now to be completely fair about this, the other fishermen in the club were all very nice and although obviously competitive, not in any sort of aggressive way. The pool itself was perfectly square and I suspected it was man-made: two banks were completely devoid of any features, both bankside and in the water, and the other two had some willow trees with branches trailing down to the water. I drew the last peg, which was in the middle of one of the featureless banks. I set up my usual float fishing tackle, the same as I'd use when fishing for tench on Tabley Mere, but noticed that most people were setting up to fish on the 'pole'. Hemp, caster and bits of chopped worm were being 'cupped' into swims while I was mixing some groundbait. In addition to this, it was an afternoon match on a hot and sunny day, the sort of conditions in which you'd never normally find me fishing. Talk about being out of your comfort zone. While most other anglers steadily caught carp, roach and the occasional tench, I struggled to get a bite until, four and a half hours into the five-hour match, I hooked and landed a small crucian carp. Rather than put it in my keepnet, I put it straight back to spare me the ignominy of 'weighing in'. When the scales turned up with the match secretary I told him that since I wasn't eligible for any prizes I'd put 'all' my fish straight back...

My last new experience of this era was a much more pleasant and rewarding one. I'd often read about barbel in the angling press and although 'barbel literature' was still very much in its infancy – in those days it hadn't yet achieved the cachet associated with the carp – I had often wondered what it would be like to catch one. When one of my angling club cards arrived prior to the 1989 season, I read that the club had just acquired the rights to a stretch of the River Severn in deepest Shropshire, a stretch noted for its barbel and chub fishing. Interesting. But the summer arrived and tench fishing took over my life until the August Bank Holiday weekend arrived. The weather was good and Lorraine and I decided that we'd have a drive out somewhere for a long walk and then stop at a pub for something to eat. She knew me well enough by now to know that 'long walks' would involve water of one sort or another, so there was no objection when I suggested that we try and find this new stretch of river on the Severn.

The drive down to the Severn was encouraging: a mixture of the A49, country lanes, small villages with names such as 'Preston Gubbals' and not a motorway or dual carriageway in sight. I could already see myself driving down there early in the morning or returning late at night, trying to avoid the badgers and rabbits that would inevitably try and cross my path. The portents were good even before I'd seen the river itself.

The River Severn was like a cross between the Dane and the

Ribble. It had the intimacy of the Dane but a size more approaching that of the Ribble, and as the stretch twisted and turned it boasted both shallowish runs filled with waving green strands of streamer weed and slower, darker runs with pools overhung by trees. We walked the entire stretch, but I was clueless as to where exactly I would have my first cast for a barbel. However it had only taken me seconds to decide that I would be returning the following weekend to fish. There were a couple of other anglers there, but they hadn't caught much and the fact that there were so few people there on a Bank Holiday Monday in good weather was also encouraging. In the end, I decided that I would be fishing at the bottom end of the stretch for no other reason than the swims were heavily overgrown with trees on both banks and this resembled a bigger version of some of the swims I'd felt comfortable fishing on the Dane.

We found a lovely country pub for a sandwich and a cold beer. While enjoying our meal, my wife remarked that I'd 'gone quiet' … indeed I had. I'd already started daydreaming up barbel-catching scenarios.

Lorraine often complains that I suddenly go quiet and start staring off into the distance. I still do it and it's usually a sign that I've returned to a favourite swim or that a random angling-related thought has just occurred to me, one which needs nurturing into a full-blown fish-catching scenario.

The drive to and from work on Tuesday was spent developing just such barbel catching scenarios; the drive into work on Wednesday likewise. On Wednesday afternoon, I could stand it no longer and sought out my boss to see if it would be possible to have Thursday off: no, not the full day, was the reply (we had an important meeting scheduled for 9 am, although in my view it was an insignificant affair compared to a potential meeting with a barbel) but I could have a half-day if I wanted. That would do.

Thursday dinnertime saw me out of work like a shot and home via the tackle shop, where I picked up hemp, casters and maggots. I already had a permanent stock of sweetcorn and luncheon meat in the cupboard in our kitchen. Home, changed, tackle in car and back on the road by early afternoon. The drive down to the river was made with some excitement, although, truth to tell, I didn't really know what to expect.

There was only one car in the club car park when I arrived at the river – great, it would have been pretty soul-destroying if there had been a dozen cars there – and I soon arrived at my chosen swim to find it empty. Thank goodness for that, although why I was so keen to fish this one swim when there were several similar ones, Lord only knows. I set up my tackle; I was using my father's rod, as it was a little sturdier than mine and a large swimfeeder into which I packed a mixture of hemp, casters and maggots. A combination of maggots and casters were placed onto a size 14 hook and swung out close to a fallen tree about halfway across the river. The river itself, still at normal summer levels, was moving very slowly in this area and I had no trouble in holding bottom; there was no breeze either, although the trees on both banks would have sheltered me from all but the strongest of winds. It was a mild, overcast afternoon but not oppressively so; it didn't feel like it was going to rain but neither did you feel like the sun was suddenly going to break through.

There were no breakthroughs on the barbel front either and by tea-time I decided to wind in and have a wander. I'd heard someone coughing further along the bank from me and guessed it was the angler whose car was in the parking area, so I decided to find out if he'd fared any better than me. I was just about to ask him if he'd caught anything when his rod hooped over and he latched into what was obviously a barbel. After a minute or two of steady pressure I saw the golden outline of a barbel appear just below the surface in the middle of the river, and soon after that it appeared in his landing net. I can't remember the size, but I'm guessing it was around the six-pound mark, which I would come to realise was an average sort of size for this stretch of the Severn.

'Is that your first one?' I asked,

'No, it's my seventh,' he replied.

Seventh! (A footnote: it might have been seven, six, eight or even nine or ten, I can't recall. I do know that it was a lot of barbel.) 'Unfortunately,' he said, 'I've got to go now so if I were you, I'd drop straight in here as there are still plenty of fish out there'. It was a tough decision to leave my fishless swim and move into his barbel-stuffed one…

Now the strange thing is that I know that I caught two or three barbel that evening, but I have zero memory of actually doing so. I don't know why I can recollect a small crucian carp being caught at the age of four but can't remember catching a six-pound barbel – it might have been five or seven pounds, I just don't know – my *first* barbel to boot, at the age of nearly twenty-eight. It also proves me to be a liar for saying that you remember all your 'firsts'.

What I can clearly remember is that I went back to that same swim every Saturday morning until the weather changed in early October and the river flooded. It was, to me at least, the perfect River Severn barbel swim, the near bank being a mass of willows and willowherb with just enough room for my chair, rod and landing net, with enough overhead clearance to enable a cast to be made. A large tree had half-fallen in on the far bank so that a canopy of branches just kissed the water, which flowed at a steady enough pace so that a swimfeeder cast in front of these branches would settle just underneath them in what 'felt' like a much deeper depression on the bottom of the river.

Each Saturday I would arrive at first light and fish through till dusk. I always caught barbel, usually at least ten of them, with the biggest fish being just under eight pounds. If this sounds a bit soulless then I guess it's a true reflection of how I felt about this little period of barbel fishing. Despite my initial enthusiasm, and don't get me wrong, I really enjoyed catching these lovely fish, I wasn't obsessed with them.

I didn't fish for them during the winter months, and it was late July of the following season when I next ventured back to the Severn during my annual two-week summer break.

The first thing I noticed on arrival at the little car park by the Severn was that it was full. Not a good sign. As I wandered along the bank of the river down towards my favourite swim I noticed that all of the swims were much wider than the previous autumn and contained anglers' debris: luncheon meat tins, sweetcorn tins, beer bottles and other assorted debris. There were also two cars parked down on the bottom bend, their tracks highly visible in the grass – the field was used for growing turf – and their windows down to allow their erstwhile occupants to listen to music while they fished. Definitely not a good sign.

I was surprised to find my swim empty. It soon became obvious why it was unoccupied. Bankside vegetation had been cleared away to make it three times bigger than the previous year, big enough to fit a bivvy, and lying amongst the beer cans, bait tins, sweet wrappers and newspapers was an enormous pile of fly covered, stinking, human excrement. I'm assuming it was human excrement as I couldn't see a dog or fox carrying toilet paper with them.

I walked back to the car, pausing only to ask a heavily tattooed, shaven-headed angler if he'd caught anything. 'What's it to you if I have?' was the reply. I never went back, and the angling club lost the rights to this stretch of the Severn before the end of the year. Of course, the club blamed a private syndicate for 'outbidding' them which was disgraceful as far as they were concerned.

Our 'Big Game' boat – or 'Water Taxi'

Shark on!

Blue shark – 120lb. Or less.

Barbel to 7lb 12oz from the River Severn in September 1989. NB This was the last time I used a keepnet for these lovely fish.

The 'other' pond at the bottom of the garden!

A Mirror carp of 12lb caught from the Trent and Mersey canal in July 1991

Lorraine accompanies me on a day's fishing in August 1990.

A 14lb mirror carp from the Trent and Mersey canal in June 1992, the second day that fishing was allowed on the 'far side' of the wide. This was one of more than twenty carp caught that day.

CHAPTER TEN

THREE PERSONAL BESTS, TWO CHILDREN AND ONE BOAT

We were happily married, had a nice house in the Cheshire countryside and were financially stable, so we decided to start a family. Fortunately for us, this was achieved without any great dramas. Within a few months of deciding that the time was right we were sitting side by side on the bed waiting for a blue line to appear on the pregnancy test. It's the opposite of float fishing really: instead of waiting for your float to *disappear* you're waiting for something to *appear*. The adrenaline rush is just the same though.

Maybe I should clarify that a little. Imagine you've been trying to catch a tench from a particularly 'habitual' pool for years and you've not even had a bite when suddenly the float stirs, then very slowly sinks away, you strike and realise you've just hooked the tench of your dreams. Multiply the buzz by ten and you're almost at the same point as seeing that little blue line appear.

Alec arrived in September 1991 and Becky in October 1993. I was present for both of their births and I won't even attempt to put this alongside a fishing analogy... well, maybe just a little one. Suffice to say that holding your newborn son or daughter is a bigger thrill than cradling any big pike or tench... even a British record one.

By the time my son was born, pike fishing as an obsession had dwindled away considerably, partly because I didn't have access to a water that, firstly, held big pike and, secondly, that I actually wanted to fish. All that suddenly changed with the discovery that the Bridgewater Canal in Cheshire not only contained pike – I'm not sure why I thought it didn't – but also big pike. I'd started to hear rumours of large pike being caught but thought they were just that – after all, doesn't every water have a 'monster pike' story to tell? Then I heard of multiple pike captures from a completely reliable source and decided that this was worth pursuing.

I took a week off work in early October when my wife returned from the hospital with our son, and by the last Saturday of that week I'd changed enough nappies to earn an afternoon off. I raced down to a stretch of the canal that I knew had produced pike in the previous weeks with nothing more than a bag of sprats, two pike rods (I'd purchased a couple of Terry Eustace pike rods some years earlier) a landing net and some basic pike fishing accoutrements. The sprats would be fished underneath small red floats, one just in front of me but close to the bank and the other about twenty to thirty yards away but also close to the bank. Why? I had a theory that went as follows. The canal had just witnessed an explosion of pole fisherman, anglers who had swopped running lines for poles, and who were now more adept at catching small and medium sized fish which would be put into keepnets for the duration of the session. At the end of the session, or a match, these fish would be tipped back into the water close to the near bank. Some of these fish would be virtually dead, or dazed, and would provide easy pickings for a lazy pike swimming along this bank. There's nothing like easy food with minimum effort for promoting rapid pike growth – that's why trout reservoirs have the biggest pike these days.

It was a cool afternoon with a strong wind that put a considerable chop on the water. Every hour and a half, I would move a little further along the bank in order to cover as much ground as possible; you would be right to think that this might be a little at odds with the 'roving pike theory', but I surmised that a pike would still rove fast enough to find my baits, and by moving I might pick up a non-roving fish. Why was I using a float as opposed to legering? If a canal boat came too close to the bank I'd have to bring my line in, whereas if I was legering I could leave my baits out. The simple reason was that I liked watching a float more than I liked watching a dropback indicator or other such device.

When seated, I lined up my far float with a bush on the near bank – I was fishing on the inside of a large, slow bend in the canal – and poured myself a cup of coffee. An hour and a half passed without any signs, or even approximations, of pike, and I decided to have another cup of coffee before I put my flask away and moved further along the canal. I looked down as I balanced the coffee cup between my knees and poured the coffee. On looking back up to check my float, I noticed that it had moved, not much, maybe a couple of feet but it had definitely moved. This didn't necessarily mean pike; the canal had sufficient current to ensure that branches, plastic bags and other flotsam moved through with enough speed to catch your line and drag the float out of position. I stared at the float, willing it to move again... which it did, drifting slowly into the middle of the canal, where it finally vanished. I walked along the bank, winding in the slack line until I reached the point where the float had last been seen. I tightened up to the invisible float and struck. There was enough resistance to tell me that I'd hooked a pike, not a huge one but at 7½ lb it was my first canal-caught pike, and it re-ignited my obsession with pike fishing.

Having a pike fishing obsession is not entirely compatible with having a baby in the family and a working wife, so I did try my best to limit my trips to just the half-day at weekends, the half-day beginning initially at about noon but then moving to eleven, before... well, you get the drift. To be fair to Lorraine, she rarely complained even though there must have been times when she felt that she was playing second fiddle to a fish, and I know I must have pushed her patience to the limit on many occasions. Every now and again she would put her foot down and say 'no, please don't go out fishing today'. Most of the time I would agree to her pleas: when people ask me, 'who is the boss in your house,' I reply, 'I am, as long as I do what my wife tells me'.

For the rest of that autumn and winter, and the following year as well, I spent as much time as I could, or as I dared, fishing the canal for pike. I knew it had produced some big pike, fish well over twenty pounds, but although I caught some double-figure fish, the 'big 'girls' eluded me. Pike fishing in the canal could be a soul-destroying affair though, you rarely caught more than two fish in a full day's fishing and could quite easily go five or six trips without having a single run, especially in the middle of winter. Of course, we were still in the last era of 'proper' winters and it was not uncommon to lose days, or even weeks, of fishing time as the canal froze over, a phenomenon that at times seemed to happen exclusively at weekends.

You might think that the lack of runs would have reduced the level of my obsession, but the opposite was the case; the less action there was, the more I needed it. I went fishing with a couple of friends, one of whom was an occasional pike angler, and had to witness him hooking and landing a superbly marked twenty-five-pound fish; 'That should have been yours,' said the other friend, and he was right. It should have been mine from the hours I'd put in, but of course, fishing doesn't work like that and truth to tell, I'm glad it doesn't. If it did, then fishing would be nothing more than a science; a mathematical algorithm of time, dates, weather, water temperatures and locations designed to tell you exactly when and where to fish. (Having said all of that, you will see later on in this book that I use just such an approach to my sea fishing!)

So, what would my ideal pike fishing day look like? It would be late autumn, say the back end of October or early November and it would have to be heavily overcast, misty and still, the sort of grey day that my parents would have associated with smog and chesty coughs. The sort of grey stillness that means you can line your pike float up with the bankside reflections on the surface of the canal and know that even the slightest of movements will result in your float giving off tiny circular ripples of water that can be seen from yards away. You look away, maybe distracted by the call of a pheasant or oystercatcher, and turn your eyes back to your float, which hasn't moved, but, now has a small circle slowly emanating from it and your heart misses a beat, then starts to pound, because you know that something has just picked up your bait. Think of the float as the 'a' in the @ symbol and trace the movement as it moves round the central point: this is how your float moves before sinking slowly away. Your strike meets with an unyielding object which then pulls your rod tip down and pulls line off a lightly set spool...

It was just under two years after catching my first canal pike – and quite possibly more than fifty trips - before I had my true red-letter day. Conditions weren't as described above though; it was warm and reasonably sunny, one of those days when the sun came and went, but there was never enough cloud to seriously suggest rain and I was comfortable sitting there in just a jumper. A gentle breeze put enough of a ripple on the water to reduce the possibility of seeing any 'emanating ripples' from my floats, but, it was a pleasant enough day, a Sunday at the beginning of October, and I had the rarity of a full day's pass. I'd arrived at the canal before ten o'clock but had promised to be back by sixish to help with tea and other son-related duties.

I soon had two of Tesco's finest sprats in the water and settled back in my chair with a cup of coffee and a book. No more than twenty minutes had passed before I looked up from my book to see my far float making tracks for the centre of the canal. Wonderful – a run within the first hour! I quickly tightened up to the float and struck. The strike was indeed met with an unyielding object which proceeded to pull the rod tip down and pull line off my lightly set spool. I wouldn't say that the fight was spectacular, it was more stubborn than anything else and a good five minutes elapsed before I got my first sight of the fish. I knew straight away that it was the biggest pike I'd ever hooked; this ensured that the fight lasted a lot longer than it should have done, as I was terrified of putting too much pressure on the fish in case the hookhold was light. There were no untoward dramas in the landing of the fish and I held my breath as the scales settled on... 20lb 4oz. Yeehaw! A 'twenty' at long last! A passer-by turned up at exactly the right moment to take a photograph, and with a last adoring look I slipped the pike back into the canal.

An hour later I moved further along the canal and history repeated itself. After another twenty minutes my far float again made moves towards the centre of the canal. Another strike, another 'stubborn' fight and another pike was lifted onto the canal bank. This one 'only' weighed 17lb 8oz but still merited a photograph and another little bit of adoration.

Two moves later I was contemplating the fact that I only had about an hour and a half of fishing time left. Should I stay put or should I move again? I decided to stay put, mainly because I was fishing a spot which had a special significance for me, being the exact place where I'd caught plenty of carp in my late teens and early twenties. I also remembered losing a plastic bite indicator there, so I spent a few minutes looking for it on the basis that it might have miraculously reappeared from the undergrowth; after all, two big pike were a minor miracle, so another one was not entirely out of the question. There was also a part of me that by then was quite happy to just sit there and read or daydream; to put additional efforts into catching another pike would be classed as greedy.

But it was a day for miracles. For the third time that day, I looked up from my book to see the far float moving out towards the middle of the canal, although this time it decided to double-back on itself until it was no more than a rod-length out, bimbling slowly along just in front of me. And for the third time that day, a strike was met with an unyielding object that pulled the rod tip down and took line from the spool.

This time the fish continued to take line as it moved away from me at a steady pace. I followed it along the canal bank for some fifty yards before it abruptly turned and headed back from whence it had come. Which was just as well, as I'd neglected to bring the landing net with me. It went past where it had been hooked and beyond where my chair had been before once again doing an about-turn and heading back along the canal. At no point had I moved the fish away from the bottom of the canal and I was in no doubt that this was the biggest fish of the day.

Its movements became slower, the distance between the about-turns shorter, until eventually I felt it rising up from the bottom of the canal. It surfaced just in front of me and stared at me for a few brief seconds before diving back down to the bottom of the canal.

This time, it didn't take long to work it back to the surface and, with all the practice I'd had that day in the art of landing big pike, it was slid into my net. Well, most of it was; I had to rely on it 'folding up' as I lifted the net, the whole fish being considerably longer than my net was wide or deep. This was a seriously big pike, but just how big?

The weigh sling was remoistened, the scales zeroed, the pike placed within the sling before being hoisted into the air. A combination of the weight and shaking hands made establishing a true weight somewhat difficult but eventually I settled on 28lb 6oz (I think it was the same one that John had earlier in the year). Fortune was yet again on my side, as another passer-by turned up at exactly the right moment and obliged with a series of photos. Three pike for over 65lb in little more than six hours of fishing, two personal bests; surely it didn't get any better than that! (I was correct, it didn't; I've never had a bigger pike, or a bigger catch of pike, to this day.)

Having children and a demanding job drastically reduced my fishing time, to one session per week with the occasional day off for special days such as the 16th June, and maybe the 17th and 18th too. I accepted this reduction stoically, as Lorraine had gone back to work and it wouldn't have been right for me to disappear for days on end. Summer weekends would revolve around an early morning trip to Tabley Mere with me getting back home for lunchtime, but even this was proving difficult to organise as I had to get from my new office in Kirkby in Liverpool to south Manchester on a Friday to collect the boat keys. If I got stuck in traffic I had to call my father, who had by now retired, and ask him to dash into town to collect both bait and said keys.

There was only one thing for it: I'd have to get my own licence for

Tabley Mere and buy or make my own boat. I spoke to the Estates Office at the Mere and was told that, yes, I could have my own licence, although at hundreds of pounds per year it was extremely expensive. I looked at a few boats in various boatyards, but most were just rowing boats of dubious stability. It was my father who suggested we make one. My father, being a fitter by trade, was an immensely practical man who could turn his hand to most things, and in turn he had expected me to follow suit. By the time I left home for university I could just about lay bricks, sort of plaster a wall, service a car or motorbike (no on-board computers in those days) and repair a washing machine. I'd also helped my father and an electrician friend of his completely re-wire our house: my help was especially important as my father was colour blind, which was a bit of a drawback when doing electrical work. My father viewed these as essential life skills and was very dismissive of any man who was deficient in these areas. Yes, you had to have qualifications, but why then waste money on paying someone to do something that you should be able to do yourself?

When my father suggested we build our own boat, it seemed a very logical thing to do. I bought a boating magazine and found an advert for a company which produced plans, technical drawings, for a variety of boats including a flat-bottomed fishing punt. Perfect. The technical drawings duly arrived and my father set out to interpret them, which was quite easy for him as that was what he'd spent most of his working life doing. The wood we were to use was keroin, a hardwood, and marine-grade plywood, which was a more waterproof version of standard plywood. A trip was made to a local timber merchants and the wood procured; my father spoke to someone at his old workplace and a couple of wooden trestles soon appeared in the garage at Timperley. We decided that we'd make the boat at my father's house for three reasons: one, because most of the tools were there, two, he'd be doing a lot of the work and three, we could put the boat onto the pond at the bottom of the garden to test for leaks. Because the boat was over fourteen feet long, it was to be made in two parts, which would be bolted together at the waterside.

The skeleton of the boat soon appeared, supported on the

wooden trestles, and held together by copious quantities of brass screws; not the easiest things to work with, because although they were rust proof they were soft, and if you weren't careful the screw heads would disintegrate under the pressure of the screwdriver.

I actually enjoyed the whole process of building the boat and working with my father. It was an easy relationship, he was the master craftsman and I was the apprentice. The sides and bottom were eventually added, along with rowlocks and duck boards, until finally the boat was ready to be painted. I was undecided whether to paint it black or green, but eventually decided to go with the green, two coats of which were applied on top of a special primer and two undercoat layers.

The final pieces of the boat jigsaw were two of the greatest inventions known to man. Well, maybe not *man* per se, but boat-fishing-man, or maybe just me. These were firstly, an adjustable rod rest embedded in a lump of concrete shaped like an upside-down flowerpot, thus being heavier at the bottom and more stable, and also because I'd used a flowerpot as the mould. The second invention was a piece of polyurethane foam pipe insulation which would clip onto the top rail of the boat and into which was cut a 'V' section which would serve to hold the rod in place.

Even though I took some random days off work and tried to spend at least some time each weekend helping my father, the construction of the boat took a lot longer than expected and it wasn't ready for the beginning of the fishing season. I therefore had to start the season on the old club boat. Shortly after this, my father and I decided that the time had come to launch her. Both sections were carried down to the garden pond and placed in the water. I then put on my waders, climbed down into the water and manoeuvred the two sections together before inserting four bolts through eight sets of holes – which thankfully still lined up – and adding the washers and nuts. We didn't have any champagne handy to complete the launch, so we made do with a can of Boddingtons instead. We stood there, my parents, my brother, my wife and infant son, and waited for signs of a leak. Miraculously, there wasn't one, and she was deemed ready for use.

The following Saturday morning I borrowed a Transit van from work and transported the two sections of boat to Tabley Mere, where the process of putting them in the water and bolting them together was repeated. Sturdy chains and padlocks were used to attach the boat to bankside trees. The van was returned and a trip to the tackle shop made to procure bait for the Sunday morning, which would see the boat's maiden fishing trip.

I asked my father to join me, but he declined. Over the next twelve years I would often ask him to come with me for a morning on Tabley Mere, but he always found an excuse not to: he had stuff to do in the garden, his back was hurting, and so on. I often wondered why he didn't come with me. I think he still liked me and enjoyed my company, as he was always ready to come to the pub with me, and I can only conclude that by then, as previously described, he found my boundless enthusiasm a little overpowering, or, that he'd fallen out of love with coarse fishing.

A quick aside: although my father and I were completely different characters, it always worried me slightly that one day I might also fall out of love with coarse fishing too. If that happened, what would fill the void? As fate would have it, I did eventually fall out of love with many aspects of coarse fishing, but found another piscatorial activity to fill the void. It was only when writing this book that I realised that the turn-offs for him – the increase in the seriousness, the competitiveness, the 'intensity' of my fishing – were the same turn-offs for me in respect of my carp fishing, and to some extent the reason why I didn't become completely obsessed with my barbel fishing. Maybe I'm not that different to my old man after all.

I christened the boat on a beautiful, smoky and sunny Sunday morning with a catch of five tench, and the boat got used at least once per week from then all the way through to September. It was a superbly stable fishing platform; you could jump up and down and lean over the side without it even coming close to tipping over. One of the reasons for the stability was its weight, but the downside of this was that rowing in anything other than a moderate breeze was difficult in the extreme, as once the wind caught the boat there was nothing you could do to stop it turning broadside and being blown towards the nearest bank. If Sir Steve Redgrave thought winning the odd Olympic medal was difficult, he should have tried rowing my boat on Tabley Mere in a gale force wind!

Once late September arrived, thoughts started to turn away from tench – it never felt quite right fishing Tabley Mere on an autumnal day with the trees turning golden brown and leaves covering the water – and back to pike fishing on the Bridgewater Canal. This pattern was repeated for the next few years.

At some point towards the end of 1997, it started to freeze. By Christmas Day the canal had several inches of ice on it and it was clear that there would be no festive pike fishing for me that year (just to be clear, we're talking between Christmas Day and New Year, not Christmas Day itself!) I needed an alternative venue, a river venue, but preferably one with bigger chub than those present in the River Dane. I'd heard rumours emanating from a stretch of the River Severn right up in the Welsh hills about big chub, many of which were allegedly over the magical five-pound mark, and with other options being somewhat limited I thought I'd give it a go.

The upper reaches of the Severn are not much bigger than the Dane and the stretch in question was relatively short with banks and fields covered with a thick layer of snow. The day itself was bitingly cold and grey; snow wasn't forecast but I wouldn't have been at all surprised if it had snowed again. If it had started to snow I would have had have a tricky decision to make, as my route to the Severn had involved some small lanes which clearly never saw a 'gritter'.

I decided to fish just upstream from a line of trees, partly because I couldn't see the bottom beneath them, which indicated deeper water, and also because it resembled one of my favourite River Dane swims. However, I wouldn't be able to float fish it, as the water between where I was to sit and the target area was significantly shallower and the bait would snag on the bottom before I could get it into the required position. By using a small quarter-ounce 'bomb' I could cast downstream and away from the trees, and by slowly tightening up to the lead I could let the current swing the lead and bait into the deeper water below the trees. I was very impressed with my own ingenuity. I was less impressed when I fluffed a cast which flew straight into the trees and required me to tackle up again from scratch.

Bait was a small pinch of bread-flake; groundbait was a very sloppy mixture of mashed bread which, when thrown in upstream, produced lots of little bready-particles which drifted enticingly into the deeper water where my own bait lay. Making the bread-mash was a finger numbing affair but essential to the task of getting the chub to feed in the sub-zero conditions.

It was dusk before I started getting the first discernible indications on the rod tip. I was using a light chub rod; it was meant to be a multi-tipped barbel rod but was ridiculously underpowered for this application, but with the lightest tip it was perfect for small river chubbing. The little taps on the rod tip were, I assumed, chub starting to nip at the bait – they could also have been small fish, but I was expecting chub, so chub they were – and eventually the rod tip pulled round in an altogether more convincing fashion and my strike was met with a solid resistance. I let the rod take the fight out of the fish and as soon as I felt it begin to tire, I worked it back towards me against the current; it was a chub and a big one to boot, which soon nestled into the folds of my landing net. At 5lb 2oz it was by far my biggest-ever chub and fifteen minutes later, with it almost too dark to see my rod tip, I caught another fish an ounce smaller than my first. With the line now freezing to my rod, fishing became impossible, but I was more than satisfied with the result. Importantly, I now had somewhere to fish when conditions were too bad, too icy, to fish elsewhere. Somewhere that was challenging and capable of producing big fish (by my standards).

Once again though, I never became obsessed by this little piece of the Severn. I never failed to enjoy myself there and fished it a lot over the next few winters, even fishing it in milder conditions in February, when I could have quite easily gone to the canal and fished for pike. As long as the river wasn't carrying any excess water I caught chub, and they were rarely less than four and a half pounds in weight, with most being around the magical five-pound mark. One December day was especially memorable as I caught seven chub, six of which were over five pounds with the biggest weighing in at 5lb 4oz. But despite trips like this, these little ventures were no more than sideshows to my main obsessions.

Life was good: we had two lovely, and more importantly healthy, children, and we enjoyed our jobs. I spent my summers fishing for tench on Tabley Mere and my winters chasing pike on the canal with the odd trip to the upper reaches of the Severn for a bit of variety. We'd also started to return to Benllech on Anglesey every October with the kids and my parents. At Lorraine's insistence we had eschewed the caravans and found a lovely cottage – actually a town house, but we always called it a cottage for whatever reason - to stay in just off the beach which had fantastic views of the sea. It was also just a few yards away from the pub, which pleased my father no end. From my point of view, it was a case of completing the circle; having spent so many happy holidays there myself, it seemed only natural to go back with my kids and have my parents there too, giving me the added bonus of going fishing with my father again. We only ever stayed there for four or five days, but these were some of the happiest days of the year. We would set out along the M56 and the A55 with Oasis blaring out on the car stereo with me, Lorraine and our two children all singing tunelessly along, the excitement generated by Britpop being a mirror of how we all felt. We'd also play a little Lloyd Cole for old times' sake.

The holiday would really start with us meeting my parents, and sometimes my little brother too, in the car park of the Little Chef at Penmaenmawr; no sandwiches this time though, we'd all head inside for a variety of full English breakfasts. The Olympic breakfast was a favourite of mine. For the uninitiated, an Olympic breakfast consisted of sausages, bacon, black pudding, fried eggs, hash browns, baked beans, mushrooms, tomatoes and fried bread. Add to this a large mug of coffee and some toast, and you had a feast fit for any angler.

Mornings, often pre-breakfast, would be spent on the beach with my father and son digging for bait and then, when sufficient worms had been dug, damming streams with me doing all the work under the instructions of my son and his grandad. Sometimes Lorraine would come down with our young daughter to join the fun while my mother prepared the breakfast which would be waiting for us on our return.

Late afternoons and evenings would be spent fishing, either in the Menai Straits or at Dinas. My father would come with me and sometimes my son as well. We caught codling, nothing big, but codling nonetheless, the occasional dogfish and plenty of whiting. I enjoyed the time spent with the pair of them and my father enjoyed going sea fishing again, although I know that what he really liked was the post-fishing trip to the pub next door. Sometimes Lorraine came with us while my mother looked after the kids and prepared something for us to eat on our return.

The pub, which was often nearly deserted at that time of the year, had a quiz machine based on the 'Who Wants to Be a Millionaire' format and we would spend hours playing on it. It gave us a focal point and ensured that the conversation never faltered before we headed back to the cottage for a large supper and a glass or two of wine.

However, dark clouds were looming on the horizon. The next chapter deals with the more serious one but first, I have to mention an event that provoked a divorce. No, not me and my wife, but me and my first angling club. I had all but stopped fishing ADAC waters. Booths Mere had been supplanted in my tench fishing obsessions by Tabley Mere. It had also been stocked with carp, not deliberately but in panic due to a pollution incident at a nearby pool and a shaven-headed, cammo-wearing, bivvy-using type of angler had started to appear which, for me at least, spoiled the ambience. Astle Mere had been relinquished as the remedial works hadn't stopped the water gradually re-silting again. Doublewoods was the only water I still fished, and even then, only maybe once or twice per year when I fancied float fishing for the carp therein with a piece of luncheon meat. It was a tactic I'd seen Keith Crowther use there to great effect: find an overhanging bush or tree, throw in a few large cubes of meat and wait. More often than not you would get a bite and hook a carp; I caught wildies, commons, mirror and leather carp doing this, the best being no more than twelve pounds, but it was easy fishing and tremendous fun.

Then someone decided that Doublewoods needed stocking with two-pound roach acquired from a reservoir somewhere in Wales, roach that had grown up in tens of acres of gin clear water. Those roach took one look at the muddy water of their new home and went belly-up (that's died, to any non-anglers reading this book). The whole pool had to be drained and 'disinfected' before being re-stocked... with barbel, amongst other things. Enough was enough, and I didn't renew my membership.

The original wooden punt in the back garden at Timperley.

Pike 20lb 4oz caught from the Bridgewater Canal in October 1994.

Pike 28lb 6oz caught on the same day as the previous fish.

In serious 'Specimen Hunter' pose with a chub of 5lb 2oz from the upper reaches
of the River Severn in 1997.

CHAPTER ELEVEN

STRESS, MORE STRESS, AND ANGLING SALVATION

I loved my job, loved the company and loved the people I worked with. Unfortunately, the transport company which owned us decided that a waste company no longer fitted their portfolio and promptly sold us to our main competitor. Don't worry, we were told, it's a merger, not a takeover. I was too naïve to realise that it was no such thing. My own little unit was shut down, and although most of us retained our jobs we were split up and cast asunder to other parts of the new organisation. I didn't like the new company and sulked like … a sulky thing. Had I been a little more mature I would have realised that I had two options: move on or move out. Ultimately, I decided to move out, although this decision was made not out of an increasing maturity but a desire to move to a new house. While at a dinner party – look, I know what you're thinking, yuppies and all that, but I promise that this was an isolated event – someone remarked to us that there was an old cottage for sale not far from us. A couple of days later I drove the half mile or so down the lane to look at the cottage and thought, wow, what a fantastic place. I spoke to the estate agents and found that although we couldn't quite match the asking price we could make a realistic offer, albeit one which would stretch our finances to their limits.

Lorraine and I went to view the cottage. We weren't through the front door before we'd both decided we wanted to live there. It was beautiful. Run down in places – what the estate agents term as having 'character' – but set in large gardens and with a view over the Weaver valley. The main bedroom had two large windows and I doubted, and still doubt, that any house in Cheshire has a better view. We'd always wanted to be able to see fields from our bedroom window and now we could see countless fields, and a canal and a river too.

The problem was that this was going to push us right up against our financial limits. But I'd recently changed roles within the new company and still had a redundancy offer on the table. If I could find a new job, a better-paid one, I could take the redundancy offer and at least have a little back-up money.

I also wanted to be a 'director'. In the same way that I could be obsessed with my fishing, I was obsessed with becoming a 'director'. When I heard about a vacancy for a Sales and Marketing Director at a solvent recovery company based in the north west it seemed the perfect way to kill two birds with one stone. There was one slight drawback; the owner of the company had a reputation for hiring and firing sales directors at an alarming rate; he was a salesman himself and basically found everyone else distinctly inferior. I met up with the owner for lunch and we got on well enough; he explained that his wife was ill and that this time he needed to really let go of the reins a little. I believed him and arranged to meet the rest of the directors for a formal interview, which went well and I was offered the job. I immediately accepted their offer and tendered my resignation to my erstwhile employers.

I started work with my new employer on the 1st February 1997, and immediately found it very stressful. I'd swopped a short commute along mainly country lanes – I'd been moved to a new location about twenty minutes' drive from where we'd lived – for a round trip of between two and a half and three hours of mainly motorway madness. I also had a crisis of confidence which was completely alien to me: business and business decisions came easily to me, I enjoyed making them, it was what I did. Suddenly, matters weighed heavily on me: had I bitten off more than I could chew? Was I going to let my wife and my family down? We had a big mortgage, what would we do if I failed? I was also working in a completely different culture: in my previous job, any dissatisfaction would be expressed in a slightly shitty memo. In this job the owner expressed his displeasure by screaming at you, often at close enough range to leave your glasses covered in flecks of spittle. The stress built up to the point that on Monday mornings I wondered if I'd get through to the end of the day, let alone the end of the week, and a full mental breakdown loomed on the horizon (I didn't see this coming, but Lorraine certainly did).

In the end, three things saved me. Firstly, Lorraine: she kept me talking and assured me that if I stuck with it, everything would work out OK in the end. Secondly, the people I worked with, especially my fellow directors John, Chris and Paul, were immensely supportive, although I'm sure they had no idea of the turmoil I was going through. The third thing that saved me was the simple act of going fishing.

I set myself a target: get through to the beginning of April, take the week off before Easter and go to Benllech with my parents. Which was what we did. We dug bait, dammed streams, went fishing. We caught nothing of note, but I managed to see that there was indeed light at the end of the tunnel. Work still had its bad days, but they became more manageable, and I gradually stopped living in fear of losing my job. The owner still had his eccentricities, but outbursts of emotion would be followed by pay rises or cases of wine, his way of apologising. He never said sorry; the closest he ever came to it was on a long slow drive across the M62 with him to see a customer.

After he'd worked himself up into a frenzy, I just asked him, 'David, what do you want me to do different?'

'Nothing,' was the reply, 'you're doing a good job.'

I'm giving the guy a bad press here, so I should restore the balance a little. He was a brilliant businessman, and by that I mean that he understood that it's all about the customer. The technical stuff on the plant was easy as far as he was concerned (it wasn't!), it was just science, but keeping your customer happy was an art; a happy customer was loyal and would pay you more than your competitors. Simple. He also understood that the four directors were a united team; he didn't need any business bollocks talk about the power of teams, he just understood that we all worked well together. There were good times and there were bad times, and in the bad times we all pulled together and got through them.

It was during a summer fishing trip of that year that I had another moment of supreme happiness. John had got into barbel fishing in a much bigger way than I had ever done, and he suggested that we head down to a new stretch of the River Severn that had been acquired by an angling club of which we were both members. It overlapped, albeit on the opposite bank, the stretch of the Severn from which I'd caught my first barbel, so I readily agreed.

He turned up at my house in his new car in the middle of the morning; it was already a 'scorchio' of a day with a humidity that hinted at possible thunderstorms later. I think he'd only picked up his new car the previous afternoon and was keen to see how it performed on the winding roads that would take us down to the Severn.

We'd got two-thirds of the way there when without warning, the car conked out. Not good, but not a disaster, especially as we'd broken down at a petrol station and the car had come with a warranty. We were both AA members and took the opportunity to eat some ice cream as we waited for the arrival of the breakdown truck; if the AA guy could affect a repair, we'd be back off to the Severn, if not we'd be back home without wetting a line.

After less than an hour, the AA man arrived, diagnosed an electrical fault that had blown a fuse and performed the necessary repair. He thought he'd made a permanent repair, but left us with a healthy stock of spare fuses 'just in case'.

Buoyed by this news, we turned up at the Severn in good spirits and proceeded to walk the length of that particular beat. We settled on a couple of swims in a section that was wooded on both sides; my swim was especially nice. Although steeply banked and overgrown, there was just enough of a flat ledge near the water for me to place my chair with the rear legs folded underneath and resting against the steep bank and with my feet resting on flat ground. Willows grew above and around me with branches that trailed into the water on my left, the upstream side, and a canopy that formed a sort of 'cavern' to my right, the downstream side. Willowherb grew all around me and had to be flattened to accommodate bait boxes and tackle box: I was careful to minimise the amount of damage I did to the undergrowth though. Our modus operandi was to fire copious quantities of hemp, sweetcorn and luncheon meat into our swims before retiring to a safe distance and letting the barbel move in following the minnows, dace and chub. By leaving the swims for an hour we wouldn't spook the barbel by catching small fish first, or so my friend's theory went.

We retired to the shade of a large tree in the middle of a field for that hour. Lorraine had made us a large chocolate cake, which we'd somehow managed to keep from melting, and we just sat there and ate cake and talked. We didn't talk about anything special, we just talked bollocks and recalled fishing trips that we'd had together. We drank coffee, finished the cake and I realised that I was happy, very happy. I was sure I'd survived the worst the job could throw at me, the sun was shining and there were barbel to be caught.

We did indeed catch barbel, and plenty of them too. I don't recall exactly how many, but I think we both had between fifteen and twenty fish with a few good ones that might well have gone to over eight pounds. We were also treated to a late-afternoon thunderstorm; searing forks of lightning and huge thunderclaps which rolled around the valley. I'm not normally fond of fishing in thunderstorms but I felt quite safe sitting down by the water, as there were far bigger trees around than the ones I was under. The storm soon passed, everything 'steamed' in the evening sun and the barbel came back on the feed again.

Life was good again. Summers were spent in the boat on Tabley Mere, with occasional barbel trips to the Severn, and winters were spent piking on the canal with chub trips to the Severn. There were also the now bi-annual trips (Easter and October) to Anglesey too.

Work was hectic, demanding, stressful, but manageably so, and financially rewarding. The owner gave the directors the opportunity to buy shares in the company and put us on rolling twelve-month contracts, as a prelude, he said, to him selling the company at some point. This didn't worry me too much. Lorraine's job had taken off dramatically to the point where she was earning more than me anyway: she would continue her rise to the top in Local Government, provide evidence to select committees in the House of Commons, meet Ministers, the Queen and other assorted 'minor royals'. Not bad for a girl who grew up in the 'care system' in Birmingham.

The time came for the owner to sell the company. In late 1999 he sold it to a cement company (it's a long story) who merged us with a competitor of ours that they'd also just bought. I did well out of this merger and was now the Sales and Marketing Director for the new company, which was twice as big as the original. However, the most important thing that happened at this point in time was that Lorraine and I had to sit down with a financial adviser for the first time. Primarily this was to make sure I paid the right amount of tax on the profit on my shares, not a big profit you understand, but still enough to require payments to be made and payments about which I knew nothing. In addition to this, he asked us what our long-term financial goals were. We hadn't really thought about this. Did we like having fancy holidays? Errrm, no, not really. So, what did we want? Well, it would be nice to be able to retire in our fifties, I said. My father had worked right up to his sixty-fifth birthday and was doing overtime, including weekends, right up to that point in an effort to boost his pension savings. Neither of us believed we could maintain our current pace of life till then; it would kill us. Excellent, he said, and a plan was born. A new millennium, a new company and a new plan. A retirement plan.

Life settled down again and for the next four years, summers were spent in the boat on Tabley Mere and winters pike fishing on the canal. We did, however, for reasons I can't remember, stop going to Anglesey, and eventually I stopped going sea fishing completely, mainly because I just didn't have the time. The kids got older: Alec played rugby, football and cricket and Becky played football, learnt to play the guitar and changed her hairstyle almost as often as I changed my clothes.

Did my kids come fishing with me? Yes, they did. I'd take them down to the canal just below our cottage and set them up with a rod each and some maggots. It was competitive stuff, neither wanting to catch less than the other with Becky, bless her, usually catching more than her brother. She had no qualms about plunging her manicured hands into the maggot box or baiting up her hook. Roach, perch and gudgeon formed the bulk of their catches. When he was thirteen, I took Alec with me to Tabley Mere one morning and managed to get him to catch a tench of about four pounds. I've no doubt that he enjoyed himself but he didn't express a desire to go back. I wasn't going to force fishing on either of them and these days Alec has no interest in fishing whatsoever, although Becky will often accompany me on sea fishing trips in Ireland (we'll get to this soon enough), which is brilliant, as she's good company and takes great photos.

Do I regret not trying to involve them more with my fishing? Yes, just a little, although there's no saying that this would have made them any more enthusiastic about it.

It was either late summer or early autumn in 2004 and I'd called back home in Timperley to see my Mum and Dad. I think I'd had a meeting in Manchester and with having an hour of free time I'd stopped by for some lunch. My father was sitting in his chair complaining about his back, 'I must have pulled something while in the garden,' he said and I thought no more of it.

A few weeks later, I saw him again and he was still complaining about his back; go to the doctor, I said. Maybe, he replied, I don't really want to bother the doctor just yet.

More weeks passed: still his back was bad. Have you been to the doctors yet, I asked? Yes, he replied, he thinks it's just muscular but he's sending me for a scan, just in case. The scan appointment came through for something like January of the following year.

A couple of weeks elapsed again before I next saw him and this time I was shocked. He looked ill, very ill. His face was gaunt, the skin slightly yellow and almost translucent and his clothes hung off his emaciated body. Sod waiting for January, I got him an appointment at the BUPA hospital – ironically the one where my mother finished her nursing career – for later that week. This confirmed the worst: he'd got cancer and it had spread throughout his body, infiltrating his spine, kidneys and various other organs. I was with him when he got the diagnosis. What do you say to someone, anyone, when they get what amounts to a death sentence? What do you say when it's your own father? All I could think of saying was 'I wish we could go back to Anglesey for one last holiday'. 'Yes,' he replied without a hint of sarcasm, 'I could just do with a holiday right now'. I am never sure if he was being ironic.

My father wanted to die at home, in the back room, looking out over his garden and down to the pond. Which is what he did, surrounded by his family, just before Christmas 2004. This was the first time I'd lost someone close to me, and his death was tough on all of us. Life goes on though, and eventually a sort of normality returns; deep down you know that it is highly likely that you will see your parents die at some point. I dealt with the pain and the stress by talking to my wife and doing what I always did; I went fishing.

The following spring, a lovely Tuesday morning in early May, I was driving down to Milton Keynes for a business meeting. I was making good progress, there were no holdups on the motorways and I didn't anticipate the meeting to be anything other than cordial. I listened to the weather forecast on the radio and heard that the sunshine and associated warmth was going to last all the way to the weekend. As I was hearing this I was passing the series of lakes beside the M1 not far from the Milton Keynes exit; I looked across as much as I dared and saw anglers sitting by their rods fishing. It had been a couple of months since I'd last ventured out fishing, but

I started to mull a few things over in my mind. I quite fancied a trip out at the weekend, but where to go and what to catch?

I daydreamed up a few scenarios, as was, and is, my way. There weren't that many choices to be honest, as most waters were still closed in accordance with the old Close Season for Coarse Fishing rules. Eventually I settled on Pickmere to try and catch a tench. I then left the M1 and re-joined it again heading north having realised that I had sailed a considerable distance past my intended exit.

I have very mixed feelings about Pickmere. It's the only place I've ever fished that I could be totally obsessed with one minute and yet loathe the next. I will endeavour to explain why.

Pickmere lake was, and is, no more than ten minutes' drive from where I live just outside Northwich. Set deep in the Cheshire countryside, it is shaped like a pear and some fifty acres, or thereabouts, in size. I first started fishing it in the late eighties when I moved out to the Northwich area. In those days, the far bank from where I fished still contained a lot of old wooden chalets which had been built during the Second World War to house families from Manchester and Liverpool who had been 'bombed out'. To my left, at the fat end of the pear, was a funfair and a landing stage from which a motorised launch, the *Princess Irene,* would leave to trundle around the edge of the lake. You could hire rowing boats there and the lake was also used by water skiers and eventually jet skiers too. I'm sure you're already thinking why the hell I would want to fish a place like this. The simple answer was that Pickmere contained some very big tench; at one point in time, back in the sixties, it was thought to be capable of producing the next British record tench. Of course, if you fished from dawn to mid-morning you missed the worst of the funfair and assorted watercraft and the place could almost be described as 'habitual'. There was one drawback with fishing these hours: you didn't catch many tench. Pickmere tench, for reasons known only to them, tended to feed best between the hours of two in the afternoon and dusk. Maybe the *Princess Irene* stirred the bottom up, and this encouraged the tench to feed; who knows. What I did know was that in between the passing of the motor launch, the water skiers and the jet skis I could catch tench on a swimfeeder set-up, including what became my best ever tench of 6lb 14oz. However, the thrill of catching large tench was soon totally negated by the noise of the funfair and the disturbances caused by the assorted watercraft. It was tench fishing, good tench fishing, but not tench fishing as I knew it, and after a couple of years I left Pickmere with absolutely no regrets.

Fast forward to 2005: the funfair, the motor launch and the jet skiers have gone. The water skiers remained though. I'd heard rumours that there had been some big tench caught at Pickmere, but didn't take them too seriously; I was getting older and more cynical when it came to that sort of thing. The Thursday following that little jaunt down to Milton Keynes saw me heading back to Pickmere for the first time in over a decade for a quick look-around. I was pleasantly surprised by what I saw. The banks, which had previously consisted of lightly grassed peat, now possessed a healthy cover of vegetation and trees had sprung up to be the size of large saplings. The water looked less peaty and the whole place had a decidedly more 'habitual' feel to it. Suddenly I couldn't wait for dawn on Saturday morning. Why was I going to arrive there at dawn and fish through till early afternoon when previously nearly all of my tench had come post-lunch? Quite simply, I wanted to be there at dawn to experience a proper tench fishing atmosphere, something which would disappear the moment the water skiers arrived. If this cost me some tench, then so be it.

I nearly didn't go in the end as the warm spell came to a premature end and the Friday evening weather forecast predicted ground frosts for the following morning. Cold, frosty mornings and tench fishing don't go together – but I'd already bought the maggots, sweetcorn, hemp and groundbait and had also dug some fat lobworms from the compost heap. Therefore, I got up before first light and with the temperature gauge on my car showing three degrees Celsius I headed off to Pickmere.

My enthusiasm wavered as I made up my groundbait mixture; it was cold! At least it was still, as any breeze would have made life pretty unbearable. Using my trusty 'Whopper Dropper' – that name still brings a smile to my face – I deposited twenty to thirty small balls of groundbait out around a marker float which was maybe thirty-five yards from the bank. I was using two matching rods and reels and yes, I was also going 'all-Optonical' with bite alarms too. On one rod, I had three maggots and a swimfeeder and on the other a large lobworm and a piece of plastic corn to try and keep the worm above the weed on the bottom; the presence of this weed around the weight attached to my marker float was a bit of a surprise and I guessed that the improved water clarity had encouraged it to grow. A tube feeder filled with small worms and corn, with the ends blocked off with groundbait, completed the set-up on my second rod.

By half past five I was sitting next to my rods warming my hands on a cup of coffee. I had intended to read a book while I fished, but it was too cold to do so and when not wrapped around a cup of coffee, my hands remained buried in my pockets. A tench-fisher's dawn was the very last thing this morning reminded me of.

Two hours later a very strange thing happened; one of my bite alarms emitted a series of little 'bleeps' before line was pulled off the spool at an alarming rate in what, I believe in modern angling parlance is known as a 'one toner', a nasty, horrible phrase which reflects the very worst of today's angling world. I would also include 'slack liner' in this litany of shame, although the use of this phrase is perfectly acceptable in sea fishing. While we're talking about litanies of angling literary shame can I just say that I go fishing or angling: I don't go baggin' or haulin'!

I stared at the reel for a couple of seconds before deciding that there was every chance that a fish had taken my bait; it took those few seconds to come to my senses because I just didn't believe that there was any chance of catching anything that morning. I lifted the rod, engaged the spool and tightened up to a fish. The fight itself was what you'd describe as steady, if unspectacular, with the only real alarm being when the tench, yes, it was a tench, decided that it quite liked the look of the tree in the water to my right. I was using eight-pound line so was comfortably able to keep the fish away from the roots and branches of that tree and soon had it on the bank. At 7lb 12oz it was my biggest-ever tench, and another obsession was born.

Three hours later a group of water skiers appeared and ploughed straight through my swim. The obsession was strangled at birth. I vowed never to go back. I broke the vow the following weekend, caught a few more tench and then re-affirmed the vow, all before dinner time. This pattern repeated itself every weekend until the beginning of the coarse fishing season, when I headed back to Tabley Mere and the boat.

I went back to Pickmere for the next three springs, always in early May when there had been enough warmth to raise the water temperature and more importantly, put leaves on the trees and make the bankside vegetation grow. Each year, my mind highlighted the tench and diminished the impact that the water skiers made: surely, they weren't that bad, were they? Yes, they were. Every morning would follow that same pattern: a dawn start, the unbridled joy of being by the water on a spring morning; coffee; biscuits; a good book to read and if a tench was caught then this was merely the cherry on the icing of a very large cake. Whisper it gently, but I rather enjoyed using my old Optonic bite alarms. I could bury my head in a book and that first little 'bleep' of the bite alarm would almost – but not quite – give me the same buzz as the first dip on the float or the little ripples that would emanate from my pike floats.

And then *they* would appear, the water skiers with their huge motorboats which should have stayed by the seaside where they belonged, and I would be filled with an antipathy which grew into a murderous rage. I'm actually getting pretty damn angry just thinking about it as I type these words. Of course, I should simply have packed up and gone home as soon as they arrived, but I was always convinced that there were more tench to be caught.

I caught some big fish there too, huge fish by my standards. A double figure bream, just, it weighed 10lb 3oz and a colossal tench of 9lb 12oz. The fact that I can nonchalantly throw these fish into the conversation in the same way that I'd mention 'plain Digestives' when discussing a list of favourite biscuits (custard creams, chocolate Hobnobs etc.) shows just how mixed my feelings for Pickmere are. I can remember catching the seven-pound tench very clearly because it was prior to that first appearance of the water skiers; after that everything is just a jumbled mass of memories and conflicting emotions.

Eventually, I started to catch fewer tench and the water skiers started arriving even earlier, so I walked away from Pickmere, vowing that this time it really was the end.

We didn't fish on Tabley Mere in the winter, so every autumn we were faced with the task of baling the boat out, splitting it in half and lifting/dragging it out onto the bank. The following spring we would return to the mere to inspect the boat, carry out any minor repairs and re-assemble it back in the water. Each year that passed saw more work needed to maintain its integrity; it also seemed to get heavier every year. I'm sure that was partly due to us getting older, but the boat most likely was getting heavier as the paint layers, despite our best efforts, gradually allowed water to reach the wood underneath. By the end of the 2005 season the boat was showing its age, in fact, it was starting to get dangerously fragile, and when rowing in a strong wind it was starting to flex in places it shouldn't. This was quite alarming, especially when you knew you had over ten feet of water below you.

There was therefore no doubt about it; a new boat had to be sourced. I thought about making a new one, but decided against it. Without my father's help and by now having two children, there just wasn't enough time to build another boat and, to be honest, I had no inclination to do so anyway. I went online and found a company on the banks of the River Thames that made aluminium punts, indeed they had a picture on their web site of two anglers fishing from one of their vessels. However, I wondered if the boat would be wide enough to accommodate our chairs, and I had a nagging doubt about that photo as both anglers were sitting there with their rods pointing at forty-five degrees up into the air, a classic mistake by people who don't know how fishing works.

John and I arranged to go down to London one Saturday morning in early spring to water test one of these punts on the Thames itself. It was a good job we did, as these punts were the most chronically unstable vessels we'd ever encountered and I doubt we'd have managed a single trip before one of us leaned back in our chair and caused the whole boat to turn turtle.

I then saw a John Wilson fishing programme during which he pike fished from an aluminium boat-cum-punt that had the maker's name on the side. A quick look online soon identified the place in question, which was in the Midlands, not too far away, and John and I went down there to order a replacement boat. The people there were very good and we were able to specify exactly what sort of boat we wanted, even including the position of the fixed seat to ensure that we could get two collapsible chairs in place. The up side of the boat being made of aluminium was that it was very light, easy to row, rustproof and therefore would not require to be removed from the water every year. The downside was that it was significantly less stable than our previous one.

Our old wooden boat was removed from the Mere one last time. I felt quite emotional as I thought of the time my father and I had spent making it as well as all the good times I'd had fishing in it. I got busy with an axe – I almost wondered if I should have placed a blanket over the bow first – and reduced it to firewood. It was then cremated and its ashes sprinkled onto the fair waters of Tabley Mere.

I'll end this chapter with a lament: a lament for the death of the close season for what seems to be the majority of canals, ponds, lakes and meres in this country. For those who don't remember, it used to be illegal to fish with rod and line on still waters and rivers during the period between the 15th March and the 15th June; on rivers, the close season still remains. The reason for this was to protect spawning fish from disturbance. 'Oh, you hypocrite!' I hear you cry, and this won't be the last time you think this either. Yes, I did fish in my own little pond when I was young in the closed season and I've just finished talking about catching tench from Pickmere in the close season! I therefore owe you an explanation, so, here it is.

Christmas Day is special because it comes just once each year. As a child, you started to get really excited from a point in mid-December until by Christmas Eve you were positively bursting with excitement. The 16th June enabled that same child to emerge from every angler. At the beginning of June, you'd start looking longingly at your tackle in the garage; a week or so later you'd be thinking that it might need its once-per-season clean. You would have been planning your opening night or dawn session for months, possibly from the end of the previous fishing season, and the 15th June becomes your Christmas Eve. That's how it was for me anyway. It still is; I can't fish from my boat on Tabley Mere until the 16th June and the night of the fifteenth will see me giddy with excitement and struggling to sleep. The longer the wait, the more the excitement builds. But nobody wants to wait for anything these days; we live in an age of instant gratification, an age where waits are measured in seconds, not months. Angling has not been immune from this and it was inevitable that with the advent of commercial fisheries (for the uninitiated, small ponds overstocked with fish which are very easy to catch because they have to eat your bait as there's not enough natural food in the water... phew) the days of the old broad close season were numbered. I feel both sad and angry about this; sad that a generation of anglers will not have that giddy Christmas Eve feeling and angry that it has been allowed to happen, on still waters at least.

A very quick aside. I'm currently reading *A Man Called Ove* by Fredrik Backman, as Lorraine had read it and started calling me 'Ove' whenever I switched into rant-mode. Ove is a grumpy old Swedish man who is obsessed by life's minutiae and prefers his own company to that of others. Shockingly, I have to concede that she has a point...

Pickmere with 5lb tench in May 1981 – with a funfair in the background.

Pickmere plus 4lb 8oz tench – with a water skier in the background

Pickmere and my best ever tench at 9lb 10oz

Pickmere and my best-ever bream at 10lb 3oz

CHAPTER TWELVE

A RETURN TO SEA FISHING

I had been perfectly happy spending my springs on Pickmere ('happy' as qualified in the previous chapter), summers on Tabley Mere and my winters on the canal, with a few trips to the Severn thrown in for a little variety. What happened next was my buddy John's fault. He suddenly found a love for sea fishing and bass in particular; lure fishing at first, swiftly followed by bait fishing. This in turn rekindled obsessions in me which by then had lain dormant for many years. Sea-fishing tackle was dug out from the back of the garage and plans made to catch some cod again.

There was a sub-text to this return to sea fishing in that my pike fishing had become increasingly stale, which left me open to a new obsession. I'd caught a few more twenty-pounders, but this class of fish soon died out, to be replaced by a larger quantity of smaller fish. I went from a situation where I only caught a pike every couple of trips, but most of the pike I caught were over eight pounds in weight – indeed many were ten-pound plus fish – to a situation where I caught regularly, but the fish were generally less than five pounds in weight. I was therefore not approaching these trips with the obsessional enthusiasm I once had.

This being 2006, I went onto the Internet and did some fairly random searching to see if I could find some better cod fishing closer to home. I was fairly sure that the cod fishing in the Menai Straits wouldn't have got any better in the years I'd been away and soon found two options that seemed to offer the potential for some proper cod fishing; by that I mean a possibility of catching a six-pound plus fish, this being the accepted size at which a 'codling' becomes a 'cod'. The first option was the River Mersey, now clean enough to support a mixture of sea fish but lacking in all the other ingredients that I would find conducive to enjoyable fishing. I would be fishing in the middle of either Liverpool or Birkenhead with a skyline dominated by office blocks, scrap metal heaps or dockside cranes.

The second option looked more promising; the River Dee. I spent a day looking at a variety of places to fish on the Dee, from Connahs Quay all the way through to Talacre, but one spot stood out with a reputation for producing codling and the very occasional cod too. This was Mostyn. Muddy Mostyn.

First of all, the plus points. The skyline was fine, a distant view of the gentle hills on the west side of the Wirral peninsula. There was also deep water close to the shore, easy parking close to where you fished and a little Portakabin nearby that sold both fresh and frozen black lug. There were some down sides. Firstly, the mud; secondly, you were fishing from a man-made embankment constructed from 'spoil' from the old steelworks at Shotton and thirdly, there was a sewage works behind this embankment from which odours spewed out across you when the wind was at your back (which was normal, as this is where the prevailing wind came from). Thirdly, fourthly, fifthly - you get the drift - the mud! It was grey and very fine. In fact, doubtless it wasn't just mud given the proximity of the sewage works and its outfall, which was virtually at your feet. And Mostyn mud gets everywhere. Whatever steps you take to minimise its spread, you *will* get it on every piece of exposed clothing and when you remove this clothing you will get the mud on your hands and then transfer it to your car, sub-clothing and anything else you touch that was previously uncontaminated.

But my old cod obsession had returned with a vengeance, so I fished at Mostyn and tried to ignore the mud. I started fishing there in October, but by Christmas Day I'd yet to catch a cod of any description; plenty of dabs and whiting, but no codling. On my very first trip there, I'd hooked something on my last cast which could well have been a codling but managed to lose it when the line got caught around the cinder blocks at my feet. Although I was disappointed to lose the fish, I was encouraged by the fact that I'd hooked something decent and didn't think that nearly three months later I'd still be codless.

Fishing the Dee for codling was a unique experience for me. I knew it was a predominantly low water venue but hadn't realised how much bigger an impact the weather had there compared to the Straits or other beach marks I'd fished. Wet weather not only sent megatons of fresh water hurtling down the river – which pushed the codling well out to sea – it also ripped out weed from the bottom of the river, removed bankside vegetation, and then concentrated this all up, with the result that you'd be happily fishing away one minute and then 'weeded out' the next as the muddy water turned into a vegetable soup of weed, grass, brambles and branches, with the odd sanitary towel and condom thrown in for good measure. This all wrapped around your line until eventually your end tackle would be too heavy to retrieve and your line would snap.

The day after Boxing Day arrived and I was 'allowed' to go out for a late afternoon and evening's fishing trip. I arrived at Mostyn just as it was getting dark. It had started to rain, a cold wind-driven rain with a bit of sleet mixed into it. The first two casts resulted in me losing both of my rigs. I was cold, wet and totally disgruntled and would probably have gone home if I hadn't started catching a few decent-sized whiting, bigger than any I'd had previously there. The hours passed, the whiting gradually vanished, it stopped raining, the sky cleared, the wind dropped and it started to freeze. I much preferred still, freezing conditions and was happy to sit there watching the shooting stars slide across the night sky (I should have added this to the plus points of Mostyn – it's a great place to watch meteors).

On my return to sea fishing I'd made some subtle changes to my gear. I'd bought some top of the range Zziplex rods, a couple more multipliers, a headlamp (LED technology and rechargeable batteries had meant that a paraffin lamp was no longer needed) and some 'tip lights'. These were small LED lights that you could attach to your rods, powered by hearing-aid type batteries. There is one very important thing you need to know about tip lights: *they have to be red!* I will brook no argument here and will engage in verbal fisticuffs with anyone who says otherwise!

So, there I was watching the shooting stars while also keeping an eye on the red lights attached to the end of my rods. The rod tips were slightly bent over as the outgoing tide put pressure on the line. Every now and again there would be a little nod on one of these rod tips as bits of weed bumped into the line. Then suddenly, one of the red lights sprung upwards into the night air; I lurched towards the rod and picked it up, only to discover that my line was completely slack. I'd read about these 'slack line' bites but had never experienced one. I quickly wound like mad until I connected with a significant weight and felt something shaking its head. Determined not to lose this fish in the same way that I'd done previously I wound like a dervish until the white belly of a fat three-pound codling appeared at my feet. Obviously, by the time I had retrieved it from the mud at the bottom of the embankment, there was not a hint of white to be seen, the fish having turned grey', but at 3lb 10oz it was one of the biggest codling I'd ever caught and a lovely late Christmas present. The next cast produced a smaller codling of 2½lb. I was happy that I'd started to unravel some of the secrets of Mostyn cod-catching.

From that point until early February, I caught codling consistently at Mostyn, but from February onwards the larger codling disappeared, to be replaced by a spring run of much smaller fish, and my interest waned. I also associated cod fishing with cold winters' days at Mostyn and sitting or standing there in shirt sleeves on a lovely spring day just didn't seem right. The eye-watering smell from the sewage works in warmer weather did not add to the ambience either.

I was enjoying my return to sea fishing and also managed a few trips to the north Wales beaches, which produced whiting and dabs but little else. As May approached, I needed something else to sea-fish for, another little obsession to feed – and that obsession turned out to be bass fishing.

It had been over twenty years since Lorraine had caught those bass at Dinas, and although I'd made a couple of half-hearted attempts to catch one in the intervening years, I'd failed miserably. But since John had developed a serious obsession with bass (an obsession far greater than mine will ever be) I now had someone who could act as my mentor. I was shown how to find and identify peeler crabs, an essential bait for spring time bassing in the Menai Straits and river estuaries, and learnt that distance casting in the Straits is not usually conducive to catching bass. I also learnt that different marks, beaches included, fished best on different states and sizes of tides but despite all of this education, the bass eluded me from spring until mid-summer.

How did I catch my first bass? In the second week of our summer break, Lorraine kindly agreed to come with me for a day out in North Wales and Anglesey. It was agreed that I could have two fishing sessions in exchange for a nice lunch and a proper meal in a restaurant at the end of the day, a fair exchange. Having bought some black lug from a tackle shop near Rhyl – there would not be an opportunity to dig any bait that day – we headed onto the beach at Abergele a couple of hours before high water. I would have liked to be there much earlier, but that would have been pushing my luck a bit too far and might have resulted in the contract for the day being extended to include a shopping trip at a later date.

The beach here consists of relatively flat sand, interspersed with gullies all the way up to a steep bank of shingle. Depending on the size of the tide, the water might barely creep over the bottom of the shingle or it might get to the top, particularly if backed by a strong northerly wind. I was using an old carp rod and fixed-spool reel loaded with braid, having already learned that where fixed-spool reels and sea fishing are involved, braid is vastly superior to nylon.

I used a simple running ledger and a single worm, cast no more than thirty yards and stood on the shingle by the water holding my rod. After about forty-five minutes, I felt an aggressive tap-tap-tap on the rod tip, then nothing, then another series of 'taps' which grew in intensity until I was confident of striking into the culprit. The culprit was a bass, and at less than a pound in weight a very small one, but it was my first bass and as is often the way after such a long wait – twenty years in this case – my next one wasn't too far behind.

We didn't catch any more fish there, so we moved on to Beaumaris on Anglesey, where we enjoyed a pleasant lunch before departing for the next phase of our little adventure, which involved finding peeler crabs or 'softies' (essentially peeler crabs that have just shed their shells). I had been taught well by my friend and we soon found enough crabs for the four or five hours we'd be fishing. I say 'we' only because Lorraine carried the bucket while I turned the stones and found the crab. While she refused the offer of a fishing rod, she was happy to offer moral support while simultaneously reading a book.

A couple of hours later I had another series of knocks, substantially bigger knocks, and a slightly bigger bass of maybe 1½lb soon lay on the kelp beside me. Both bass I caught that day were returned, slightly to my wife's annoyance, as they were below the minimum size that would have allowed me to legally keep them. Since then I've caught a lot of bass, and a few more cod and plenty of other sea fish too, but have only ever taken one bass for the table, at Lorraine's insistence. Even then, I regretted killing the fish as soon as the deed had been done. I must have started to go soft in my middle age.

At first, this change in fishing habits was slight; I still occasionally pike fished on the canal in winter but started to spend an increasing amount of time on the coast, particularly Mostyn, after the codling. Summers still saw me spending much of my time in the boat at

Tabley Mere, but much less so on the Severn, with my non-Tabley-tench-fishing time being spent on the Menai Straits or the beaches of the North Wales coast.

We revived the family trip to Anglesey, but headed for Beaumaris, as without my father it wouldn't have seemed right going back to Benllech, especially for my mother, who came with us. Beaumaris guards the eastern entrance to the Menai Straits, quite literally, as the imposing castle on the edge of town was commissioned by Edward I in 1295 as part of a chain of castles around the North Wales coast. The castle inadvertently gave the town its name – it was built on a marsh and the French builders called it 'beaux marais', which translates as 'beautiful marshes'.

I didn't do a lot of fishing on this trip but did manage to catch a lovely bass of 6½lb, the catching of which demands a little explanation. Since the kids were still at school I couldn't plan this little trip around the tides, as I would have done previously, so I was faced with what I considered to be less than ideal tidal conditions: very small tides, albeit with a late afternoon low water. I'd purchased and then found a reasonable number of peeler crabs, and on the afternoon of our first day I headed down to a lovely isolated little mark just outside Beaumaris itself. It was a mark that had produced some nice codling in previous years (and had been the venue for the 'engagement bet') but had changed significantly since then. It had been a mark of predominantly sand with the occasional rock; now the reverse was true, which made it a perfect spot for bass fishing. Another angler had given me some important advice about fishing in the Straits: 'if you're after bass in the Straits and you're not losing tackle, you're fishing in the wrong place.'

I was fishing from a rocky outcrop, which in truth was no more than a foot or so higher than the surrounding area, and to my left was a shallow crescent-shaped bay. It was a grey, overcast afternoon with a strong south-westerly breeze howling along the Straits as low water approached. Casting was difficult, but eventually I managed to catch a couple of blank-saving dogfish. However, through the foam-flecked waves I was sure I'd seen some 'disturbances,' possibly mullet, but also potentially bass. These disturbances had been quite close to the shore, with one being inside the shallow bay to my left in what must have been no more than two feet of water.

I returned the following afternoon to find that conditions were much the same except that the wind had dropped completely, to leave the Straits eerily quiet with a surface unruffled by nothing more than clumps of weed travelling in the current and the odd 'boil' close to the shore denoting boulders underneath. I took two rods with me and my tripod. By now, my accepted way of bass fishing in the Straits was to stand there holding the rod; as soon as I felt the rod tip move, I'd follow the bite with my rod until I was sure that whatever had taken the bait was serious in its intention before striking. This afternoon, however, I wanted to put a bait into the shallow bay to my left, effectively casting parallel to the shore, and for this I used another of my old carp rods and one of my old Baitrunner reels which could be left in free-spool mode on the basis that I wouldn't have to worry about losing my rod if a decent bass took the bait.

It didn't take long for me to catch my first bass on the rod I was holding. Tap, bigger tap… and the rod tip slammed round before I could 'follow' the bite. The fish only weighed about two pounds, but the force of bite these fish can give is quite out of proportion to their size. I was still at the stage of my bass-fishing career where the capture of a bass of any size marks the trip down as a complete success (truth to tell, it still does!) and I was quite happily standing there with a silly grin on my face when the Baitrunner suddenly growled out as line was taken from the spool. It took me a few seconds to put the rod I was holding onto the other arm of the tripod and then pick up my other rod. I engaged the spool and lifted into something that by now was out of the shallow bay and very angry. The line went slack. I wound in quick and the fish was still there, it had just shot back towards me. My heart started beating again of its own accord as the fish tore around the shallow bay and as it passed in front of me I piled the pressure on and dragged it into the shallow water, where it bounced around as I tried to get hold of it. I placed two hands underneath it and scoop it out onto the rocks.

It was big, fat and beautiful (a bit like me) and after a weighing and a quick photo, I got it back into the water as quickly as I could.

Now this was a useful lesson for me; I knew that bass fishing in the Menai Straits could be carried out at close quarters, but not that close. It was about this time that I started to do the one thing that has made the biggest difference to my sea fishing: I started to keep a detailed angling journal into which I recorded the minutiae of every trip. This would include weather (sunshine or cloud, temperature, wind direction and strength); time of day I started and finished fishing; the times of low and/or high water; the size of the tides (in metres relative to Liverpool Gladstone Dock); the size of the swell (how big the waves were); the length of the swell (how far out they broke); and time of capture of any significant fish and bait employed in said capture. If I'm catching lots of small fish such as whiting, then I won't record individual fish but numbers caught over a period of time.

However, when it comes to interpreting this mass of data I am very aware of the 'Homer' school of thinking. That's Homer Simpson, not the Greek poet, who once said 'facts are meaningless, you can use them to prove anything'. Let me explain: unless you have tried to fish a mark in all tide states, heights and weathers, the data will be scientifically worthless, as you will usually have gravitated towards only fishing when you expect to catch, normally based on the results of your first few trips or information from other anglers (who may have fallen into the same trap). It's only recently that I've had the time to deliberately target the times, tides etc when I wouldn't normally expect to catch and therefore to build up a more complete picture. But if, like me, you believe that fishing is as much an art as it is a science, you will sometimes ignore the data and go fishing simply because you want to, and just every now and again that will produce a magical moment. As the saying goes, it's called 'fishing' and not 'catching' for a reason.

The precursor to the first cataclysmic change in my fishing habits occurred in February 2008. I was cod fishing at Mostyn on a cool and very windy day, not catching much, and was aware that time was running out as far as that winter's cod fishing was concerned.

Two other anglers turned up and we got talking. See, I'm not completely anti-social. It turned out that they were only fishing Mostyn because they couldn't get onto their favourite rock mark on the west coast of Anglesey, where they had been intending to catch thornback rays. Interesting, did they often catch rays there? Yes, they did. Something stirred deep inside me, and you'll have to indulge me as I tell you why.

The significance of a particular day's fishing may not become apparent for years later, maybe even decades. For me, this was the case when I recall a fishing experience I'd had over 40 years ago. An occasional fishing friend and his mother turned up on my doorstep one day in May, when I would have been about twelve, and asked me if I wanted to accompany them on a 'works outing' – a day's sea fishing aboard a boat running out of Fleetwood. I never turned down any offer of a day's fishing so obviously I said 'yes' and proceeded to dust off my rudimentary sea fishing tackle from the back of the garage (the tackle that was only ever used once a year during our two-week summer holiday on Anglesey). The boat in question was the 'Viking II' skippered by Frank Bee, and the idea was that we'd be running up to the sandbanks of Morecambe Bay to catch thornback rays.

Some aspects of the day remain quite vivid in the memory. I can remember the smell – that mixture of stale fish and diesel fumes that you seem to get on all fishing boats, not that I've ever done much boat fishing – and I can also see the look on the skipper's face when he saw the tackle I'd brought on board. It was a look of pure disdain and said tackle was quickly consigned to the wheelhouse, amid much head-shaking and muttering, before being replaced by a much heavier rod and multiplier set up. The terminal tackle consisted of a single large hook (maybe a 4/0) and a cube of lead that must have weighed about a pound.

It didn't take us long to get to the chosen mark and we soon anchored up in surprisingly shallow water. In fact, the skipper said that there was little more than twenty feet of water below us and if we looked carefully we might even see the rays on the seabed. I did indeed look, but couldn't see a thing in the murky water. Out came the bait: frozen herrings that were sliced into chunks which were unceremoniously impaled on the hook. Hook, line and sinker were then dropped overboard until the bottom was reached (about three seconds later), the ratchet set and the spool disengaged. 'You'll know when you've got a fish because you'll hear the line being pulled off the spool,' I was told. Interesting: I wasn't going to be looking for little taps on the rod tip then, the sort of bite that the small flatties I was used to catching gave.

I think there were about 12 of us on board that day and as fate would have it, the first bite was mine, a short run which took about five yards of line. I engaged the spool and started to wind in ('no need to strike, son'). There was definitely something there, something that was sort of fighting back although to be honest there was so little 'give' in the tackle I was using it would have taken a ray of gargantuan proportions to put a bend in that rod. A few seconds later a white belly popped up onto the surface, the skipper grabbed the trace and my first ever thornback ray was swung aboard. At around five pounds in weight it was easily the biggest sea fish I'd ever caught, in fact it was by far the biggest sea fish I'd ever seen. However, this fish was dwarfed later in the day by a thornback ray of over 16lb that my friend's mother managed to boat. This was particularly impressive as it was taken during the main tide run when we were all struggling to hold bottom, even with a pound of lead, and when I realised how ridiculously under-gunned I would have been with my own tackle.

Impressive beasts, these rays, I thought and a small obsessional seed was sown, one which would take many decades to germinate before finally flowering. It was a shame, I thought, that there was no way you could ever catch these fish from the shore...

The skipper said that if we wrote a report on the trip and sent it in to the *Angling Times* along with a photo, they would publish it. My friend's mum duly wrote the report and sent it to the paper along with a photo (sadly, it was a photo of the three youngest anglers standing behind a pile of dead rays) and it appeared in the following week's edition. I thought that was the coolest thing that had ever happened to me; in hindsight, it shows what a relatively dull life I was living!

Fast forward those decades. While driving through South Wales on business I get a call in the car from John. He's fishing a beach on the north Wales coast in daylight and I'll never guess what he's just caught: a thornback ray of about 5lb. The seed germinates into a young plant. 'Wow, brilliant,' I said and I agreed to return with him to that same beach a few days later. That trip was an unmitigated disaster: a beautiful, warm, sunny, late February day that saw me spending most of my time unpicking birds' nests (when you mess up a cast and your multiplier overruns, you end up with a huge tangled mass of line which resembles... a birds' nest) as my casting technique disintegrated in a quest to blast oversized baits to the horizon. The plant wilts and looks like it could die.

Fast forward another year and I'm talking to those anglers at Mostyn. I pick their brains for more information and with this, supplemented by a trawl of the internet, I start to understand the rigs and baits I would need to employ to catch a ray.

The following week I headed off to the Cable Bay area on Anglesey, arrived just after nine o'clock on a still, grey morning and found three anglers there before me. Thankfully, these guys couldn't have been more helpful and were happy enough to identify themselves as ray fanatics. I set up my tackle on the next rocky outcrop and watched in awe as after no more than an hour, one of them *actually caught a small thornback ray!* It may have weighed no more than 2lb, but it was a ray and proof that they could be caught from the area I was fishing. Over the next few hours they caught two more rays of a similar size. I didn't catch anything and to be honest, I wasn't too bothered; after all, it should really take years of effort before you finally catch your first ray from the shore.

They packed up late in the afternoon and, gentlemen that they were, they told me to move into 'their' spot as it would give me a better chance of catching a ray. They also showed me the best rig to use for ray fishing, a pulley Pennel rig, and the best way to mount a sand eel on your hooks (remove head and tail and slide hook from tail end to head end) First cast, using a now-streamlined frozen sand eel for bait, a gentle pull down and my first shore-caught ray was hooked. It was only about 2½lb in weight, but that little obsessional plant burst into life, and in true Jack-and-the-Beanstalk style it shot up into the grey Welsh sky and opened the door to a little bit of heaven and a world of ray fishing. At the same time the switch on my cod-fishing obsession flicked instantly from 'on' to 'off'.

My first Mostyn codling weighing all of 3lb 10oz

...and my biggest Mostyn codling at 4lb 14oz. In fact, somewhat pathetically, it's my biggest-ever codling.

My very first bass – caught over twenty years after Lorraine caught hers!

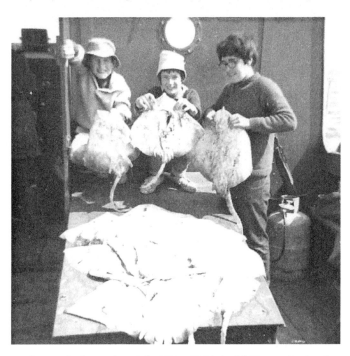

A fine catch of rays aboard the Viking II. Little did I know then just how significant this day would be in future years.

A lovely bass of over 5lb from Pensarn in North Wales.

ANGLESEY ROCKS, AND RAYS OF SUNSHINE

Of all the changes to my fishing life, this was without doubt the biggest. It was the point at which I started to become a sea fisherman first and a coarse fisherman second. A distant second, too. There would be another cataclysmic change to come in a couple of years, but first I need to entertain you (?) with a few tales from the rocks of the west coast of Anglesey.

Before I do that however, I need to thank a group of people without whom none of this would have happened. They are the unknown warriors who conceived, planned and executed the mighty A55 dual carriageway. Without this road, which links the M56 motorway to the Isle of Anglesey and reduced journey times from nearly two and a half hours in those first trips in the 1960s in my parent's car to a paltry ninety minutes, I could never have contemplated regular fishing trips to Ynys Mon (I'm showing off, that's 'Anglesey' in Welsh). Having a company car and a Fuelcard helped too, of course.

Having caught my first ray, you might think that I'd be quickly catching dozens of them. You'd be wrong. Remember the Homer Simpson story? Well, I was only just beginning to collate all the information that I'd need in order to understand how to catch rays on a regular basis. Compared to freshwater fishing there are infinitely more variables in sea fishing, well maybe not infinitely more, but a lot more. In coarse fishing, you have time of year, time of day and weather, maybe moon phase too if you really think that this makes a difference; personally I don't, but that may be why I've never caught large numbers of specimen coarse fish. In sea fishing, you have all of the above plus tides (same as moon phase) and all of the other factors previously mentioned. These days, you could of course just go on the internet, log into one of a number of angling forums and try and short-cut the hard work by asking for information from 'people in the know'. My experience is that this information varies from good to well meaning through complete bollocks to utter drivel, which I suspect is deliberately designed to mislead the unwary angler, who just doesn't know what he doesn't know, and therefore has no way of distinguishing the good information from the bad.

Easter of that year fell in the middle of April, and I persuaded John Woodhouse to accompany me to the island on Good Friday. We didn't have a set plan in mind but wanted a mixture of rock and beach fishing, the final mix being decided by the weather and how big the swell was. The rock marks would be unfishable in big swells, but this would better suit the beaches.

We got to Anglesey reasonably early in the morning, certainly by nine o'clock or thereabouts, which was just as well as the day dawned with clear skies and a sudden promise of hot weather; proper hot weather too, with temperatures forecast to climb past the twenty-degree mark. We headed for the rocks on the west coast and weren't too surprised to find our favourite spots taken, but to be honest, we were happy just to be there. From the size of the swell, our best chance of catching a fish would be while bass fishing on a nearby beach later that afternoon and evening.

I did manage to hook a dogfish but got it snagged on the rocks below me. In trying to retrieve it I got a bit of a soaking from a rogue wave: very symbolic, a baptism of seawater heralding my impending conversion to a full-blown sea fisherman.

By mid-afternoon, the angling incumbents in 'our' spot had surprisingly failed to catch anything and packed up, complaining bitterly about the lack of fish. We moved straight in as soon as they left, partly because we were more comfortable and optimistic in fishing that spot – it was the only spot where I'd ever caught a ray – and also because we were losing a lot of tackle in the spots we'd chosen to fish. We were, without the need for advice from any other angler, to discover that fishing tackle-hungry spots were not linked to the catching of rays.

As the afternoon wore on and low water approached, the wind dropped a little and the swell started to reduce. We were a little alarmed about this as we'd hoped that the swell would bring the bass in, having already decided that bass were a much better bet than the rays, and in truth, we were doing little more than kill time in preparation for the evening ahead.

I was sitting there, literally burning in the late afternoon sun, when one of my rod tips slowly pulled down before straightening again. There was no slack line but, by the same token, the line was not as tight as it had been. Was it a fish, I asked John? Only one way to find out, he replied, so I gently wound down to find that everything was stuck. Nothing would move. Very strange indeed. I lowered the rod tip, increased the pressure and leaned backwards. Slowly and surely, I got a couple of yards of line back onto the reel. I then repeated the process. And again. And again. You get the idea. Over the course of what seemed many minutes I gradually dragged 'the thing' closer to the rocks when suddenly whatever it was lifted off the bottom and came up in the water towards us. John saw it first. 'It's a ray,' he said, 'a big ray'.

I took advantage of an incoming wave to guide it on to the rocks below me. Now there was still a significant swell and I take my hat off to my friend for a superb piece of gillying that saw him plunge down to the waterline and emerge holding a thornback ray of what to us then was gargantuan proportions. The scales were produced and we settled on a weight of exactly 10lb 6oz. To say I was ecstatic would be an understatement. Photographs were taken and the fish released none the worse for its ordeal; there's no finer sight than that of a ray slowly flapping its wings as it returns to the depths. My first ten-pound plus ray, what a day!

We finished the day on a nearby beach, where I blanked but my friend caught a nice plaice and a bass, so we both went home contented.

It took me another month before I caught my third ray, a fish of about 5lb in weight caught on a warm day in early May. I'd spent the morning catching dogfish, dogfish and more dogfish, sometimes two dogfish on one Pennel rig (a Pennel rig is one with two hooks and one bait; one hook goes into the bottom of the bait and the other into the top) and didn't even realise that I'd hooked a ray until it surfaced in front of me. I also started to retrieve my rigs with not only the bait missing, but the hooks too. The culprits turned out to be spider crabs (*Maja squinado*) – large crabs with long legs and claws easily capable of snipping through thirty-pound hook-lengths. If you've ever watched 'Deadliest Catch' on the Discovery Channel, then these beasts are the closest thing we get in this country to the ones that Sig Hansen and his mates catch. Further trips produced similar results, but without the ray, and taught me that ray fishing from the rocks on Anglesey should be a winter and early spring affair.

Even if I had caught the odd ray, I would still have stopped going there because this level of continual action was at odds with what I already considered to be 'pure ray fishing'. It's worth exploring what I mean by this, and why I was already so obsessed with these fish.

There are so many things I like about ray fishing from the rocks, it's difficult to know where to begin. First of all, I like the waiting: ray fishing is rarely frenetic, although it can have its moments when fish follows fish, but for the most part you sit there waiting for your rod tips to move. The waiting is important' it allows the tension to build in the same way as in pike or tench fishing where you sit there waiting for the float to stir into life but rarely have mornings or days where bite follows bite. As long as the weather is dry, I can also read while I fish, drink coffee and eat biscuits. Thus, I can do four of my favourite things at the same time, although these days I have to forego a lot of the biscuits for reasons you will discover shortly.

I fish with my rod tips under tension so that there is just enough of a curve in them to spot a slack-line bite, one which would lead to the straightening of said rod tips. I also have the line clipped into a line clip and the reels in free spool mode with the ratchet on. So I get an audible sign of a bite when a fish takes the bait. The bites that a ray gives are also quite magical: there's nothing hurried about them, it's either a slow slack-line affair or more usually, a slow pull down on the rod tip until the line pulls out of the line clip and pulls a bit of line of the spool with a corresponding noise from the ratchet. Many is the time when I've been engrossed in a book only to hear the ratchet sound out and realise that a ray has taken my bait. These slow pull-downs are especially enchanting at night when you have two rod tip lights side by side; one slowly drops down below the other before springing back above it as the line pulls out of the clip. At the same time you hear the ratchet on the reel and know that something of note has grabbed your bait.

I like describing bites; when I phone John to tell him how I've got on if he's not been with me, I'll be about to describe the bites I've had when he'll interrupt me by saying, 'yer gonna start describing yer ray bites again aren't yer?' I would point out in my defence that he's never shy in describing his bass bites…

Ray fishing can be a solitudinous affair (there's no such word, I've invented this one as it fits the ray fishing mood perfectly) in that a lot of the rock marks can only accommodate one angler and often you are out of sight of any other human being. It's not that I dislike other anglers or am especially anti-social, but I'm more than happy with my own company or the company of a few good friends when I'm fishing.

Being on the rocks at dawn or dusk, but especially at dawn on a still winter or spring morning, is almost beyond description. You get surprisingly few mornings when there is absolutely no coastal breeze whatsoever, but when you do get such a morning and the sea is truly like a mirror with no discernible swell you cannot fail to be happy, and catching a ray is of purely secondary importance. On mornings such as these you may be fortunate enough to see schools of porpoises venture past, sometimes within yards of where you are fishing. I can remember one such morning when they gallivanted about in front of me for several minutes and at one point one of them stopped and looked straight at me for a good five seconds before slowly sinking away again. I should have asked him or her if there were any rays down there.

I have so many happy memories of fishing Anglesey's rock marks, and I'd like to share a few with you.

The first tale is a strange one in that it doesn't involve any fish, but it remains etched in my consciousness as if it only happened yesterday. It was early spring 2009 and I'd arrived at my favourite rock mark on a Sunday morning just before high water to find it deserted. A good start. I had two baits in the water and was just about to open my flask of coffee when another human being appeared beside me. He was in his fifties or maybe early sixties, I'm not much good at judging people's age, and had a canvas bag around his shoulder similar to the one my father used for his flask when he cycled to work. He said hello and asked if I minded if I joined him: at least he'd had the courtesy to ask so I said yes, no problem. It turned out that he was a fellow angler but more of a lure fisherman and was pleasant enough company; he asked me if I wanted some of his coffee – he had a flask in that canvas bag – and I said yes. I offered him some custard creams in return and we talked in some detail about spots that we'd both fished. He told me that he often went fishing with his son and asked if I had kids and whether or not they came fishing with me. Yes, I did have kids and no, they didn't come fishing with me. He complimented me on my casting – unusual, most people are very rude about my casting ability – and I complimented him on his coffee.

During the course of an hour's amiable conversation it dawned on me that this guy just needed to talk to someone, anyone, and it also occurred to me that maybe he was recently bereaved. His wife possibly, god forbid not his son. Another thirty minutes passed, during which time he started repeatedly looking at his watch before finally announcing, 'I'd better get back, she [his wife, I presumed] will need me now that he's gone. My lad goes back to Afghanistan this morning, I've said goodbye to him but I couldn't be there when he left the house... thanks for everything, I hope you catch something.' And with that he was gone, and the fishing didn't seem quite so important any more. I've often wondered if his lad returned home safely.

I'm sure you're wondering if I ever managed to improve on that first double figure ray. Yes, I did, and here's how I did it.

I would like to say that it was a beautiful still winter's morning, but it wasn't. Conditions were forecast to be distinctly borderline: a nasty bitterly cold wind which would be blowing straight into my face, a mixture of sleet and rain and a swell of between two and three feet in height which did not exactly fill me full of confidence. If it wasn't for the fact that the weather had prevented me from going out for the previous two weeks with the forecast for the forthcoming week looking no better, I wouldn't have gone. Ever the optimist, I was hoping that conditions wouldn't be quite as bad as forecast and that maybe, just maybe, I would be able to find a ray or two. It turned out that conditions were worse than forecast, but having travelled for an hour and a half I decided that I might as well give it a go and embarked on the ten-minute walk from the car park to my intended rocky platform. I soon had two baits in the water, although the wind had reduced my casting distances considerably and I sat there slightly disconsolate in the knowledge that I was surely wasting my time. I couldn't even read a book. I decided that as soon as I'd finished my coffee and biscuits, I'd be off home.

Matters got even worse when a larger than average wave hit a rock in front of me and showered me with freezing cold sea water, which I could feel running down the back of my neck all the way to my underwear. Disconsolation turned to anger, and I cursed myself loudly for being so stupid as to have let my hood drop down, and even to be there fishing in the first place.

Three hours later I finished the last of the coffee and decided that three hours' fishing almost justified three hours' driving and it was time to go home. I wound in the first rod and was about to remove my rig when I noticed that it had stopped sleeting; in fact, the wind had dropped a little too. Maybe just one last cast? After all, it was an hour after low water, which was my favourite time for catching rays from this spot.

I made up another squid and sand eel wrap, which for the uninitiated is a large frozen sand eel with head and tail removed around which is wrapped with what remains of a squid when its head, tentacles and insides have been removed. The end result looks something like a squid cigar. Taking advantage of the lull in the wind, I launched it further than any other cast that morning and almost felt a glimmer of hope.

Ten minutes later the rod tip pulled down, the line came out of the clip and line was slowly pulled off the spool. Normally the line coming off the spool would stop almost immediately, but this time it kept on going, only slowly but steadily, as something swam out to sea. I engaged the spool, wound down to the fish and set the hook.

For a couple of seconds there was nothing but an immovable object before suddenly it sprang to life and started to take line of an admittedly lightly set clutch. A ray had never done this to me before, and the adrenaline started to course through my veins. I moved down closer to the water to a point where I could land the fish and immediately got another soaking: this time I didn't feel it. The fish kited hard to my left and then to my right but I was able to gradually work it back towards me until I got my first glimpse of it and knew straight away that it was the biggest thornback ray I had ever hooked. It obligingly allowed itself to be grounded on the sloping rocks in front of me and I knew I had to make a split-second judgement as to when to grab it before the next wave came.

I *nearly* got it right. I managed to get hold of the fish but couldn't make my escape before the next wave arrived. I felt the water surge up my legs towards my waist; I started to rise up in the water (I should point out that I was wearing a flotation suit and wellington boots with metal grippers in their soles) and just as I thought I was going to lose my grip the water subsided and I was able to climb back up the rocks with my trophy in my hand. What a trophy too!

At 12lb 10oz it remains my biggest thornback ray, and like all the rays I catch, it was returned to grow even bigger with an instruction to come back and find me in ten years' time.

A note to my wife, who will doubtless read this last paragraph in horror unless she has taken out some life assurance on me that I don't know about. I have exaggerated the dangerousness of landing that ray for dramatic effect. Honestly.

Six months later I returned to that very same spot for a rare bit of summer ray fishing. As I've previously stated, the volume of dogfish and spider crabs usually means that I see sense before even thinking of returning there in the warmer months. However, I'd just returned from a successful trip to Dingle in Ireland (more of which to come) during which time I'd enjoyed catching lots of thornback rays to the extent that I decided I would risk the Irish Sea dogfish and spider crab bouillabaisse in order to hopefully further this enjoyment. It was a rare mid-week trip for me and I arrived late morning to warm sunshine and light winds to surprisingly find 'my' spot free of other anglers. This spot has two platforms, a low water platform and a high water one, and it was the high water one I found myself fishing from to begin with. Thankfully, the fishing was slow and the first few hours produced only a couple of dogfish and no spider crabs, which enabled me to open a book, a flask and a packet of chocolate Hobnobs.

I was thoroughly engrossed in the book (a re-read of Clive Gammon's 'Castaway') when the sound of the ratchet on my multiplier interrupted me. I looked up to see line pouring off the spool at an almighty rate and dived towards my rod while at the same time looking around for seagulls, who have an annoying habit of tangling with fishing lines as they fly past. There were no seagulls about, so I engaged the spool; it's a good job I always leave my reels in ratchet/free spool mode, otherwise the rod would have disappeared before I could have grabbed it. I tightened up to whatever was on the other end of the line and for the first and only time in my sea angling life I found myself attached to something that I could make no impression on whatsoever. Line disappeared off the spool at an alarming rate, so I used my thumb to try and slow the spool down...

stupid idea, cue one burnt thumb. I tightened the drag on the reel, a much better idea but ineffective... tightened it some more and leant back to brace myself against the fish... still ineffective... line nearly all gone, all 240 yards of it, so I locked the spool completely and the line goes slack. Was the fish running back towards me or had it gone? Unfortunately, the fish had gone, the hook link having been neatly bitten through.

I've no idea what it was, although the prime suspect would have to be a tope. I didn't catch a ray that day, but I could go home and legitimately tell people about 'the one that got away'.

Once I got the measure of fishing off the rocks in daylight, I started to fish into the hours of darkness too. By 'getting the measure of' I mean building up a mental picture of the immediate landscape to a point where I could fish with a relative degree of safety. In the same way that darkness added another dimension to my coarse fishing, I found that the same applied to my ray fishing. Actually, I would say that the enhancement is greater. For a start, the nights are darker – less man-made light – and the stars, planets and moon are therefore more vivid; the sense of isolation is greater too, as your whole world consists of the one circle of light from your head torch and the two red (red!) tip lights. The magic of hooking into a big fish in darkness is also much more intense as you wait for it to first appear in the light beam of your head torch... is it a ray?

Obviously, it can be a little more dangerous at night, especially when fishing by yourself, hence the reason for making sure you have a good mental map of the area you're fishing and is also why I wear a flotation suit when fishing at night. I usually wear one during the day too, unless the weather is warm.

When fishing for rays you inevitably catch other species too. The most annoying of these are whiting with even the smallest whiting, known as pin-whiting, seemingly able to swallow the largest of baits and hooks. Many is the time I've sat there waiting for a ray only to discover on retrieving my bait that a tiny whiting has been nailed on, one too small to give a bite, meaning that I've wasted precious ray-catching time.

The other species I commonly encounter is the bullhuss or greater spotted dogfish. Many people think they are fantastic fish to catch; they fight well and grow as big as rays, if not bigger. For me, the clue is in the name... dogfish. However you dress it up, they are nothing more than overgrown dogfish, regardless of size. I find them intensely irritating for a whole variety of reasons which I'm happy to list below.

Firstly, they aren't rays.

Secondly, although they usually give huss-like bites – violent pulls on the rod tips followed by slack-liners – they can also imitate ray bites, which gets you all excited until you get that first glimpse of the fish and think, damn, it's a huss.

Thirdly, they are masters of holding onto baits, but not getting hooked. They will hold onto your bait until they are right at your feet, at which point they will simply spit the bait out and swim off while nonchalantly giving you the proverbial fin(ger). So, you don't even have the option to say you've caught the little beggar, although this does relieve you of the fourth issue.

Fourthly, have you ever tried unhooking an overgrown dogfish – sorry, huss? They refuse to open their mouths; when holding them they twist and turn in an attempt to break your wrist and if they can't do that they try and wrap themselves around your wrist or arm and remove as much of your skin as possible.

Fifthly, to repeat, they simply aren't rays, and when you are obsessed with rays, as I am, then huss just don't cut the mustard.

Aside from the west coast of Anglesey I also made a nostalgic return to the east coast and to the rocks at Benllech. Not the rocks I usually fished with my parents, but the next fishing rocks along, rocks which we only rarely fished but which are still classed as Benllech. A fellow angler had mentioned to me that thornback rays could be caught from these rocks, and although more than a little sceptical about this information I was sufficiently intrigued to give it a go. I turned up on a Tuesday morning in the middle of the school holidays, bought a day-pass for the campsite below which the rocks are situated and headed down there. I soon realised the big drawback with these rocks, something I should have remembered: they were full of people fishing for mackerel with strings of feathers. Most of these people were holiday-only sea fishermen (and fisherwomen too) and as such struggled to cast straight, meaning that I spent most of the morning disentangling my line from other people's. I shouldn't be too sniffy about these people as I too was once a holiday-only fisher-boy who enjoyed feathering for mackerel at times, but, even at the age of ten, I could cast in pretty much the direction I wanted to! I'm sure you're getting a good enough idea of my character by now to realise that being surrounded by semi-competent anglers would drive me nuts, and you'd be right. Mr (In)Tolerant packed up and returned home in a huff.

The following summer I was browsing through an online angling forum (something I've virtually stopped doing now: the information contained therein varies – with a few exceptions – between garbage and as previously mentioned, I suspect an attempt to deliberately mislead) when I stumbled across a photo of an angler I knew holding a ray. It wasn't a big ray but I'm sure I recognised the background as the same rocks that had driven me to distraction during the previous year. I mulled over the possibilities in my mind: the cynical part of me said that the rocks would be covered in fluff-chuckers again and I'd only last ten minutes before regretting it. The optimistic part of me was very excited about catching a ray at Benllech, our family's spiritual home on Anglesey, and thought that with it being outside the main school holidays I might have the rocks *almost* to myself.

In the end, the optimistic side of me won the day and I headed back to Benllech on a scorchingly hot Saturday afternoon with the intention of fishing from a couple of hours from before low water right up to high water. Conditions were exactly as I wanted them when I got down onto the rocks: no swell, very little breeze and a bright sunny day. Baits were soon sent out to the horizon (OK, not quite that far, in fact, nowhere near that far) and rods placed onto the tripod to await some action.

The first cast produced a dogfish, which alarmed me a little, but I needn't have worried as the following few hours didn't produce any more of the buggers. It did, however, produce a few mackerel fishermen, and I started to get a little fidgety as strings of feathers started to land near my line. So, when the ratchet on one of my multipliers suddenly sounded out I assumed at first that someone had crossed my line - a set of mackerel feathers cast over your line and subsequently retrieved gives a very good imitation of a ray bite. But a quick look around indicated that there was no one winding feathers in and I assumed it must be a fish.

I wound down to the fish and felt a weight. So far so good, and the weight started kiting to my right as I wound it in. Even better. As the weight came closer to the rocks it rose up threw the water and appeared in front of me; a fine thornback ray of about 5lb. For once, size wasn't important, nor was it important an hour later when I caught a slightly smaller ray. These fish meant more to me than specimens twice their size caught on my usual ray marks, and my only regret was that my father wasn't with me to share the moment. It wouldn't be the last time I felt like that: the more I learnt about sea fishing, especially some of the easier to fish marks, the more I regretted not getting more into my sea fishing at a younger age. My father would have loved to catch a ray or a bass but never did so, something that would be easy for me to rectify with the knowledge I now have.

In September 2011, the company I worked for was sold – yet again – to a Spanish-owned competitor that had grown steadily in the UK, mainly by acquisition. This meant that I now worked for the UK's largest hazardous waste company, but what role, if any, would I be fulfilling? The company decided to bundle all the core hazardous waste services into one group and put all the non-core activities into another called the 'Field Services Division' or, as it was more commonly known, the 'Waifs and Strays Division'. Each group would have its own Managing Director, and I was asked to take on this role for the Waifs and Strays Division: I liked the title but not the job, so I declined, right up to the point when I realised that there might not be another role for me. The Waifs and Strays included Industrial Services, Mineral Recycling, Clinical Waste and being Country Manager of our Turkish Operation, which was essentially another industrial services company based in refineries over there. I was used to visiting refineries in the UK but wasn't used to seeing refineries with armed guards and multi-lingual signs reading 'Please leave all mobile phones, lighters, matches, guns and knives at Reception before entering the refinery'.

A couple of years later we were re-organised again and I got the job I really wanted; Commercial Director for the whole of the UK. This was a fascinating, if stressful, job that took me to places as diverse as Barcelona, Chicago, Kiev and Newport.

A 10lb 6oz thornback ray from the west coast of Anglesey.

Anglesey meets 'Deadliest Catch'. Maja squinado, aka a spider crab.

The smile is forced as I gaze at a double figure huss and wish it was a ray.

Sunset and a small thornback ray on a lovely spring evening.

An emotional return to the rocks at Benllech and a small thornback ray. I wish my father could have seen this.

An 11lb thornback ray from the rocks at night (in case you hadn't noticed!)

A glorious early spring morning on the rocks on the west coast of Anglesey.

A bitterly cold winter's day is warmed up by the arrival of a double-figure ray.

CHAPTER THIRTEEN

WELSH BEACHES, AND MORE
RAYS OF SUNSHINE

My conversion from coarse fisherman to sea angler (predominantly) became complete in the autumn of 2010. I was happily fishing away for bass on a sunny Sunday afternoon in late September on the Menai Straits. Life was good, I was happy, my wife was happy and my kids were happy: a full house of happiness. I'd caught a few bass too, so when my equanimity was disturbed by what turned out to be a fellow angler, I reacted with less than my usual grumpiness. To be fair, I soon realised that this guy was a decent sort; no random boasts and a careful choosing of his words led to a decent conversation and the swopping of intelligence on various local marks. He liked his ray fishing just as much as his bass fishing and asked me if I'd ever tried to catch the small-eyed rays that turned up at this time of year on the beaches around Rhosneigr, especially at Cymyran Bay. No, I said, I'd never really heard of small-eyed rays before, do they grow to any size? He nodded his head and added, 'I've heard rumours that they've been caught there well into double figures, although the biggest I've ever caught is 9½lb'.

We parted company after he'd given me some loose directions on how to get to Cymyran and I sat there thinking. Beaches, rays... it was my road to Damascus moment. I vowed to go straight to find this Cymyran Bay as soon as I stopped bass fishing, but in the end, I packed up early and went to find this magical place. His directions were good enough and I walked through the sand dunes to be confronted with a huge swathe of beach which stretched all the way round to Rhosneigr. It looked a very shallow beach though, surely too shallow for rays?

I spotted a number of people fishing on the main beach and a man and his wife fishing into what they told me was the Cymyran Strait, a narrow piece of water that separates Holy Island from Anglesey itself. This couple, Stu and Wendy, couldn't have been more helpful to me and explained all the various permutations in fishing both the beach and the little Strait too. They also explained that although rays could be caught in daylight, especially in early evening, more rays were caught during the hours of darkness. I could suddenly think of no better place to be than a beach at night with those regular lines of creamy surf rolling towards you, and walking out of that surf with a ray would be even better than emerging with a codling.

I was desperate to fish there, so I went into work the following day with the intention of booking the following Friday as a day's holiday; to my immense relief, my boss agreed. I spoke to John Woodhouse, and he agreed to come with me. I Googled Cymyran Bay during the week and found a link that led me to an angling forum on which a couple had reported catching some small-eyed rays the previous Sunday evening after dark – they were Stu and Wendy!

The week passed extraordinarily slowly, as all I could think about was Friday, Cymyran and small-eyed rays. What would small-eyed ray bites look like, did they fight well and should we fish the main beach or the Strait?

Eventually, Friday arrived and by mid-afternoon we were parked up in front of the sand dunes at Cymyran. It was before low water, so in terms of where we fished we had no option but to start on the main beach, as the Strait was virtually devoid of water. There was a small surf, but this meant nothing to us as we had no benchmark as to what constituted 'good conditions' for ray fishing off a beach.

Three hours later we hadn't had a bite between us despite fishing at various distances, and as we'd seen a steady stream of other anglers arriving, well, three anglers, which by our standards constituted a crowd, we decided to move back up the beach to the Strait to the place that we considered to be the 'hotspot'. We had to wait another hour or so for the Strait to fill up with enough water to make fishing practical, and on our first casts there we soon discovered a slight problem. Stu and Wendy had been fishing there on a small tide and were able to comfortably hold bottom; we were fishing there on a very large tide, one of the biggest of the autumn, and found that a combination of weed and tide was ripping our leads out and depositing them virtually on the shore some thirty yards or so 'downstream'. Despite this we persevered well into the hours of darkness, until just before high water, when fishing became truly impossible. We had a quick conflab and decided to move past the other anglers – by now there were seven or eight of them – to the far end of the beach. A rather sweaty ten-minute walk later we found ourselves a piece of beach well away from everyone else and set up tight against the sand dunes; being such a big tide the waves were pushing right up to the top of the beach.

Just after high water, two things changed. Firstly, the swell started to increase dramatically. Waves which had been no more than two or three feet in height suddenly became four or five-foot monsters with tremendous power which pushed us right back into the dunes themselves. (I came to realise fairly quickly that this is a common phenomenon here, as swell and current oppose each other on the ebb.) Secondly, the water was full of weed, thick kelpy weed which caught our lines and made fishing difficult and then impossible. I wound my lines in and wondered if this would bring an early finish to our quest for a small-eyed ray. It did, but not in the way I'd imagined. One minute I was sitting on my box, the next I was aware of a monstrous wave rushing towards me, a wave which lifted my box with me still on it clean off the dunes before depositing me back down onto the beach ten yards away. The lid of the box flew open as I tumbled off it, instantly filled with a mixture of sand and water with its contents spewing everywhere. I quickly scooped up everything I could see before the next wave arrived, thankfully a smaller one, and dropped the box further up in the dunes. Both rods and my tripod had also been dragged out onto the beach and covered in weed: although one of my rods was bent over at a hideous angle, both rods and reels were still there. Unfortunately, both reels were completely clogged with sand and unusable. John had undergone a similar fate, so we packed up, defeated on our first attempt.

We walked back to the car past other anglers who were also packing up because the weed had made fishing impossible. We stopped to talk to one angler who gave the opinion that the arrival of the weed was a great shame as there were definitely rays 'out there'. How did he know this? Because he'd caught one just before the weed arrived. The angler was also kind enough to tell us that the first two hours of the ebb were often the best time for rays on this beach. This put a whole different complexion on the evening. We never thought that we would just rock up and start catching rays, in fact it would have devalued the whole process had we done so, but rays, or more accurately, a ray, had been caught, so we were making progress.

We had to wait two weeks before we returned, until the tides were 'right' once again. You can look at this one of two ways: it can be really infuriating having to wait for the right tides, but the wait makes the anticipation all the greater and success all the sweeter. I will return to this theme on later pages, but sea fishing is the antithesis of 'angling' (is it really angling?) in commercial fisheries where gratification is virtually instant. On the plus side, commercial fisheries keep anglers off the beaches and rocks, allowing me to fish more or less in solitude.

We went back to Cymyran on a Saturday in mid-October. Once again, we drove down the heavily rutted little track, across the sands that get covered in sea water on a large tide and parked up on a little grassy knoll in front of the sand dunes. It was a grey afternoon with a hint of rain in the air when we stepped out of the car; a brisk south-westerly breeze pushed against the car door and in the background, we could hear the roar of a distant surf. We donned waders and waterproof jackets, gathered our gear and headed across the sand dunes, the noise of the distant surf getting louder with every step.

My heart rate started to increase, not just because of the exercise, but also with the excitement of reaching the top of the dunes and seeing the sea for the first time. It looked perfect with parallel lines of white surf rolling onto the beach at the low water mark. At that time, I didn't realise that these were the best conditions for catching small-eyes (NB: Just so you know, proper ray fanatics call them 'small-eyes' and not small-eyed rays!) but what I did know was that when it was dark these conditions would be very similar to *that* photo in the old *Angling* magazine. The beach was devoid of other anglers, which was a bonus, and we set up at the low water mark in a direct line from where we believed the ray had been caught two weeks previously. A little obvious, maybe, but we needed all the help we could get and if this meant copying other anglers until we'd got a better feel of the place, then so be it.

There's often nothing relaxing about fishing at Cymyran to begin with; no sitting on your box reading a book or drinking coffee and eating biscuits, because as soon as the tide starts to flood you're continually moving back up the beach towards the high-water mark. You get into a routine of moving your box back a good hundred yards, then moving your rods and tripod back fifty yards: of course, there's only just over 240 yards of line on your reel, so every couple of moves you have to wind a rod in, re-bait and recast. We soon learned that the trick is to stagger the distances you cast so that you're never in the position of having to wind in two rods at the same time.

Darkness fell a couple of hours before high water, by which time the tide had reached a part of the beach which had enough of an incline to enable us to sit on our boxes and have time to take sustenance in the form of coffee, biscuits and sandwiches. We also caught our first fish there in the form of small to medium-sized whiting and a couple of dogfish.

High water came, and with it the weed again. Not quite as bad as on the previous session but bad enough to make life difficult, albeit not unfishable, although my friend said he'd had enough and moved further down the beach in an effort to get away from the worst of the weed. I was mindful that the weed was bad all the way along the beach when we were last there and really wanted to stay put in the 'ray hotspot'. However, the weed got steadily worse, so I decided to wind my baits in and walk along the beach to see how my friend was faring. The weed's fine here, he explained, before making a dive for one of his rods. 'That was a good bite,' he said. He waited a few seconds before winding down and pulling back on his rod. 'Anything there,' I asked? 'Maybe a dogfish,' he replied.

No more than twenty or thirty seconds later with the fish approaching the surf, it became obvious that this wasn't just a dogfish. Something was pulling back strongly and I could see a fish of some sort making a disturbance on the flat tables of water between the waves. My friend saw the fish first. 'It's a ray!' he exclaimed. It was too. He reached into the water and emerged grinning from ear to ear and holding a beautiful small-eyed ray. It weighed just under seven pounds, and was quickly photographed and returned. I say 'quickly' because before the ray was back in the water I was off, sprinting back to gather my tackle and set up about thirty yards beyond where my friend was fishing.

By now we were nearly an hour into the ebb and I wondered if my chance had gone. I soon had two baits in the water, but with the tide retreating fast I had no more than fifteen minutes' fishing time before having to retrieve the baits and move everything back down the beach, doing the opposite of what we'd done on the flood.

Just when I thought my chances were over for that night, I noticed that one of my tip lights had moved so that it was slightly higher than the other; a definite loss of tension but not a slack-liner by any means. It was now or never for this evening. I took a deep breath. and wound down to make contact with the lead. The lead had been 'broken out,' a good sign, and with my heart thumping away I connected with a weight on the end of my line, not a big weight but something other than a whiting. The question was, dogfish, weed… or ray.

About half-way in something started pulling back – not weed then – and by the time it was in the surf I could feel it making powerful surges parallel to the beach. It had to be a ray.

I put my head torch onto full beam and pointed it in the direction of where I thought the fish was. Initially, I couldn't see anything, but then out of the mixture of sand and sea water the most glorious small-eyed ray in the world emerged. I plunged my hand into the water, grabbed it and walked out of the surf, holding it aloft in the same way that John Darling had done with his cod in *that* old photo.

I took one look at that ray and decided immediately that they are the most beautiful of all the ray family. Being sandy in colour on their upper side with exquisite white lines, they are a more subtle form of ray than the thornback, whose thorny upper sides give them a much more aggressive appearance.

It weighed 6lb 5oz and my friend, who, on hearing my scream of joy – I think half of Anglesey heard that scream - had correctly surmised that I had caught a ray and came across to take the photos. I waded well out into the surf to release the fish and watched it in the beam of my head torch until it was no longer visible.

Although we had a few more casts, the sea was now retreating at a rate that made fishing too difficult, so we packed up and headed back to the car, being careful not to tread on the legions of toads that had appeared out of nowhere and covered the sandy track through the dunes. I always keep a can of Red Bull or similar caffeine-based energy drink in the car in case I get tired on the way home – it was by now well after midnight – but there was no need for that on this particular night as the adrenaline carried me home and kept me awake till dawn.

Yet another little aside: the Irish call small-eyes 'painted rays' and I've often wondered if this is because the white lines on their upper surface look like they've been painted on with the sort of thick paint brush that I used when I was in Infants school.

We fished a few more times that year and caught a couple more small-eyes. Over the next few years I started to get the measure of the place, while my friend gradually lost interest as his serious bass obsession took hold. The first small-eyes would be caught in September and I would catch them intermittently through till the first spell of really cold weather in November. It was not only small-eyes I caught there: each year I'd always catch a couple of bass, including one of over 5lb which ripped my rod off the tripod and had I not been standing nearby would have taken it out to sea too.

This was the final piece in my fishing calendar jigsaw. The winter would see me fishing for thornback rays and occasionally for pike, mainly when the weather was too bad for me to get onto the rock marks of Anglesey. Spring would see the arrival of the bass on the beaches of North Wales and in the Menai Straits. Summer would see me in my boat on Tabley Mere, fishing for tench as well as having a few more bass trips. The autumn would be spent chasing small-eyes at Cymyran before the cycle started over again in the winter. Of course, there were also random trips to other places when the fancy took me.

As always, some afternoons and evenings at Cymyran stand out more than others. After a long spell of warm, sunny and windless weather I was just desperate to get back there, so I embarked on the long drive – always an hour and a half – to Anglesey in conditions that couldn't have been any worse. I walked out onto the beach in hot, bright sunshine and a sea which was devoid of surf and flat as the proverbial pancake. I'd hoped that somehow the weather forecast might be a little wrong and that there would be at least some movement in the sea but, as always, when you want the forecast to be wrong it's usually totally accurate.

It wasn't even a big tide and by late afternoon, with it still being hot and clear, the sea had crawled up three-quarters of the way towards the high-water mark. I had two baits out as usual: by this time, I would use sand eel on one rod and a sand eel and squid wrap on the other. The water was so flat and shallow that I was able to wade out more than a hundred yards before casting the sand eel, but when it came to the sand eel/squid wrap, I thought sod it and just dropped it no more than about seventy-five yards out. Ten minutes later I was standing next to my rods thinking what a complete waste of time this was, but that I just might pick up a small-eye on the ebb in darkness, when something brushed across my face. It was the line on my right-hand rod, the one with the sand eel/squid wrap, which was now completely slack and waving gently in the slight breeze. This was such an unexpected event that it took me several seconds to comprehend that I'd actually got a bite, but lo and behold, on taking up the slack line I found myself connected to a small-eye. It wasn't a big one but at just over 5lb it was the most unexpected one I've ever caught. A woman in a red dress was passing and came across to see what I'd caught. She said she'd never seen anything like it and I asked her to take a photo for me with my camera; I somewhat condescendingly showed her which button to press (I assume most women are like my wife when it comes to matters electrical, and yes, you're right in thinking that I will get all manner of grief for writing this) and assumed a pose with the fish. She looked at me as if I was an idiot and started barking out commands, 'hold the fish higher, not that high, now kneel down, close your mouth when you smile, move the fish up a bit, now hold the fish to your right, now the left,' while at the same time adopting different positions with the camera and changing from landscape to portrait mode. She then handed the camera back to me, smiled, and walked off. I looked at the photos she'd taken and had to admit they were pretty good.

Another Saturday afternoon in October saw me arrive at Cymyran in mild, sunny, almost humid conditions to find a lovely surf running, arousing expectations of a ray-filled evening. By ray-filled, I mean three or maybe four rays, I wouldn't want you to think in terms of commercial fishery sized catches. I had the beach to myself to begin with but was soon joined by two anglers I knew, Richie and Degsie; if I had to share my beloved beach with anyone apart from John, then it might as well be with these two, both good anglers and founts of good information.

Just before dusk, Richie caught a small-eye and I photographed it for him, and fifteen minutes later I too caught one and Richie reciprocated with the camera. At the near end of Cymyran Bay, on the far side of the straight, were rocks from which anglers occasionally fished and I'd caught sight of two anglers arriving there at dusk.

Darkness fell without any more small-eyes appearing, but conditions were so good that I was supremely confident of all of us catching more fish. This confidence grew when I saw a couple of camera flashes from the rocks in the distance; yes, I thought, they've just had a couple of rays. I wandered over to Richie to discuss this with him.

'Did you see the camera flashes?' I asked him.

'Er, they weren't camera flashes, they were flashes of lightning in the distance,' he replied. Just to illustrate his point perfectly, there was a double flash of lightning in the distance.

A little physics lesson for you now. We were using carbon fibre rods which, obviously, taper down to a point. Carbon fibre is one of the best conductors known to man. Now, we also have to consider what is known as the 'Action of Points'. The electric charges on the surface of a charged object do not necessarily spread out evenly and as a result, the charge density at sharp points becomes large. Since like charges repel, electrons are emitted more rapidly from sharp points than flat surfaces. This is called Action of Points. Thunderclouds carry a vast amount of negative charge at the bottom and an equal amount of corresponding positive charge at the top. When they loom over us in the gloomy sky, positive charges are induced on the objects on the ground, as a result of electrostatic induction. The induced charges accumulate at sharper points due to action of points. Then suddenly a massive electric flow takes place between such a point and the cloud in question. This is called a *lightning strike* or *thunderbolt*. In other words, we were standing on a flat beach next to two perfect lightning conductors, our rods.

'Maybe the storm will pass us by,' I said more in hope than anything else, 'after all, we haven't heard any thunder yet, have we?' Before he could answer there was another flash of lightning, a clear fork this time, which was followed by a deafening clap of thunder.

No more words were exchanged as we both gathered up our tackle and sprinted for our cars, trying to keep our rods as low as possible. The storm broke right around us in a maelstrom of lightning, thunder, rain and hailstones as big as marbles. It was both scary and exhilarating at the same time and although the worst of the storm had passed by the time we got back to our cars, the blackness of the sky – it really was pitch black – indicated that other storms were not too far away. It was a surreal moment putting my fishing tackle back into my car with over an inch of hail on the ground making it look like we'd had a blizzard, although the air temperature must have already recovered into double-figures.

Fast forward to the autumn of 2016, which was an outstanding one for me in terms of catching small-eyes. At one point, I was so confident of catching them that I thought I could just stand on the beach and whistle and they would come flapping towards me as fast as their little wings would carry them. This was partly down to the fact that there had been a lot of small-eyes around the previous year, but also because that I'm sure no one fished there as much as I did in that second autumn of my retirement (of which you'll learn more shortly), not even the locals, and I'd accumulated a vast knowledge of the place, all of which was recorded in my little angling diaries.

It was also the year that I discovered a magic sandwich. A little explanation is required here. Conditions were mixed for this trip – the weather was ideal, misty with a fine drizzle which gave very low light levels – but the surf was quite small, being less than two feet high, although quite 'long' at 150 yards. By 5:45pm I had the usual suspects in the water – a sand eel and a squid and sand eel wrap – and shortly after that had the first coffee and sandwich of the evening. Normally I would wait till closer to high water, but I was quite hungry and thirsty that evening.

No sooner had I taken a bite out of my sandwich than the line on my left-hand rod fell slack. I hastily re-wrapped the sandwich in its tin foil and stuck it into my pocket. Shortly after that the first small-eyed ray of the session was posing for its photo after being weighed in at 6lb 9oz. The ray was returned and the rod rebaited and set to work again. I took out the sandwich from my pocket, unwrapped it and took another bite. The line on my right-hand rod immediately fell slack and I went through the same process as before: rewrap the sandwich, place in pocket, wind a ray in. At 5½ lb it was a little smaller than last time but still very welcome. I took the sandwich out of my pocket again; it wasn't looking quite so appetizing by now and had a few bits of grey fluff attached to it, along with some short lengths of used bait elastic. However, it was clearly a magic sandwich,.so I took another bite – and sure enough the line on my left-hand rod fell slack yet again and a few minutes later I was returning a 6lb small-eyed ray back to the sea.

Having recast once more, I took the remnants of what had once been a sandwich out of my pocket, but there was only enough for a small mouthful and nothing happened. In fact, nothing happened until just before high water, when the surf all but disappeared and I caught a small thornback ray and a dogfish. I made a mental note to make bigger sandwiches next time.

The previous year had been a completely different story, however, and I'd made twelve trips to Cymyran without catching a single small-eye by mid-October. One of the reasons for this was undoubtedly the series of high pressure areas which settled over the UK that autumn, each one bringing spells of settled, warm and windless weather; ideal for everyone apart from the committed small-eye fisherman, or bass fisherman for that matter, both species preferring a surf to get them feeding inshore.

Having notched up twelve blanks, my thirteenth trip to the Rhosneigr area was made without a great deal of optimism although to be honest this didn't bother me too much as I am happy to just be there sometimes. Sitting there at high water on a dark, clear night counting the shooting stars with just a chance of a small-eye is often enough to make me insanely happy.

It was around four o'clock in the afternoon on a warm October day with just enough cloud cover to obscure the sun when I arrived at the parking area. I got out of the car and listened to see if I could hear the surf in the distance and this time, yes, for once, there was enough noise to indicate a respectable amount of movement in the water. I put on my chest waders, loaded myself up with rods, box, tripod and bait bag and made my way over the dunes to the beach. I broached the top of the dunes and saw the regular white lines of a good surf, a slow two-to-three-foot swell, a surfline of around 75 yards and a gentle breeze at my back, conditions which I love to fish in; maybe not the best to catch in, but conditions which make for easy and enjoyable fishing. I was slightly concerned that the light breeze at my back might cause the surf to flatten off later in the evening, but I wasn't too bothered – it was just a great day to be out on the beach.

Afternoon became evening and the time up to high water passed pleasantly enough, but with only a handful of whiting and a solitary dogfish to show for my efforts. The breeze all but disappeared, but the surf held up satisfactorily, and actually increased as the tide turned (swell opposing current again).

Having had the beach to myself for the past six hours, I was a little surprised to see the head torches of two other anglers appear just after high water. I recognised one of the anglers – Nick Woodhall – and after I had exchanged pleasantries with him, they both set up some thirty yards or so further down the beach. Not long after they'd started fishing, in fact I think it was their first cast, I saw Nick wade out into the surf and pluck a nice small-eyed ray out of the water. Great, I thought, there are rays out there, but I was also a little jealous that he'd got one first cast compared to my six-hours-plus blank, not to mention the previous twelve rayless trips!

I caught a whiting while the second angler then proceeded to catch another small-eyed ray. All sorts of thoughts go through your mind in these circumstances: are they doing anything different to me, what am I doing wrong? I went across to have a quick chat with them and found that they were doing exactly what I was doing, same baits and similar distances, so I returned to my rods with a mixture of enthusiasm and trepidation. Blanking when there aren't any rays around is one thing, blanking when you know there are rays around and when you've put so much effort into catching them is something else.

It was over two hours past high water, and to be honest I'd just about given up hope of catching anything when I thought I noticed a little bit of movement in one of the rod tips. Not much movement, just a slight loss of tension which would not have been noticeable had not both rod tips been perfectly in line with each other. The angle of the line had also changed, but this could have been due to the weed which often turns up at exactly this point in the tide. I decided to pick the rod up and see if anything was there, knowing that this was realistically my last chance of catching a ray that evening. I wound down to the lead and found that I didn't have to break the grips out – a good sign, usually this means 'fish on'. Definitely some weight there… actually, quite a lot of weight there… something's starting to pull back quite hard…

With my heart pounding, I gradually teased the fish – surely a ray – into the shallows, where it decided to run hard to my right, taking line off, as usual, a lightly set spool. I played the fish extremely carefully, desperately hoping that the hook wouldn't pull out and regretting that I hadn't changed my whiting-ravaged hook lengths. I then caught my first glimpse of it in the surf and knew straight away that it was a special fish and possibly my biggest beach-caught small-eyed ray. I waded out to meet the fish and lifted it from the surf. It felt heavy and I took it back to my box, where I weighed it at 10lb 3oz, my best-ever small-eye. Rather than use the self-timer on my camera I ran across and asked Nick if he would photograph it for me. He did so, describing it as a 'slab of a ray', which I thought was a pretty good description.

I was, and am still, truly obsessed with the small-eyed rays of Cymyran Bay. There are so many things to like about fishing there, not least of which is the fact that the season is relatively short, usually no more than a maximum of twelve weeks, so you can never catch quite enough rays. You can be reasonably sure that for some of these weeks conditions will either be too stormy – once the wind starts blowing into your face at over thirty miles an hour you struggle to stand up, let alone fish – or too calm. It is possible to catch in calm weather as proved above, but more often than not, you're wasting your time. Most of your fishing is done in darkness, watching for those elusive movements in your red (not blue, not green!) tip lights.

Which brings me on to the bites themselves. They are similar to thornback ray bites in that they are slow, unhurried affairs: a slow pull down on the rod tip, which may keep going until the rod is dragged, slowly mind, off the tripod or which may reverse into a poker–straight rod tip and a partial or full-blown slack line bite. Alternatively, the rod tip may just lose a little tension – you should always keep the tip slightly bent – and slowly straighten up. Of course, at night this once again appears as one red light slowly rising up against its partner. The rays themselves are not the sea world's greatest fighters and often they will allow themselves to be guided into shallow water before deciding to wake up and fight, but once in the surf they can give a good account of themselves.

But most of all, it's the thrill of walking out of the surf at night with your head torch on full beam, holding a large fish…

My first ever small-eyed ray. The silly grin was surgically removed a few days later.

Sunset at Cymyran Bay.

A 10lb 3oz slab of small-eyed ray. Cymyran Bay, October 2015.

CHAPTER FIFTEEN

ADVENTURES ON THE DINGLE PENINSULA

Some decisions in life are easier to make than others. For example: back in 2008 Lorraine asked me if I would mind if she took a ten-day spring beach holiday in America with her two sisters. She added that it would only be fair if I then chose our summer holiday; in fact, if I wanted, we could have that fishing holiday in Ireland that I'd been talking about for years. She even said that I could go fishing every day and she wouldn't object! So, ten days of unrestricted fishing time (work providing) while she was away in America followed by a week's fishing in Ireland. I think that's what's called a 'no-brainer'.

I then had to decide whereabouts in Ireland to head for. Again, this wasn't too difficult a decision because, as you will doubtless remember, I'd grown up reading books and magazine articles by the likes of the late Clive Gammon, who eulogised about the bass fishing on the strands (beaches) of the Dingle peninsula. Inch, Stradbally, Gowlane, Fermoyle... names that brought butterflies to my stomach. So Dingle it was.

However, going fishing to an area you've never fished before can be a daunting experience – what time of year is best, what tides, weather etc? Clive Gammon did most of his bass fishing on the peninsula in autumn and winter, but asking my wife to go there at those times of year would have been to push my luck a little too far. So, it had to be the summer, or what passes for summer in Ireland. In terms of everything else, I began an internet search of anything and everything to do with fishing on the Dingle peninsula.

The name 'Bob Moss' cropped up on a regular basis. Bob wrote two books about the fishing on the Dingle peninsula: *A Guide to Shore Angling on the Dingle Peninsula* and *The Third Breaker*. These can be considered the ultimate guides to the area, and the first book is particularly useful for its description both of what fish you can catch, and how to catch them, from nearly all the main marks on the peninsula. I quickly acquired these books from Bob himself and asked him for more information, which he duly gave me in long and detailed emails.

Over the years I had a number of conversations with him and found him to be one of the most helpful and humble anglers I've ever spoken to. Unfortunately, he died early in 2016. Whenever I mentioned his name during my visit to Dingle that summer – in bookshops, restaurants, bars – everyone seemed to know of him, with the phrase 'what a lovely man' being repeated more times than I can remember.

Just getting across to the Dingle Peninsula was an adventure in itself. We got the ferry from Holyhead, which was apt, in that it meant we were starting out on our old holiday route along the A55, passing familiar landmarks such as the old Little Chef at Penmaenmawr, now sadly closed. We boarded the ferry at Holyhead and consumed a 'full English' in homage to Little Chefs now departed. That first drive from Dun Laoghaire to Castlegregory on the peninsula was made before the dual carriageway from Dublin to Limerick and beyond had been completed, and it took seven hours to wind our way along small 'A' roads and through villages that wouldn't have changed for donkey's years. The drive wasn't a drag, it was interesting and very much part of the adventure, culminating in an afternoon stop for a late lunch at a village called Adare. On the banks of the River Maigue and overlooked by the imposing Desmond Castle, Adare is a quintessential small Irish village, known as one of the prettiest in all of Ireland with its rows of thatched cottages, Augustinian priory and two abbeys. It is also home to some lovely cafés and one such café, the Good Room, became our regular stopping point. Much in the way that the Little Chef had been part of our Anglesey trips, this lovely place has become integral to our Dingle trips. We are both creatures of habit!

Having never been to the Dingle Peninsula before, I'd booked a small place via the internet (how else?) to stay just outside Castlegregory on the basis that it wasn't too expensive and was close to Back Beach, the final strand on the crescent-shaped beaches of Brandon Bay. Fundamentally, Fermoyle, Gowlane, Kilcumin, Stradbally and the lesser known Back Beach are all one classic Irish storm beach that's over twelve miles long.

The accommodation was adequate, if a little uninspiring, but that didn't matter too much as we expected to be only there to sleep and have breakfast. Lunches and evening meals would be taken on the hoof, depending on where we'd been fishing.

We awoke on that first Sunday morning to clear skies and warm sunshine. I'd decided that we would spend that first day driving around the peninsula identifying as many of the marks as possible from the Bob Moss book. We visited all the aforementioned beaches in Brandon Bay before heading on to the Cloghane Estuary and Brandon pier. We then retraced our steps back to the Conor Pass, a drive of staggering beauty with views right across the peninsula which more than makes up for the fact that it's essentially a one-lane road with passing places so narrow that cars pass each other with quite literally inches to spare. On the outskirts of Dingle itself we took the Slea Head road through Brandon Creek, Smerwick,

Ballydavid – home of the late Bob Moss – and past small and inviting strands such as Wine, Black and Bealbawn.

Eventually we arrived back in Dingle via Ventry beach and Reen Beg on the far side of Dingle Bay, and looked for somewhere to eat. Dingle itself was glorious in the afternoon sun. It's an old fishing port which is protected from the worst of the Atlantic storms owing to the fact that it's set back from the main part of the coast. Imagine a light bulb with Dingle near the top of the bulb and the narrow part being the entrance to the Atlantic. Finding somewhere to eat in Dingle proved difficult: there were simply too many good restaurants to choose from! Eventually we chose somewhere at random, stuffed our faces with seafood, and waddled back to the car to resume our journey.

The next stop was the famous Dingle Lighthouse mark situated at the 'neck' of the light bulb, which at that point was only around three hundred yards wide but whose waters were very deep with a strong tide rip. I loved the description in Bob's book which included a line to the effect that you can 'catch specimen sized dogfish here but you may have to catch a lot of rays first'!

For the first time that day, I saw another angler. He was fishing not by the lighthouse itself but a couple of hundred yards before it in what looked like suspiciously shallow water, the bottom being clearly visible. He was using one slightly battered rod and a fixed-spool reel, and had this been Wales, I'm slightly ashamed to say that I would have dismissed him as being a bit of a numpty. But this was Ireland and if he was a local angler then he might just have had some knowledge to impart. He was indeed local and our conversation was barely one minute old when he struck and reeled in a small thornback ray of about 3lb. Who was the numpty now? To be fair to this guy, he didn't hold back when it came to imparting local knowledge; did I want to catch rays? If I did then I should head 'over there' – he pointed in the rough direction of Reen Beg. 'There's a tiny footpath down by the side of a bungalow that'll take you down to the shore. I've fished there many times this year and never failed to catch a ray'. I did wonder what he was doing fishing here then, but decided to put my cynicism to one side.

A little aside: I've not spoke to many local anglers on the Dingle peninsula, but the ones I have talked to could not have been more helpful. I commented on this to a guy called Chris O'Sullivan – you'll meet him later – who replied that there's so much good fishing on the peninsula that there's no need to keep any of it a secret!

After Dingle Lighthouse, we headed for Trabeg. Despite having never even seen the place, I'd already decided it was one of the spots I just had to fish. One of my internet searches had revealed a description of a fishing session there by a group of anglers who had caught large thornback rays, ten-pound plus small-eyed rays and eight-pound bass all in the one trip!

We left the main Dingle to Tralee road and headed down narrow lanes bedecked with orange montbretia and red fuschias until we came onto the headland above Trabeg Strand. I wasn't disappointed; the place was magnificent! Trabeg is a steep strand – there's no more than a hundred yards or so between the high and low water marks – with unusually dark red sand. It's bordered by cliffs on all sides and a small river empties into the western end of the strand, which is known as Doonsheane. I think the combination of the cliffs, its relative isolation and almost complete lack of man-made noise or light give Trabeg an almost haunted feel to it, especially at night, and Lorraine refuses to go there after dark because of this.

We walked the length of the beach – which didn't take long as it's not a long strand by any means – and went back to sit in the car and stare out to sea. There was a lovely gentle surf rolling in and I regretted not having my tackle with me. The atmosphere was slightly ruined when I tried to reverse out of our parking spot, a mixture of stones and sand, and got our car stuck. But this being Ireland, every passing motorist, not that there were many of those, stopped to offer help and advice, and eventually a tractor was summoned from a local farm and we were safely extracted.

Our next stop was Inch Strand, possibly the most famous bass beach in the entire world, and this was the only time in the whole holiday when I felt a tinge of disappointment. The upper part of the beach was covered in cars and the water filled with surfers, paragliders and swimmers; it had more of a holiday camp feel to it than the secluded bass beach I was expecting, although to be fair, Inch is known primarily for its autumn and winter fishing. I've been going to Dingle for nine years now and I've still to fish on this iconic strand.

We returned to our base via Derrymore Strand, a place noted for its stingray fishing, and the Trench, noted for its large thornback rays. We freshened ourselves up and headed back out to the top of the Magharees – the spit of land that juts out north from the peninsula near Castlegregory – to a little restaurant for our evening meal. It will not come as a shock to you to hear that we do like our food. Lorraine is lucky in that she doesn't tend to put weight on easily, but I was starting to get distinctly porky around this time.

Two momentous things happened in that restaurant. Firstly, I tried a pint of Guinness in Ireland for the first time. I'd tried it in the UK but just couldn't acquire a taste for it. I was most perplexed that it was the only alcoholic drink I'd ever come across that I didn't like: I adored the look of a pint of Guinness, but could only stomach it if I took the bitter edge away with blackcurrant and let's face it, Guinness and black isn't something I was going to ask for in Ireland. Everyone had urged me to try the Guinness in Ireland: 'it's a different drink entirely, you *will* love it,' they said. I took a sip... no bitter taste, just sweetness. I took a mouthful... that's good! I turned to Lorraine... 'er, would you mind driving back?'

The Guinness on the Dingle peninsula is now another reason in a long line of reasons why we go back there. We've been in restaurants in Dingle that don't serve Guinness themselves but will send someone across the road to get you one from another bar: it's one of our most abiding memories, that of a waiter, tray in hand, white cloth over arm, walking out of the restaurant, across the road and down the street to return five minutes later with a single pint of the black stuff on his tray.

The other momentous decision we had to make was the venue for our first fishing trip the following morning. I say 'our' because Lorraine was as good as her word and came with me on every trip, bless her. It was a toss-up between Trabeg and Reen Beg, and ultimately the 'I've never failed to catch a ray there this year' line swung it in favour of Reen Beg.

The following morning, we had breakfast (coffee and toast, not a full English, as we were still stuffed from the previous day's culinary excesses) and headed out over the Conor pass towards Dingle and Reen Beg. The traffic was slightly gridlocked on the road over the Conor Pass, but eventually we reached the summit and had that first breath-taking view of Dingle and Dingle Bay. We therefore arrived at Reen Beg a little later than I would have liked.

We found the little footpath by the bungalow easily enough and headed down towards the shore, and then along the shore, towards the narrow entrance to Dingle Bay. It was a good twenty-minute walk which burned off a good few of the previous day's calories before we stopped at a spot that I thought was as good as any, there being no real features to fish from. The morning was a mixture of sunshine and cloud with a strong south-westerly breeze which was blowing from right to left from where I was fishing.

I put a sand eel onto one of my faithful pulley Pennel rigs and launched it about sixty yards into the waters of Dingle Bay. I hadn't even had time to finish baiting my second rod when I noticed that my first rod had got what appeared to be a slack-liner. Strange, I wasn't used to getting instant ray bites; was it weed or fish? All was revealed a couple of minutes later when a thornback ray of about the 4lb mark was swung ashore: my wife took a photo and said she'd do likewise with every fish I caught. She had a busy morning as my baits were rarely in the water for more than a couple of minutes before being leapt upon by a hungry ray. After two and a half hours, at which point the flooding tide was pushing us off the mark, I had caught fifteen rays. Fifteen!! At this point in my ray fishing career I was struggling to catch fifteen thornback rays in a whole year in Wales.

The following day we headed back over the Conor pass to Trabeg. Conditions were pretty grim, from a fishing perspective, not too much surf and bright sunshine, but at least it kept Lorraine happy as she was able to sunbathe, this being one of her favourite ways of passing a few hours. Just after low water I was happy too, as a textbook slack line bite gave me yet another thornback ray. It might not even have weighed three pounds but I wasn't bothered. I'd caught a ray in magnificent surroundings and was grinning like someone who'd just won the Lottery as Lorraine obliged with the camera once again. I only had one more bite, which yielded a medium-sized flounder near the end of that session.

We had our fair share of duff trips too. I tried fishing into what I thought was the main channel of the Cloghane Estuary only to realise after a couple of hours that I'd been fishing into water that was no more than six inches deep; I also managed to blank at the Trench, that well known big thornback ray hotspot. Most disappointingly of all, I twice walked out of our 'home' and across the road to fish Back Beach and both times I blanked, despite there being a good surf. This was entirely down to my lack of knowledge of how to fish those Brandon Bay beaches; if I had known then what I know now, I would have fished at night and been confident of catching both small-eyed rays and bass. I suppose the mantra 'if I had known then what I know now' could be the story of every fisherman's life, and rightly so, as, without wishing to repeat myself, if we wanted it to be easy we'd only ever bother to fish those overstocked commercial fisheries.

The final session of the week on the Friday afternoon saw us going over to fish the Dingle Lighthouse mark. I decided to fish just below the Lighthouse, where the channel was at its narrowest and the water, I presumed, at its deepest. I had the biggest fish of the trip on my first cast, a six-pound thornback ray, and proceeded to catch another ten rays, including one of 9lb 14oz which for some years remained my biggest Irish-caught fish. I packed up at tea-time and we headed back into Dingle for our final meal of the holiday.

The whole trip had been a complete success. Even Lorraine had enjoyed it, and was more than happy to agree to return the following year. However, we both decided that we'd look for a base in, or around, Dingle itself. At that point in time I thought I'd be doing most of my fishing on that side of the Conor Pass and the quality and variety of restaurants was much better in Dingle. I spent hours poring over the internet, looking at properties and trying to work out exactly where they were, until I eventually came up with a place just outside Dingle which was less than five minutes' walk from a small strand and no more than fifteen minutes' walk from the lighthouse itself. According to Bob Moss, that little strand was good for bass to lures early in the morning with a possibility of rays, both thornback and painted (small-eyed) at distance. A 'possibility' was good enough for me, so this clinched the deal and we booked the cottage.

The following year we returned to Dingle and drove up to our chosen cottage, perched just above the cliffs overlooking the entrance to Dingle Bay. The views were simply stunning. The inside of the cottage was lovely and modern with internet access being the only mod-con that was lacking (this was remedied a couple of years ago). We got up on that first Sunday morning, cooked ourselves a 'full Irish' and then walked out to fish at the lighthouse. It's a novelty I'll never tire off, walking out to go sea fishing as opposed to driving for at least an hour. It was nice easy fishing in warm sunshine and I caught seven rays, although the biggest was no more than seven pounds in weight.

On the Monday morning, I got up early to wander down to the little strand below our cottage. The strand was no more than thirty yards wide at low water and closer to ten yards wide at high water with cliffs to both sides which tapered down to long jagged fingers of rock that that ran perpendicularly from the shore and out to sea. I took my beachcasters and an old carp rod that I used when going on my very occasional lure fishing trips. I set my beach rods up and cast out a couple of sand eels and then left these rods to fish away with the reels set in free-spool mode while I flicked lures out into the channels between the fingers of rock. I am not by any means an accomplished, or even half competent lure fisherman and soon got bored with what I assumed would be a thankless task.

On returning to my rods I noticed that both of them had what could possibly be slight slack liners. I wound down on the first rod to find that, yes indeed, I'd had a bite and soon pulled a thornback ray of about four pounds onto the beach: a similar sized ray was on the other rod too. I didn't catch any more fish that morning but, once again, I wasn't too bothered about the size or quantity of the rays. It was just tremendous fun being able to get up at five or six o'clock in the morning, wander down to the beach for a couple of hours' fishing, catch a few rays and then return in time for breakfast. This also enabled me to have at least one more fishing trip later in the day, as Lorraine generally stayed in bed and gave these morning sessions a miss.

Later that week, the calm and sunny weather was replaced by grey skies, rain, wind and yet more rain. The swell increased and the sea started to fill with weed. Having not fished the beach in these conditions I thought it was still worth a try, and took my bass rod with me along with my usual beach rods. There was a reasonable surf running onto the beach when I got down there but thankfully, not too much weed. I set up my beach rods just as I had done on the previous mornings, but this time I also put a large sand eel on a simple running ledger rig on my bass rod on which I had a fixed spool reel loaded with 30lb braid. I positioned this sand eel at the side of the nearest line of rocks, about 40 yards out. There was no room on the tripod for the bass rod, so I leaned it against a large rock some yards behind me and to my right.

Nothing came to the beach rods, which wasn't entirely surprising as it didn't feel a particularly ray-like morning, and I was contemplating an early finish and another cooked breakfast when I noticed a javelin fly past my right-hand ear. Of course, it wasn't a javelin, it was my bass rod, and I just managed to grab hold of it as it slid along the beach into the water. The rod doubled over as soon as I picked it up and there was a horrible grating sensation as I dragged a powerful fish around a submerged rock. I quickly got it into open water, where it charged around spectacularly for a minute or so until I managed to beach it on the back of a large wave.

I knew straight away that not only was it my first Irish bass but my best. I gently placed it in a shopping bag and weighed it: the pointer on my old Avon scales settled at 7½lb. After a few quick photos, it was returned to the water. My only slight regret is that five minutes later my daughter, who along with her boyfriend and my son had accompanied us on this trip, turned up with her expensive camera. If she'd have been a little earlier I would have had some better pictures. Breakfast never tasted better than it did that morning!

Over the following years we returned in July or August to the same cottage and my knowledge of how to catch fish on the peninsula increased with each visit. Every year I'd visit Trabeg, usually twice, once for an afternoon session and once to fish either a low water at dusk or one in the early hours of the morning. I never blanked there but never caught another ray, catching bass, dogfish and sea trout. It also provided me with my best haul of bass when I caught six of them, all weighing between three and four pounds, just before dawn on a surprisingly cold morning.

There's more to the Dingle peninsula than just fishing, eating and drinking. The whole area has a rich heritage and I would recommend a visit to the Blasket Islands. This group of islands, three miles off the coast, is famous for memoirs written in the Irish language by many of the inhabitants who documented the harsh realities of rural life there before the Second World War. The Slea Head drive takes in views that cannot be matched anywhere else in the UK, and the dry-stone beehive huts at Fahan are well worth a visit along the way.

One year we arrived to find that the little strand below our cottage had changed completely. A catastrophic storm had ripped away a lot of the sand, so that at high water you were effectively fishing twenty yards further back than previously; this meant that the rays were now beyond the range of my casting ability. I didn't give up on that little strand though and it did provide me with my first Irish bass caught in the traditional Irish style: standing waist-deep in the surf, legering a large sand eel and holding the rod waiting for it to pull round. It is exhilarating fishing; you're watching the surf, mindful of any approaching wave that looks capable of knocking you off your feet – which have to be braced against both the incoming waves and their returning riders while at the same time you're holding your rod and waiting for the tap, tap, BANG of a bass hitting your bait.

Our most recent visit to Dingle provided me with two firsts, and two of the best moments in my angling life.

Over the years, I'd fished a few times on the strands of Brandon

Bay, but with only a solitary bass to show for my efforts. This was partly due to conditions not always being entirely conducive to good fishing from these beaches, but also to my lack of knowledge. However, a chance meeting with an angler at Gowlane one day changed all that. It was the evening that I caught that first bass, a small one of less than two pounds, but the discussion I had with him was an eye-opener. The previous night had seen some pretty stormy weather which had kicked up a decent surf and, so he said, a large number of bass to eight pounds in weight had come out at low water and in darkness. I didn't have a chance to fish in those conditions that week – that's the one big downside of only having the one week, you're totally at the mercy of the weather – but this information was stored away for the following year.

The weather at the beginning of this trip had been diabolical and I'd struggled to catch anything. Fishing in heavy rain – especially rain that drives into your face when you're a glasses-wearer like me – is not pleasant, and by the time we reached Tuesday, the wind and rain was once again so bad that I'd decided against going out during the day. Instead, I decided to go for a night-time sortie with the destination for the night's session being Gowlane in Brandon Bay, on the basis that there was some surf there and the westerly wind would drive the rain across the beach. This meant that I could for the most part stand at the side of my rods with the rain at my back.

As previously described, Gowlane is one of the surf beaches that make up the crescent-shaped sweep of Brandon Bay with all of them being relatively flat and backed by sand dunes. The sand on the beach itself is almost silver in colour, nothing like the colour of the sand at Trabeg, and very firm to walk on. Behind the sand dunes, the Brandon Mountains, through which the Conor Pass cuts, rise up into what seems like perpetual low cloud on all but the sunniest of days.

I arrived just before darkness, which was about an hour before low water, to find a surf of around the three-foot mark, small by Brandon Bay standards. It was still raining but not quite as heavily as the previous evening and the wind had abated a little too. The Brandon Mountains were completely invisible behind a blanket of misty cloud as I put on my waders and waterproof jacket before striding out onto the hard silver sand. I didn't really know what to expect from the evening's fishing: the sea could be filled with weed, making the session an extremely short one, or it just might be filled with rays and bass. I felt that strange mixture of nervousness and excitement that accompanies a first cast into new waters. My only other sessions here had been during daylight with little surf running, and therefore not comparable with a night-time trip complete with surf.

I made my first cast and retrieved it shortly afterwards to check the weed situation. There was some weed, but thankfully not too much. I felt quite at home on this strand, as it was exactly the sort of fishing I was used to doing on the Welsh beaches, and decided to fish one rod at maximum distance and one in the surf itself. Amazingly enough, there wasn't another angler or person of any description within sight and I had literally miles of strand to myself. I'm not particularly anti-social (you will have made your own mind up on this one by now), but I adore this sense of isolation and loneliness. It adds another dimension to the fishing. It's just you, all alone on a pitch-black night; there's no one there to help you photograph a fish or come to your rescue if you suffer a sudden illness or get caught by a rogue wave. It's just you, your head torch, the sand, surf and, if you're lucky, a few fish too.

After an hour or so, I noticed some movement on my right-hand rod which did not look like weed; there was a slight release of tension in the rod tip, which suddenly developed into a full slack-line bite. This was the rod that was fishing at short distance, so it didn't take me long to tighten up to the fish as I walked out into the surf with my head torch on full beam. The powerful lunges, interspersed with kiting sensations, led me to think that this was not a bass but a ray. It was indeed a ray – a small-eyed ray – and as soon as it saw my headlight it charged off along the strand, ripping yards of line off the spool. It ran back and forth along the beach, but at the turn of each run I was able to get it closer to my feet. I eventually got it close enough for my head torch to pick out the finer details of the fish and I realised that it wasn't just a nice one, it was a superb one.

I reached down into the warm waters of Brandon Bay, picked up the fish and strode out of the surf holding it aloft. It turned out to weigh 10lb 7oz – my first double-figure Irish ray and my best-ever small-eyed ray. To say I was pleased was an understatement. In fact it was a good job the strand was deserted, as I literally whooped with joy.

Having weighed, photographed and returned the ray I recast both rods into the surf (having disentangled a spider crab, of all things, from the rod fished at distance). Unfortunately, within minutes, both rods were straining to the right, not with fish but with copious quantities of weed, which brought an early end to proceedings.

Overnight, the wind picked up again and it was Thursday before I could return to Gowlane. With the wind dropping, the surf there in the evening was due to be between three and six feet in height, and just as importantly, the distance between these waves would be around ten seconds. This would create the perfect 'tables' of water between the waves for both bass and rays.

I arrived just before dusk to find exactly these conditions. Although the tops of the mountains of the Conor Pass were still shrouded in cloud, at ground level it was dull but dry and reasonably still. I almost ran from the car to the beach, I was that excited, although again somewhat surprised to see that no one else had come up with the same idea.

I fished both rods with sand eels at varying distances within the surf, although to be honest I couldn't have cast beyond the surf line anyway, it was that long. As the daylight ebbed away with the tide I couldn't stop smiling. I couldn't think of anywhere I'd rather be than standing on the hard silver sand of an Irish surf beach with my headtorch picking out the regular white lines of breaking surf. There was no weed around either, and after only twenty minutes I had my first bite, which came from a small-eyed ray of 5½lb. By the time I packed up at just after 2 am I had beached four more rays, the best going just over 9lb. A magical evening on a magical beach with no one else in sight. Perfect.

The second event of note owes more to an Irish friend of mine, Chris O'Sullivan, than it does to any angling prowess on my part. En route to the cottage we had got into the habit of stopping in

Tralee to see Chris at Atlantic Tackle. Having struggled to source peeler crabs in the UK in previous years, I stumbled across Chris on an Irish angling forum and found him to be an excellent source of both quality bait and information.

We collected our crabs from Chris, and after a chat about current fishing conditions he casually remarked that he was having a trip after the stingrays on Tuesday morning and would I like to come along? Another not-so-difficult decision! I'd always wanted to catch a stingray, the biggest ray that offers a realistic chance of capture from the shore, but had never really worked out what to do about it. Bob Moss wasn't really a stingray fisherman and his books were a little short on information in this area. It also offered me a chance to do something unusual – after all, how many sea fishermen do you know who can claim to have caught a stingray from both UK and Irish waters? Not many, I'd venture to guess.

It was a dry but windy morning when I met Chris near the strand at Derrymore. From there he took me in his 4x4 across the sand to a mark in Tralee Bay – the same mark from which he'd caught a fifty-pound-plus stingray which had appeared in various sea angling magazines. (Fifty chuffin' pounds!!! How on earth do you land a fish of that size?) I asked him what our chances were and his reply fired me with more than a little enthusiasm. If the weed wasn't too bad, we had an excellent chance of catching both stingrays and undulate rays. However, the first look at the fast-moving water confirmed our worst fears, as we could actually see the weed in the water; in fact, the water was black with it. We did try and fish, but the weed ripped out our leads in seconds, apart from a ten-minute window at slack water which didn't produce anything. Never mind – the time spent with Chris was very informative and as we parted he urged me to try another strand later in the week from which he said I also had a very good chance of catching a stingray if the weed wasn't too bad.

The final day of our 2016 trip to Dingle arrived and with a warm, sunny afternoon forecast I decided to take Chris' advice and head for the edge of Tralee Bay to try for the stingrays. The beach at Derrymore is a mixture of sand, shingle and slightly rougher ground, and as the tide floods into the bay you're fishing into pretty shallow water. End tackle was to be pulley Pennel rigs with bait being peeler crabs, cut in half and mounted on 2/0s to give narrow baits – Chris told me that stingrays have surprisingly small mouths. One rod was cast at medium range and the other was lobbed out around the forty-yard mark, as Chris said that the stingrays can come in extremely close to the shore.

I've said before that, once in a blue moon, I get a feeling that something momentous is going to happen, and I had that feeling on this day. It's irrational, but as the session progressed I almost expected to catch a stingray, despite never even having had a sniff of one before. Of course, this didn't mean that the adrenaline rush was any less when after only an hour of fishing the rod tip straightened and yards of slack line billowed in the breeze. I had my bait about 70 yards out, but I'd regained 20 yards of line before I tightened up to the fish. As I did so there was a noticeable eruption in the water as something shot to my right, ripping yards of line of the spool. The tension then completely disappeared from the rod and I thought I'd lost the fish, only to realise that it had run towards me. Then, wham! Off it went again, and this cycle repeated itself until I gradually worked the fish closer to the shore. I still hadn't seen it and my suspicion was that it was a big bass, until I saw a large flat black shape zoom past me in the shallow water and knew I really had hooked a stingray. I managed to get it into the shallows and then dragged it up onto the beach, while being mindful of its stinger, which it was thrashing around in an attempt to spear me.

Chris said that stingrays fight quite well. That's an understatement of gargantuan proportions!

With its stinger covered with a damp cloth, it was unhooked, weighed ('only' 9lb 4oz), photographed by Lorraine and returned to the water. By the way, if you ever wondered why most stingrays are photographed lying on the sand, it's not just because of the stinger, it's because they are incredibly slimy and difficult to pick up.

What a way to end that year's holiday. My heart is racing as I type this and recall just how I felt on catching my first ever stingray.

Trabeg – one of my favourite Irish strands.

First cast in Irish waters results in a 4lb thornback ray. The next couple of hours
resulted in another fourteen rays of a similar size.

Trabeg, and another small thornback ray.

Walking out of the surf with yet another thornback ray, this time caught from the little beach below our cottage.

The 7lb 8oz bass also caught from the little beach below our cottage.

Standing in the surf, fishing for bass.

A 4lb bass caught minutes after the previous photo was taken.

A 3lb bass from Trabeg.

Gowlane at dusk on a wet and windy day. Brandon Mountain and the hills of the Conor Pass are obscured by low cloud and there's not another angler in sight. Perfect.

At 10lb 7oz, this is my best small-eye. Gowlane, August 2016.

At long last, a stingray! 'Only' 9lb 4oz, Derrymore, August 2016.

TALES FROM THE BOAT

It's only right that I devote a full chapter to fishing from the boat on Tabley Mere. After all, having fished there every summer for more than thirty years, it is without doubt my most longstanding angling obsession. The timing is good too: I'm writing this a couple of days into the 2017 season on the mere. My angling buddy John and I have been there at dawn on both mornings, and although we've seen plenty of tench roll and had them bubbling on our groundbait and around our hookbaits, we've only managed a single bite between us. Even then I suspect this was just a line bite, since I missed it but brought back a couple of tench scales on the hook. The two blanks have occurred despite us both adhering to all of our opening day rituals; no new tackle on opening day, it's bad luck, and the cake consumed being either coffee or chocolate cake. Despite this lack of fish, I'm already having palpitations at the thought of going back there in a couple of days' time after a vicious low-pressure system has moved through; maybe the tench will then be more inclined to look at our hookbaits?

Tabley Mere is a curious place, and its tench even more so. It was formed in 1790 by extending an old mill pool into a 47-acre lake to improve the parkland landscape for the nearby hall and provide yachting for house party guests. Most of the mere is only a couple of feet in depth, apart from the old channel formed by the stream which used to exit the mill pool; depths here can exceed twenty feet in places.

In years gone by we've had summers when we've had regular multiple captures of tench, even hauls of up to thirty fish, summers when you arrived in the morning expecting to catch tench. These have been followed by years when we've failed to catch a single one; in fact, at one point I nearly went two whole seasons without catching one, times when, were if it not for seeing them spawn, you could be forgiven for thinking the mere was completely devoid of tench. The beauty of boat fishing is that there is no hiding place for the tench: if they are feeding somewhere on the mere, then one of the boat anglers would eventually find them. So why don't we catch them?

There are a number of theories. It could be that they are preoccupied with natural foods such as bloodworm, tiny snails, or daphnia; the clouds of daphnia in the water can be huge and you can imagine that the tench would only have to swim around with their mouths open (which is exactly what they do) to get a pretty good feed. Likewise, the mooring posts are often coated with bloodworm and small snails after being in the water for some hours.

The water quality is variable, but often gin clear, and this may also play a part in their apparent disappearance. Like many Cheshire and Shropshire meres, Tabley Mere suffers from high levels of phosphates, which encourage excessive weed growth, especially surface weed. However, when a tench is caught in one of these lean years it is always in good condition, showing that whatever is happening to them, it isn't causing them any great stress. I don't really subscribe to any particular theory, although if I had to, I would choose the 'natural food' option.

In recent years the trend has been that we're catching fewer tench, but much bigger ones. From six-pound fish being exceptional in the eighties and nineties, we started to break the seven-pound barrier, and then a small number of eight-pound fish appeared. Of course, we are catching the same fish over and over again, which possibly makes me look a little hypocritical when I'm criticising other anglers catching 'named' fish from other waters, the only difference being that we've never resorted to calling these tench anything other than tench. Actually, that's not quite true as John and I call all tench 'Terry'.

Time for another little aside. John and I got fed up of reading about 'Heather the Leather' (that's a large leather carp, if you hadn't worked it out), 'Two Tone' and 'Red Belly', so decided that, in a minor act of petulant rebellion, we'd name all the fish we caught. But to make it easy we'd only use one name per fish. Hence Terry the tench, Barry the barbel, Bertie the bass, Donald the dogfish and, of course, Raymond the ray. This explains why I might get a text from my friend saying something like: *Went to Anglesey and had 2 Raymonds, 4 Donalds and lots of Williams. Nothing of any size.*

A William? A whiting, of course.

Let's return to those tench in Tabley Mere and another reason for me to have a little hypocritical squirm. There are three reasons why the tench have continued to grow beyond their historical norms: firstly, the fish density in Tabley Mere is quite low, partly due to predation on the silver fish by cormorants; secondly, there are fewer tench, and thirdly (hence the squirm), a handful of carp anglers, who fish on the mere from a boat owned by a large angling club, have been using vast quantities of pellets and boilies, which have been avidly consumed by the few remaining tench. The carp population in Tabley Mere is also growing, unfortunately, and although the carp anglers would have you believe that there are secret thirty-pound plus fish in there, I have not yet seen anything that would even hit the twenty-pound mark.

The number of successful trips has declined in proportion to the size of the tench. If I had twenty trips there in the summer, I would now expect at least a dozen blanks. Does this bother me? Not really, it just makes each tench caught an even better achievement, and it's the antithesis of today's angling 'instant gratification' culture. I'll be going to Tabley Mere at least twice next week and I've no idea if I'll even get a bite, but if I do, it could be a float-caught eight or even nine-pound fish, which to someone of my generation would be a staggering achievement, as the British Record tench was less than eight pounds when I was growing up. Of course, catching such a fish on the float, not legering and sitting behind a bank of bite alarms, would make this even more special.

We've had mornings when, a bit like the last couple of mornings, the tench flaunt themselves in front of you but you can't buy a bite, and other mornings when you don't see a roll or a single bubble but catch consistently.

Another oddity is as follows. Imagine, if you will, two anglers sitting no more than four feet apart, using identical floats, hook lengths, hooks and bait. Those floats and bait are likewise sitting no more than four feet apart in identical depths of water. You would expect from a statistical point of view that, in terms of tench caught, the most common ratio would be 50:50. At Tabley Mere we never, ever, catch equal numbers of tench. Indeed, I've sat there and watched as my friend has caught tench after tench, sometimes as many as nine, and missed bites too while my own float has remained motionless. In these situations, there is nothing you can do but sit there fuming and hope that at some point your luck will change. The converse has also happened and left me smiling and my friend cursing. We have come up with many theories to explain this anomaly: Tabley Mere just doesn't like you today, God doesn't like you today or is punishing you for some recent misdemeanour, or the successful angler has been using some secret additive (as if!) that the tench are finding irresistible. The only real rational explanation we have come up with is that the tench swim in small shoals of fish that circulate around the edges of the deeper water... and some days they circulate in a clockwise direction and some days in an anti-clockwise direction. When a fish is hooked, the other members of that shoal swim back from where they've just come before resuming their previous circulation. Anyway, it's just a theory and I'd love to hear a better one.

Some four years ago, the managers of the estate told the five owners of the private boats on the Mere that they wanted us to group together to form a syndicate so that they could deal with one person, or organisation, as opposed to five individuals. At the same time, a large angling club had made some efforts to secure bank fishing on the mere. The thought of bank fishermen filled us all with dread: before we knew it, the banks would be manicured to provide bivvy-friendly pitches, trees that lay rotting in the margins would be removed and zip leads would be flying around our ears wherever we fished. Most of all, it would destroy the very soul of the place. Thankfully, English Nature objected to any plans for bankside fishing due to the presence of nesting herons, but this threat did galvanise us into agreeing to form a syndicate. We did so on the back of one of the worst seasons ever for tench fishing on the mere, and one of our number decided to remove his boat from the mere and leave before the syndicate was officially recognised. My friend took his place as a full paying member of the group, even though we'd be sharing a boat. Since no one else wanted the job, I took the role as Secretary, Treasurer and General Factotum.

From being threatened with physical violence by a pair of anglers in the 'angling club' boat (apparently, I was fishing in 'their' spot) to watching an osprey diving for fish no more than a hundred yards in front of us, fishing Tabley Mere was, and is, never dull. We caught other fish as well as tench, including bream to eight pounds, carp to thirteen pounds and last year for the first time in my thirty-odd years of fishing the mere I caught a pike while fishing for tench. It was only about four pounds in weight and took two maggots on a size 14 hook. The following week I almost repeated the feat with a pike more than twice as big that took a small piece of bread flake, also on a size 14. Having played it to what I thought was a standstill, which took nearly twenty minutes, the pike took one look at my undersized net – perfectly adequate for tench but not for pike of that size – and leapt clear of the water, only to fall on my line and sever it instantly.

We've fished in heatwaves, gales and thunderstorms, and all were less than pleasant in their own ways. An aluminium boat reflects the sun's rays and leaves you feeling like a fried egg and looking like a poached salmon; gales create tremendous currents, so that your float trots through the swim as if you were fishing a river; thunderstorms leave you with nowhere to hide as you can't go and shelter under the trees. In the days when I worked for a living, I would spend the summer months driving out to one of my offices, or to a meeting, thinking, *it's wet and windy out there – great conditions for catching tench on Tabley Mere*, or *it's hot and still out there, not great for catching tench but it would be lovely to be sitting there fishing*. It was a very, very rare day when I thought I was glad to be going to work as opposed to sitting in my boat.

The opening day of the 2016 season gave me my best ever Tabley tench. Like every opening day for more than twenty years, I was there as first light broke through on the eastern horizon, but unlike previous years I was by myself as my angling buddy had something important to do which just could not be put off. I rowed across to the far end of the mere in what were hardly classic tench fishing conditions; although it was far from cold, there was a brisk north-easterly breeze which made it feel chillier than it really was. I moored up at the edge of a steep drop-off which would leave me fishing into about ten feet of water. A groundbait was made up which consisted of brown breadcrumb, hemp, small pellets – yes, the whiff of hypocrisy once again – with a shot of molasses to sweeten the mixture. I firmly believe that this is one thing Terry and I have in common: we both have a very sweet tooth. By four-thirty in the morning I had my float sitting in the water over the baited area and was savouring many things: the start of the season, the first season in which I wouldn't have to return to work (see next chapter!), the cup of coffee in one hand and the large piece of coffee cake in the other. All I needed for a perfect start to the season was a tench.

Over two hours later, I hadn't had a bite or seen a tench. Glynn had turned up not long after me and was fishing in the Deep Hole. I turned around to see if there was any indication that he was catching fish at exactly the same time as the wind dropped sufficiently for me to see a large one roll on the opposite side of the hole from where he was fishing. Decision time: should I stay or should I go? I decided to go, which turned out to be the right decision. I moored up on the far side of the Deep Hole opposite Glynn, and not long after I'd started fishing again he hooked into what was obviously a very big tench. On landing it, he called across to me and asked if I would mind coming across to weigh and photograph it for him. No problem, I replied and was delighted to take multiple shots of him holding his best ever tench, a lovely fish of 8lb 3oz.

With anticipation reaching fever pitch, I rowed back to my posts and started fishing again. Less than an hour later, I had my first bite of the new season and hooked into something which stayed deep, and although it didn't run too far from the boat, it radiated 'substantial tench'. Or was foul hooked. After five minutes of dogged fighting, I got my first glimpse of it; not foul hooked and very substantial indeed. I just managed to get it into my landing net – if the tench grow much larger I am going to need a bigger net – and knew straight away that this was my best-ever Tabley tench. With trembling hands, I watched as the pointer on my old Avon scales settled at 8lb 13oz. Photographs were taken and the old girl slipped back into the fair waters of Tabley Mere, where, with a strong kick of her tail, she disappeared into the depths.

I had five more tench that morning, including one of 7lb 8oz, to make it one of the most special mornings I've ever had there. More special than the morning when I had my first two six-pound tench, or indeed, the morning when I caught my first tench there? Possibly the equal of those mornings, but more special? No.

Incidentally, over the next ten days I had five more trips to Tabley Mere and caught eleven more tench, but after this I didn't catch another all summer despite many, many more trips.

Glynn started fishing Tabley Mere in 1953 when he was just fourteen years old and still fishes there several times a week in the summer and autumn in the same punt, which must be nearly as old as he is. He told me a story about an old gamekeeper who worked on the Tabley estate, so these words are his, not mine.

On my introduction to the Mere in 1953 I met Mr Hart, then aged seventy-eight years old and still the resident gamekeeper. He told me the following story. The owner of a large neighbouring estate, a Lord of the Realm no less, had heard tales about a great pike in Tabley Mere and set aside a fortnight to catch this monster. He was a renowned big game hunter and decided the fish would look well set up in his own hall, along with the hundreds of game trophies brought back from Africa and two splendid tunny caught off Scarborough.

He wrote to his neighbour at Tabley for both permission to fish and to have the expertise of Mr Hart as gillie. The answer came back 'Help yourself – Mr Hart is at your command'. His Lordship then sent his own bailiff to check the two Tabley estate boats, both lovingly maintained by Mr Hart. Unfortunately, much to the chagrin of the gamekeeper, both boats were pronounced unsuitable.

His Lordship then requested permission to use his own boat, complete with velvet cushions and awning. 'By all means,' came the reply. His Lordship's bailiff then tried to deliver the boat to the Mere by horse and cart, but found the only bridge up to the lake was unsafe. His Lordship proceeded to write to his neighbour offering to repair the bridge at his own expense. 'Delighted – get on with it,' came the reply. The bridge was duly strengthened and the boat delivered.

Mr Hart, who had been a spectator so far, was then asked to produce live bait samples for his Lordship. This he did and they were taken up to his Lordship's house. 'Too small, too weak, too puny,' came back the verdict. His Lordship would have his own large perch livebait caught in his own lake and delivered daily. The great day finally arrived and for the next fortnight Mr Hart rowed his Lordship around the lake all day and every day, barring Sundays (there was no fishing on the Sabbath).

'And did his Lordship hook the monster, Mr Hart?' I asked. A twinkle appeared in the old man's eye. 'He certainly did not – because I took jolly good care never to row him anywhere near it,' came the reply!

There are pike in Tabley Mere, as you've just read – I've caught and hooked them by accident, but never felt inclined in recent years to fish for them in winter by design. Why? Quite simply, the thought of fishing on the mere in the winter, the trees devoid of foliage, the banks bare of vegetation and the water brown and muddy, would desecrate my image of the place. To me, fishing on Tabley Mere is all about misty mornings as the sun rises, wet and windy mornings, grey drizzly mornings; in fact, any morning as long as it's summer and tench are the quarry.

A smoky dawn on Tabley mere in August 1994.

Bream 7lb 12oz – August 2005

Common carp 13lb 6oz – July 1998

A view from the boat... if you look carefully you can just see the red float!

At 8lb 13oz, this is my biggest Tabley Mere tench – June 2016.

Glynn Stockdale with an 8lb 3oz tench, also June 2016.

A fin-perfect tench of 8lb exactly – June 2015.

CHAPTER SEVENTEEN

REDUNDANCY, RETIREMENT AND FULL-TIME FISHING

You will have noticed a few references to cooked breakfasts, biscuits and cake, and realised that I do like my food. As each year passed, my waist expanded in direct proportion to my receding hairline, so I responded by getting new shirts and suits in ever-increasing sizes while promising my wife that I would look to start dieting and taking more exercise tomorrow or the day after. Days that never came. I went into the tackle shop near my office in Heysham to get a new flotation suit only to find that I needed the 'FB' size. 'Does that stand for 'Fat Bastard'?' I asked the shop assistant? 'No,' he replied, slightly embarrassed, 'it stands for 'full bodied'. Same difference.

Then in the April of 2014 I was having a shower when I noticed that I appeared to have grown a third testicle. It wasn't, of course – it was a hernia. This explained why I'd been getting a sore groin when standing ray fishing at Cymyran for long periods. A visit to my GP confirmed the obvious and I went home to Google hernias on the internet to see what the surgical options were and the recovery times associated with each option; after all, I had bass fishing to think about, not to mention rowing and tench fishing on Tabley Mere. Hopefully I could have keyhole surgery, which would only need a couple of weeks for recovery, but a meeting with the surgeon soon put an end to those thoughts. It was a bad tear and would need a full anaesthetic, a significant incision, a mesh insertion and six weeks for a full recovery. I asked the surgeon how long before I could go fishing again, and after a bit of confusion when he thought I meant big game fishing (it transpired that this was what he did, having both an estate and a big game boat in the Caribbean), he said I should be able to do some 'light' fishing in about four weeks' time. Could this include some light rock lifting and moving when looking for peeler crabs too? No!

Four weeks without fishing or any sort of physical activity, not that I did too much of that anyway, left me in a bit of a state. I had a few bass fishing trips and started tench fishing in the boat on Tabley Mere, but I didn't feel quite right; nothing I could put my finger on, just not quite right. Then one morning I got up with backache: crap, just what I wanted, but the backache got worse, an intense pain that took my breath away. I developed a chesty cough too, took various tablets which didn't help and eventually went to my doctor, who took no more than a couple of minutes to diagnose pleurisy. 'You haven't been coughing up blood, have you?' he asked. I hadn't. He prescribed antibiotics, and I went home and promptly started coughing up chunks of blood...

A phone call back to the GP resulted in an immediate referral to a chest specialist at a local hospital. He listened to my tale of woe and said that it was likely that I'd got pulmonary embolisms (blood clots in my lungs), but was there anything else of significance in my past that he should be aware of?

'Well, I would have had a greater exposure to asbestos than most people, due to my first job,' I said.

There was a long pause. 'We'll get a scan done to confirm the diagnosis,' he said.

'What if it's not blood clots?'

Another pause. 'Let's get the scan done,' he said.

But it was a Friday, the scanner was broken and I'd have to wait till Monday for the scan and full diagnosis. I had the whole weekend to consider my fate and feared the worst; in these situations, I always pick the worst possible scenario and focus on that. Lorraine, on the other hand, does the complete opposite and lives by the principle of 'don't worry, it may never happen'.

Monday came, the scan was taken and that evening the chest doctor phoned me to confirm the diagnosis: four big blood clots on my lungs, as well as double pneumonia. I may be the only person in history to greet such news with a shout of, 'Yesssss, thank f*** for that!'

This did mean, however, an immediate trip back to hospital to get a clot-busting injection and a lesson in how to self-medicate with these injections, which was what I'd have to do for the next few weeks until the warfarin that I'd also have to take thinned my blood sufficiently to reduce the risk of further clots.

I felt ill, really ill, but relieved that it was something treatable. I also lost my appetite for the first time in my life and resolved, at long last, to lose weight and get fit. Losing my appetite meant that the first stone disappeared without any effort on my part, but I did change my diet, and as my health improved I started to exercise more, walking at first then using my son's exercise bike. Surprisingly enough, eating the right food and exercising more meant that the weight fell off me. Who would have thought it? As I'm typing this now, I'm at exactly the same weight as when I first met Lorraine, which, I'm ashamed to say is over five stone lighter than I was at my heaviest.

I'm telling you all of this as part of the explanation for my decision to retire early. The weekend I spent waiting for the diagnosis confirmed to me that life was too short to spend working. Did I enjoy my work? Well, sort of. My stock answer to this question at that point in my professional career was that two days per week were good, two days were bad and one would be ok. The job was very stressful – what else would you expect at board level? – and I didn't want to be one of those people who retired in their sixties and promptly keeled over and died some months later.

I sat down and did a detailed appraisal of our finances: we would be in a position to pay off our mortgage in April 2017, so this seemed a good point to aim for in terms of my retirement. I discussed this with Lorraine, who agreed that if I wanted to retire, that was fine with her. She was still enjoying her job and planned on working for another three years or so beyond this date.

I never made it to that April. That's workwise, not life-wise, although I'm sure you would have figured that out for yourself. The organisation I worked for tended to re-invent itself on a regular basis in a quest to find the magical combination of people and business structure. When the last reincarnation saw me removed from my post as Commercial Director for the whole of the UK and moved into a role as Business Development Director, I had a pretty good idea of what was coming next. It was a classic case of being moved out along the branch away from the core business until the branch could be cut away with minimal impact on that business. Just before Christmas 2014 the company started to get rid of people, good people, people with whom I'd worked for over ten years, so when one February morning I got a call from my boss while driving along the M6 that started with the words, 'you might want to find somewhere to stop before we have this conversation,' I knew exactly what was coming.

The owner of the company wanted me out; my boss, who was also being made redundant, said that I could, within reason, choose my timing and explained that the owner didn't want me to go and work for a competitor. I started to crunch some numbers and worked out that if I could work to the end of June and get a substantial redundancy payment then there was the possibility that I wouldn't have to work ever again.

I talked this through with Lorraine on a Saturday morning in a Costa Coffee. (Can I just say that now I am retired, I am a big Costa fan – the coffee house, not the footballer – and one of the joys of retirement is being able to read the newspapers therein while enjoying a large cappuccino). Provided I could get the redundancy payment I wanted, she was happy for me to finish work completely, although she stressed that she wasn't ready by any means to retire yet herself. However, there were a few bits and pieces that we'd have to sort out. Our agreement came to be known as 'The Retirement Contract', which is relayed in full below.

THE RETIREMENT CONTRACT

1. RB to fully clean house on a weekly basis.

2. RB to do the washing and ironing.

3. RB to load and empty the dishwasher.

4. RB to ensure that there is an evening meal ready and waiting for LB's return from work, except when RB is out fishing. In these instances, RB to ensure that food is available for LB to cook, or eat, on her return.

5. RB to cut the grass and keep the garden tidy.

6. RB to be allowed to go fishing whenever he wants, within reason, *(NB Not defined!)* and preferably only once at a weekend.

7. RB to get up at the same time as LB during the week even if he hasn't got in till the early hours himself e.g. 2am. *(NB LB changed jobs about this time and started to get up at 5:45am as she was based in the centre of Manchester... quite ironic that I retired only to have to get out of bed earlier than ever.)*

8. LB to buy a puppy.

9. RB to walk said puppy during the week including the first morning walk at circa 5:45am.

10. RB to explore the possibility of obtaining some Non-Executive Director work on a part time basis or find something else to keep his mind 'active'.

We'd had a dog before, a golden retriever called Holly, which was very much Lorraine's dog. She had grown up with dogs, whereas the only pets I'd ever had were goldfish and a rabbit, which ended up being eaten by the dog from over the road. We, with our daughters' help, acquired a six-week-old Chocolate Labrador bitch that we ended up calling Billie. Why Billie? It was a name chosen by committee: me, my wife and our two kids. Originally, the pup was to be called Ruby until my wife started singing 'Ruby, Ruby, Ruby' by the Kaiser Chiefs. Now my wife has many, many talents, but singing isn't one of them and eventually the three of us decided that there was no way the dog could be called Ruby and we compromised on Billie.

Billie is two years old now and I've started to take her fishing with me; I used to watch Henry Gilbey taking his dog Jess fishing with him and thought that was pretty cool. Billie isn't quite at the Jess stage of fishing obedience, but she is as much my dog as my wife's and I love her to bits.

My formal redundancy was agreed with the company and a suitable financial settlement reached. On the 30th June 2015 at about 10am, at the age of 53, I walked into my office at Sandycroft near Chester, left my work laptop on my desk, said a few goodbyes and thirty minutes later left work for the final time in my life. I was quite happy with this situation, having achieved just about everything I wanted to in my professional life.

People ask me what I miss about work. Not much, I reply: some of the people; the camaraderie you feel with your colleagues when things are going well; my company car and Fuelcard; and the 'Friday feeling'. Although you could argue that every day is a Friday for me now, it is difficult to replicate the feeling I used to get on a Friday afternoon, especially if I was in the car driving back from a meeting somewhere. I would listen to Mark Kermode's film review on the radio and contemplate the weekend's activities: in the summer, this could involve a barbecue on Friday evening (my red-meat-treat for the week), fishing at Tabley Mere by dawn on the Saturday, followed by a trip to watch my son play cricket somewhere in Cheshire during the afternoon. If I was lucky, I might even have tried to fit a bass trip in on the Sunday afternoon and evening.

I don't miss the stress or having to work when conditions looked absolutely perfect for fishing on one of my favourite venues. This became an increasing frustration as I started to do more sea fishing. Sea fishing is far more weather dependent than its coarse counterpart, and you also need to consider the tides. Many were the times when conditions were perfect during the week – my job meant that it was rarely possible to take time off at short notice – only to deteriorate rapidly over the weekend, causing me immense frustration.

As you will have gathered by now, I am primarily a sea angler. Friends often ask me why I spend so much time and effort – not to mention money on fuel – going sea fishing when I've got so much excellent coarse fishing right on my doorstep. I tell them that sea fishing is now a 'purer' form of angling. Don't get me wrong, you will have realised that I do still enjoy various aspects of freshwater fishing such as float fishing for tench from my boat or pike fishing, but fundamentally, I now class myself as a sea angler first and foremost.

Why? There are a number of reasons for this change.

When I was young, there was still a certain mystique about coarse fishing, particularly carp and tench fishing. A five-pound tench or a ten-pound carp was still classed as a specimen fish and you could never really say 'I've just caught the biggest carp or tench in the lake'. You may well have done so, but you wouldn't know as there were no online forums, so the sharing of photographs was something you only did with your closest angling friends. These days a big fish, especially a carp, is likely to be well known and have a name. This doesn't bother me too much, but what it does do is remove some of the sense of achievement. The famous climber George Leigh Mallory, when asked why he wanted to climb Mount Everest, said, 'because it's there', and another climber, Edmund Hillary said, 'no one remembers who was the second person to climb Everest'. So, what do you do when you've climbed to the summit, or caught one of the biggest carp or tench? Climb it, or catch it, again? Yes, I am being a little hypocritical here, as the tench we catch in Tabley Mere are undoubtedly the same ones year after year, but in our defence, we haven't started giving them individual names. They are all still called Terry.

Now compare the above to sea angling. Thirty or forty years ago big cod and bass – and I assume rays as well, although not many people seemed to write about rays – were caught in good quantities from the shore of the UK and Eire. If you read the books and magazine articles by the late Clive Gammon and Anthony Pearson, you get a sense that multiple captures of eight-pound-plus bass were not irregular occurrences. Likewise, Ian Gillespie, John Darling and others would write about multiple captures of ten, even twenty-pound, cod. You also have to remember that the tackle in those days was distinctly inferior to that of today. Fast forward to the present time and eight-pound plus bass or ten – let alone twenty-pound cod, for example, are distinctly uncommon captures from the shore despite vastly superior tackle.

This is the crux of the problem for someone of my age: catching big (by my standards) coarse fish has got easier, and therefore means less, whereas catching big sea fish has become more difficult and therefore means more. And, of course, because you can never claim to have caught the biggest bass, cod or ray in the sea, you will never reach the sea angling summit!

Thankfully, no one has yet worked out how to cordon off a little piece of the sea, stock it with farm-reared, overgrown bass, cod or rays in order to sell day tickets to catch these bloated imitations of a true fish.

Despite being primarily a sea angler, I have managed to widen my repertoire of pike-fishing venues. A few years before I retired I was walking along the canal at the bottom of the field below our cottage when I came across a lure fisherman fishing for pike. Do you ever catch much here, I asked? Yes, he replied – and showed me a picture of a sixteen pounder. I'd lived within walking distance of this canal for over fifteen years and had never thought of fishing it for pike. I soon put this right and caught plenty of pike, although most were under five pounds in weight. What it did do though, was to provide me with an opportunity to go fishing for a few hours here and a few hours there, especially now that I'm retired. It also provides me with an opportunity to take Billie with me, although she does need to be tied up to stop her following my red pike floats into the canal!

Having discovered that this canal contained pike, I wondered if it contained carp too. Over a cappuccino in Costa Coffee, I questioned whether I could rekindle my love of carp fishing or if it was completely dead. I spent three nights baiting up a swim at the bottom of the field below our cottage and fished it on the fourth. It only took me four hours to realise that I wasn't enjoying it at all. There was no buzz, no anticipation, no excitement. Nothing. I sat there wishing I was on a beach somewhere or even simply sat back at home in my own chair with a glass of wine. At least retirement allowed me the luxury of this exploratory session.

Retirement has also allowed me the time to try and explore a few new places. The most enjoyable of these has been Ynyslas, near Borth in mid Wales. Bounded by the Dovey estuary at its northern end and stretching for over a mile before the wooden groynes of Borth beach begin, Ynyslas is a completely different beach from those I fish on Anglesey. It's a true storm beach on which small-eyed rays and bass are the main quarry, but here you catch most of these fish within fifty yards of the shore in water that is no more than knee or thigh deep. I remember my first trip there on a hot September afternoon in the first Autumn of my retirement; I walked the full length of the beach and bought an ice cream before even unloading my tackle from the car. There was very little surf on that day but I still managed to catch a very small small-eyed ray, in water so shallow that at Cymyran I'd have waded beyond there before even casting out.

However, it was a trip in December of that year, technically my birthday trip even though it was just before my birthday, that confirmed my love of the place. It was a wild afternoon, wet and windy with a big but slow surf, the kind both the rays and the bass loved. I had five rays to seven pounds and a four-pound bass, all caught within fifty yards of the shore from low water up to high.

There are two downsides to Ynyslas, though: firstly, the weed that can suddenly appear out of nowhere to make fishing impossible and secondly, the long drive. It's usually a two-and-a-half-hour trip to get there during the day, though less when leaving at ten or eleven o'clock at night. It can be really infuriating to spend an eternity getting there, being stuck behind tractors, tankers and caravans, only to find that within one cast the water is full of weed and completely unfishable. At least now I've managed to make contact with a local angler who can let me know if the weed is really bad, although it's not always possible to fully ascertain the weed situation without actually casting a line.

I also discovered smoothhounds, while trying to catch thornback rays from the Dee estuary one day in May. These grey mini-sharks provided me with some superb sport and in fighting terms I would rate them the equal of any bass. I wouldn't say that there's any obsessional spark there with them, but they will possibly fill a gap when nothing else is feeding.

By the beginning of 2015 I hadn't managed to find any non-executive director work. This was partly due to the restrictive covenants contained within my redundancy agreement, but mainly due to the fact that I hadn't applied for any...

Lorraine wasn't too bothered about this, but she was concerned that I was lacking 'mental stimulation' and suggested that I find something to do, even if it was voluntary work. I thought long and hard about what I really wanted to do and came up with the idea of writing an article and submitting it to various angling magazines. So how should the article be structured? Well, I looked at my angling diaries and thought, how about a brief introduction, explaining how I got into firstly coarse fishing and then sea fishing, followed by a session-by-session account of what I caught and more importantly, a description of the venue I was fishing, the weather and the very *feel* of each session. I wrote the article, then rewrote it, before finally being sort of happy with my efforts.

I submitted the article to a couple of magazines and got an immediate response from Paul Dennis, the Editor of *Total Sea Fishing*. He suggested a few amendments which I took on board, and I resubmitted the article. He said he'd like to use it and could

I do a similar one each month for the foreseeable future? Yes, I replied, I'm sure I could.

The more I wrote, the easier it became, although the same couldn't be said of my photographic skills. I had a fairly basic digital camera with a delayed action feature that gave you ten seconds from pressing the shutter button to the photograph being taken. Ten seconds in which to pick up the fish and then pose with it; rays, in particular, have a habit of curling up when you first pick them up off the rocks or beach, while asking a huss to keep still while it has its picture taken is a thankless task. If I had someone with me, then the picture taking was easier, but if I was by myself, as I usually was, then it could take numerous attempts before I got a picture I was happy with. Even then, especially at night, what looked like a decent photo on the beach could turn out to be blurred, out of focus, or corrupted by a single drop of rain on the lens when viewed in the cold light of the following day.

I eventually borrowed my daughter's camera, a much superior version which took better quality pictures and had a feature that sought out faces to focus on, but it still only gave you ten seconds to pose with your fish. I enjoyed writing these articles and, as you will have read in the foreword, decided to have a go at writing a book.

Retirement also gave me the opportunity to have a full week's holiday in Anglesey in autumn. I found a lovely place to stay, a Swiss-style lodge situated among the sand dunes just outside Rhosneigr, and last year we had our most enjoyable trip for years. The four of us, me, my wife, my mother and Billie the dog, arrived in perfect weather; unusually, perfect for both fishing and things like dog walking and sitting outside to eat. The days brought mainly warm sunshine and the evenings and nights brought enough wind to create a good surf. I also enjoyed my best night's ray fishing from a beach, in terms of numbers, and it happened like this.

A few days into our holiday, a huge groundswell appeared from nowhere to render most of the beaches in the area unfishable, and I decided that I'd have to spend a fishless evening in the cottage. Just before dusk, my wife and mother parked themselves in front of the television and outlined what we were going to watch that evening (no sport!), so I volunteered to walk the dog. One minute later I crossed the little stream that carved a deep channel into the sand in front of the dunes and walked onto the beach in front of the cottage. I immediately realised that most of the weed that had previously covered the lower reaches of that beach and made it unfishable had been pushed up to the high-water mark. In addition to that, the surf here was perfectly fishable. The beach was slightly more sheltered and flatter than that at Cymyran next door, so the surf was more spread out, producing great 'tables' of water that just screamed fish, especially bass and rays.

I ran back to the cottage, casually asked if no one would mind if I had a 'quick couple of hours' fishing', assumed the answer was in the affirmative, grabbed a single pack of sand eels and a box containing three squid, put on my waders and gathered up my fishing tackle. Fifteen minutes later I was making my first casts. The flatness of the beach meant that I was having to wade a long way out to be able to cast into any depth of water. It was well over an hour after low water and the tide was moving in quickly, producing a surprising amount of lateral movement in the sea. This meant that I had to be very careful of my footing when wading out to cast.

Within minutes of casting, both rod tips were bent over and pulling hard to the left: I assumed that weed was to blame and decided to drag one rod in to check just how bad the weed really was. There was indeed a heavy weight on the end of the line, but with nothing pulling back I assumed it was just weed, until it was no more than ten yards away from me. The 'weed' then changed into a ray and started pulling back strongly, although it only took a minute or so to drag it on to dry land. At 9lb 4oz it was a good small-eyed ray too, and I quickly returned it on the basis that my other rod was likely to have a ray on it as well. It did indeed – another cracking ray of 8lb 9oz. I recast both rods, but even before I'd returned to the tripod with my second rod, the first rod tip had straightened with the line pointing round to the left...

The next two and a half hours gave me the most hectic beach ray fishing I've ever had. I landed another eight rays and lost two more in the surf. They weren't as big as the first two – the best most likely was in the five to six-pound category – but the bottom must have been paved with rays and I never went more than a couple of minutes without a bite.

Eventually I ran out of bait, despite reworking my sand eel/squid wraps as best I could. Back at our holiday home I thought about returning with more bait, but I wouldn't have been able to get back across the channel of the stream, which was by then nearly four feet deep, having been filled by the incoming tide.

I returned there the following evening, accompanied by my wife and Billie the dog for the first couple of hours, but only managed the one ray, which may just have broken the four-pound mark. Whereas the previous evening the bottom was covered in rays, this time the sea was full of nothing but dogfish and whiting. What had changed? Very little, except that the surf was slightly smaller.

The other highlights of this holiday were pancakes for breakfast at Mojo's, sitting outside in the morning sunshine with Billie, my wife and my mother (I still enjoy my food, but now in moderation) and a trip around the old Golden Sunset caravan park in Benllech. We tried to locate the position of every caravan we had stayed in there when I was a child, and Mum was able to hobble from the car to the cliff path so that she could see the rocks we used to fish from, including 'our rock' which served as our first rod rest. I also took my mother sea fishing again. Well, sort of; she sat near the car within sight of me fishing and I was hoping that I could snare a bass to show her, as that was something we'd never managed to catch as a family in our old Benllech days. Unfortunately, I couldn't even manage to get a bite.

One man and his dog went... to catch a ray.

A 12lb pike from the Trent and Mersey canal on a very wet day in February 2015.

Ynyslas and a small-eyed ray of circa 5lb in April 2016.

A 9lb plus small-eye from Traeth Crygyll in October 2016 which was part of a catch of ten rays in a little more than a couple of hours.

CHAPTER EIGHTEEN

NOT THE LAST CAST

Phone calls in the early hours of the morning are never harbingers of good news. No one phones you at six o'clock in the morning to say, 'guess what – you've just won the Lottery,' so when the phone rang dawn one Saturday morning in early December, my only thought was just how bad the news was going to be.

It was my brother. He told me that Mum was unconscious and that it was suspected that she'd had a stroke, a diagnosis that was confirmed in hospital later that morning.

It was a severe stroke, which left her almost completely immobile and with her speech greatly affected too. Worst of all, she wasn't allowed to eat or drink anything other than a few teaspoons of food, as her swallowing reflex wasn't strong enough. This was heart-breaking to see, as Mum loved her food and drink – I definitely got my love of all things culinary from her! There were times when her clarity of thought was still apparent, especially when talking about holidays in Anglesey and days out fishing.

The doctors warned us that there would be no recovery and that the prognosis equated to a slow decline and eventual death. We got my mother into a nursing home within a few hundred yards of where she lived, which meant that all of her friends, of which there were many, could walk to see her.

When the phone rang once again in the early hours of a Thursday morning in June I had a pretty good idea of what the message was going to be and I wasn't wrong. My mother had gone to sleep the previous evening and had just slipped away peacefully without any fuss, she was 84 years old.

The following week, a few days before the funeral, I went out by myself in my boat on Tabley Mere for a morning's fishing and thought about all the good times I'd had with my mum, and my dad for that matter. I have no intention of coming across all maudlin here. As I've already said in relation to the death of my father, as you get older you know that the day will come when you have to bury your parents; it's not a tragedy, and as long as you can say they've had a full and happy life then those lives should be celebrated.

It's now early July as I'm typing this and I'm sitting here partly thinking about what to write and partly contemplating where I'm going to be fishing tomorrow. I'm torn between going back to Tabley Mere – I haven't caught a single tench there yet this season – or going across to Ynyslas for some bass fishing (I'm kidding myself there, of course, it's the rays I'll really be after).

So, what does the future hold? Will my current obsessions – predominantly rays, followed closely by tench and then bass – endure, or will others replace them in the coming years? Maybe cod, barbel or pike will climb my own Premier League table of fishing obsessions in an attempt to reclaim past glories. Or will new ones emerge, for example, tope or lure fishing? It's going to be fun finding out and one of the great things about having an interest in both sea and freshwater angling is that you never get the chance to become sated with any one species, location or method. I don't see myself ever being anything other than obsessed with my fishing, but these obsessions are just slightly less intense now and each one occupies its own relatively short-lived time and place.

Each year will start on the rock marks of Anglesey, indulging my current obsession with rays, but I will still look forward to the transition to the spring bass 'season'. As the summer arrives, I'll also be doing a lot of tench and bass fishing and a little smoothhound fishing and will therefore be spending my time in wildly diverse locations such as rocky, kelpy shore marks on the Menai Straits, clean sandy beaches in North and Mid Wales, the Dee estuary and the habitual seclusion of Tabley Mere. Final decisions as to where to head for and what to catch will depend on the weather, and more importantly, how my angling disposition takes me. Am I in the mood for tench, bass, smoothhounds, or will my ray addiction get the better of me once again and force me to brave the dogfish and spider crab-infested rock marks on Anglesey's west coast?

I also have a number of new 'marks' that I want to thoroughly explore, and I really would like to try and catch a tope from the shore too.

The summer will also bring my annual trip to the Dingle Peninsula where I'm hoping to improve on last summer's first stingray with a much bigger one, as well as indulging in my favourite form of bass fishing – standing in the surf using a simple leger rig with sand eel for bait. Doubtless I'll also have a few trips after the thornback and small-eyed rays too – given their proliferation over there, it would be rude not to, wouldn't it? I may just be able to persuade my lovely wife to have *two* holidays per year in Dingle now that she too has decided to retire at the end of the year. We might even go in the autumn or winter, which would enable me to fish the iconic Inch Strand for the first time.

I'm hoping that Lorraine's retirement will lessen my 'workload' (!) and will give me even more scope to get out fishing, although I'm not sure she sees it like that. She likes to travel, and I suspect there will be some bargaining to be done over the fishing versus travel mixture. Maybe we can combine the two?

Autumn will see me heading back to the shallow beaches on Anglesey and Mid Wales for the small-eyed rays, along with a few bass trips to the Menai Straits. I've already booked to stay in Rhosneigr again for a whole week of concentrated fishing, although with somewhat mixed feelings, as this will be the first trip where we won't be accompanied by my mother. Doubtless we'll drive there while listening to Oasis and maybe even Lloyd Cole as well. We'll stop for breakfast at Costa Coffee and look wistfully at where the Little Chef used to be at Penmaenmawr. The autumn will finish with a little cod fishing, which will hopefully continue into the winter when the thornback ray fishing will start all over again.

There's only one place to finish this book though, and that's where it all started. I went back to my mother's house to take some photos of the pond as it is now. The pond and surrounding vista has changed a lot. All the houses now boast multiple extensions (apart from ours); there's a proliferation of decking, along with an artificial island to protect the ducks and moorhens from urban foxes. Foxes – I would never have imagined that in my younger days! Trees have disappeared, some blown down in high winds, some removed for 'aesthetic' reasons, and others have started to sprout in their place. The potamogeton is still conspicuous by its absence.

I crouched down close to the spot where I used to fish and closed my eyes. I could hear my father telling me 'don't strike quite so hard' and my mother asking me if I wanted a cup of tea and some cake, but most of all, I could still see my little red float sitting in that same patch of green water.

The pond in May 2017.

Printed in Great Britain
by Amazon

83286402R00169